"I'D LIKE TO BE YOUR FRIEND, TANYA."

Wade's voice was soft. "The only thing is, it could be very dangerous to both of us."

"I don't understand...."

"You really don't, do you? I wasn't sure at first, but now I'm convinced you don't have any idea what you do to a man with that smile, that skin, that lovely mane of hair."

Fascinated by the huskiness in his voice and the warmth in his eyes, Tanya stared up at him. He slid the cap off her head, and when her hair tumbled around her shoulders, he buried his hands in it.

Tanya couldn't find her voice or the strength to pull away. With a groan he grasped her shoulders and pulled her up against his hard body. His mouth closed over hers in a deep kiss, and she realized she wanted him never to stop.

ABOUT THE AUTHOR

Irma Walker says she has always been fascinated by circus life, and writing *Spangles,* her third Superromance, proved to be more fun than work. The prolific California writer comes by her love for the circus honestly. Like the hero of *Spangles,* one of Irma's uncles ran away to join the circus when he was a young man and traveled with the show for many years as a contortionist. Among the rest of the family, Irma says, he became a legend.

Books by Irma Walker

HARLEQUIN SUPERROMANCE
104—SONATA FOR MY LOVE
147—THROUGH NIGHT AND DAY
163—SPANGLES

These books may be available at your local bookseller.

Don't miss any of our special offers. Write to us at the following address for information on our newest releases.

Harlequin Reader Service
P.O. Box 52040, Phoenix, AZ 85072-2040
Canadian address: P.O. Box 2800, Postal Station A,
5170 Yonge St., Willowdale, Ont. M2N 6J3

Irma Walker
SPANGLES

Harlequin Books

TORONTO • NEW YORK • LONDON
AMSTERDAM • PARIS • SYDNEY • HAMBURG
STOCKHOLM • ATHENS • TOKYO • MILAN

Published May 1985

First printing March 1985

ISBN 0-373-70163-2

Printed in Canada

To Ellen Grimm Froehler, Georgette Livingston and Helen Santori, who love animals, too.

CHAPTER ONE

WADE BRODERICK stood by the wide expanse of windows that filled one wall of his den, staring down at the shimmering, glittering lights of the city below. New York...the epitome, the goal, the symbol of the ambitious and the hungry. How did the song "New York, New York" go? Something about if you could make it there, you could make it anywhere?

Well, he'd made it in the great gray canyons of New York, but first he'd carved out an electronic empire in California's Silicon Valley that had helped to put him in the bracket of the very rich, successful beyond the wildest dreams of his boyhood.

So why the hell, when he had it all and had just reached the pinnacle of success, did he feel so damned let down? Why did his life seem so dull? What the devil had happened to his fine enthusiasm for each day to begin?

Remembering that he wasn't alone in the room, he tried to recall what he and Larry Glover had been talking about before they'd both fallen silent over their martinis. A woman's shrill laughter outside in the hall intruded into the room and shattered the quiet. Not for the first time that evening Wade wondered why he'd thought it would be a good idea to throw a party, to fill his penthouse with people and noise and confusion.

His dark mood deepened as his gaze fell on a two-month-old copy of *The Wall Street Journal*, which was lying on the polished mahogany top of his desk. He had been clearing out his desk drawers and had tossed the newspaper into the wastepaper basket along with other discards, but his houseman, obviously assuming it must have been placed there by mistake, had retrieved it and laid it on his desk.

His own face stared up at him from the front page above a caption that read: "Computer Whiz Kid Sells Out to Conglomerate in Multimillion-Dollar Deal."

Whiz kid—not really appropriate for a thirty-two-year-old man. Still, he *had* made his first million by the time he was twenty-six, so it seemed he was stuck with the label—until another Silicon Valley boy wonder came along with a bigger and better electronic marvel.

Curiously he studied the picture, but the man in the gray-and-white photograph, with his unsmiling mouth and his wary eyes, seemed to have nothing at all to do with his own image of himself....

Again he'd forgotten that he wasn't alone, that he'd invited Larry Glover into his den for a quiet drink, and he started when his friend, his voice tinged with irony, said, "The French call what you've got ennui. We psychiatrists have a buzzword for it. Burnout. It's to be expected. You've been working fourteen-hour days for the past twelve years, and now suddenly you have nothing to fill your time. Is that what all this sudden hedonism is about—the parties and the discos and the nightclubbing?"

Wade stared at Larry with morose eyes. His friend was in his early forties, a happily married man with three daughters. He was slightly built, several inches shorter than Wade's six foot two, an intense man with sharp black eyes, a deceptively lazy drawl and a lively curiosity about people, which, he confessed freely, was the thing that had drawn him into the field of psychiatry. That he was also an outgoing person—the opposite of Wade, with his loner instincts and his wary view of the world—was the thing that gave their friendship depth.

Larry could also be disconcertingly intuitive. Was this one of those times? Was it possible that job burnout was the explanation for his restlessness and lack of interest in everything, his feeling lately that time had suddenly become his enemy? If so, he'd better get used to it, because he had no desire to return to the rat race of the electronic industry, at least not for a while.

"I'm still celebrating my delivery from overwork," he said.

"Right. Celebrating. Which is why you grabbed me by the arm like a drowning man clutching a life jacket and pulled me in here for a drink when there must be a dozen New York lovelies out there, all dying to be alone with you. Do you realize that I've known you, oh, eight or nine years, and you've never invited me into your inner sanctum before?"

Larry paused to run an appraising look around the spacious room with its solid, masculine desk and tables, its dark red leather club chairs, its floor-to-ceiling shelves of books. His eyes lingered on a collection of posters on a nearby wall, then moved to a glass exhibit case. "I have to admit this room comes as a total surprise," he went on. "Somehow I never figured you for a collector—certainly not of circus memorabilia."

Wade fought against annoyance. After all, by inviting Larry in here he had laid himself open for his friend's probing remarks. "Everyone has his interests," he said lightly.

"But not the iron man of the electronics business. How many times have you told me that work is your hobby?" Not waiting for an answer, Larry set his martini down on a marble-topped table, got to his feet and sauntered over to examine an oil painting framed in narrow cherrywood. It was a portrait of a group of acrobats; although stylized and subtly distorted, their elongated bodies held a grace that seemed to breathe life into the canvas.

"Picasso, isn't it?" Larry said. "He must have done this during the same period he did the circus family—I can't think of their name now."

"The Saltimbanques," Wade said.

"Right. I saw that painting once at the National Gallery of Art in Washington. What museum did you steal this one from?"

"It's never been shown in a museum. I bought it from a private estate in Detroit."

"I see. And that exhibit case over there? Why clown masks, of all things?"

"I got that collection from an old codger named Wally Olds who lived in Gib'town—that's Gibsontown, Florida, a town mostly inhabited by circus and carnival people. He was getting ready to move into a retirement home, and he wanted to make sure his collection of masks would be kept together. For fifty years he was an auguste clown with Ringling Brothers—"

"An auguste clown?"

"That's the white-faced clown in a circus act whose intentions are good but who always messes up. Mr. Olds took life masks of his clown friends, then painted them himself. Each clown's makeup is as individual as a fingerprint."

Wade opened the case and took out the mask of a sad-faced hobo with a red bulb of a nose and blubbering lip. "This one is Emmett Kelly—he was the greatest of the tramp clowns. Those two over there, of Dan Rice and Grimaldi, Mr. Olds did from old photographs. Along with Kelly, they're the big three of circus clowns."

"And the posters?" Larry asked, staring at the framed collection displayed together on one wall. "Are they rare? They look very old."

"Very old and rare." Wade pointed to a yellowed square of cardboard encased in tinted plastic. "This one shows Tom Thumb's wedding—in 1863. And that one over there is a Dan Rice poster from when he was with Howes' Circus in 1846. His tricks and gags are still standards with modern-day clowns."

Larry turned his attention to a brightly colored poster that looked much newer than the others. "And this one? It looks fresh off the press."

Wade hesitated, then wondered at his own reluctance to talk about his newest acquisition. "The Peeples Circus is one of the very few shows still under canvas—you know, still performing in tents. I expect it will eventually fold, too. So many of the small circuses have in the past decades."

"Well, the artist picked a real beauty to feature," Larry said, obviously fascinated by the woman on the poster. She was facing a snarling lion, her chin tilted at a defiant angle. Chestnut hair shot with golden highlights formed a cloud around her shoulders, and her amber eyes seemed to burn with an inner fire as she stared out of the poster, as if challenging not only the lion but the whole world.

The artist had used the same tawny shades to depict both woman and lion. Wade wasn't surprised when Larry commented, "She looks like a young lioness. Too bad she isn't real—or is she?"

"I doubt it, although I understand there is a female lion trainer named Tanya Rhodin with the Peeples Circus. If this is her picture, I suspect the artist took a lot of artistic license." With the hope of changing the subject, Wade picked up the martini shaker. "How about a refresher?"

Larry watched as Wade topped off both their glasses. "I feel a little better about you now, Wade. At least you have a hobby to keep you occupied."

"That's the wrong word. I have no need for hobbies. *Interest* is more like it—and an old one, at that. Just because I happened to stumble upon a Picasso painting that intrigued me at a time when I was decorating my apartment and led to my acquiring some circus memorabilia doesn't mean I intend to go on with it. The Peeples Circus poster is the only one I've added in years."

"Uh-huh. Well, don't knock hobbies. I recommend them highly. And I advise you, my friend, to take one up. It's obvious to me that hedonism is not your thing. Your eyes were glazed with boredom tonight, even when you were dancing with our senior senator's luscious daughter."

"Not bored. Just a little tired. Monica Clarkson is...very charming."

"Right. Charming. Elegant, sleek as a seal, and she knows all the latest buzzwords, the ones that pass for conversation in our crowd. Just what you need at this stage of your life—which is why you couldn't wait to get away for a quiet drink with your old buddy, Larry."

"So what do you suggest I take up? And don't bother to push your own hobby, golf. As far as I'm concerned, there's nothing quite as useless as knocking a ball around a golf course just for the sake of having something to do. It isn't even good exercise.''

"Then take up something else. Isn't there anything you wanted to do as a kid, something that excited your imagination?''

"Such as?''

"Oh, such as going around the world in a sailboat or climbing Mount Everest or—'' Larry nodded toward the posters on the wall ''—running away from home and joining a circus?''

Wade gave him a crooked smile. "Would you believe I once did just that?''

"*You* ran away to a circus? How did that come about?''

"I was sixteen, and things were pretty heavy at home.'' Wade hesitated a moment, then added, "You've met my brothers, of course, but I don't think I ever told you about my mother.''

"No, you've never talked about your parents. I know that you come from California, but that's about all.''

"Well, my father is dead, and my mother abdicated the job of raising her family when I was in my early teens and my four brothers were still kids. We all have different fathers—I'm the oldest by seven years. My father died when I was six. I just barely remember him. Mom remarried within three months and had Bobby nine months later. Then, two years after that, she had Paul and Peter—by her third husband. Her fourth husband fathered Andy just before that marriage busted up, too.''

And after that, he thought, though he didn't say it aloud, *she didn't bother to marry them.*

"Elaine—we always called her by her first name,

her preference—worked as a secretary for a talent agency," he went on. "She had a weakness for aspiring actors. She was so busy falling in love and having these great relationships that most of the time she forgot she had a family. So I took care of the younger kids, and I was getting pretty fed up with it, when I got a temporary job scrubbing down elephants at this small circus that was doing a three-day engagement in North Long Beach. I decided that was the life for me—no responsibilities, a chance to see the country, money in my pocket that I'd earned myself and didn't have to spend on my younger brothers. I looked more like eighteen than sixteen, so when the bull-boss offered me a permanent job working as an elephant handler, I grabbed it."

He paused briefly as memories came flooding back. "It was one hell of a summer. Sometimes I wonder what my life would've been like if I'd stayed with the circus. It's funny...even now, after all this time, whenever I smell popcorn my mind flashes back to that summer."

"So why did you return home? Your conscience give you a hard time?"

"It was the man who owned the circus—Pop Peeples. When he realized how young I was and got my story out of me, he made me see that I wasn't the type to run away from responsibility. He staked me to bus fare and I went back home."

"Where you finished your education, went into electronics, opened your own company with that revolutionary modem you invented, built yourself an empire, put your brothers through school and saw that they were established in their own businesses— all at the expense of a private life of your own."

"I had no choice. Someone had to take charge."

"It's odd, you know. I always assumed that you and your brothers were orphans, Wade."

There was a question in Larry's voice. Wade, who knew his friend's curiosity so well, hesitated. No matter what his private views of his mother might be, he had already said enough—perhaps too much.

"My mother has married again and is living in Bermuda," he said briefly. He didn't add that his stepfather, a sometime golf pro, was fifteen years her junior and that both of them lived on the more than generous allowance he sent them every month on the condition they not meddle in his or his brothers' lives.

"And *you* live in New York and are something of a closet circus buff."

"Not a buff," Wade protested. "I haven't been to a circus in years."

"Well, maybe you should go more often. It's obvious you have some highly romanticized ideas about a rather sordid way of life—"

"Where the hell did you get that idea?" Wade interrupted hotly. "Circus people are highly moral. They have a code of honor that is much more rigid than some of the double-dealing the business world is capable—" He stopped, staring at his friend's knowing smile. "You've been playing the devil's advocate, I see."

"Right. And you just came up with the solution to your ennui, my friend. *There's* your hobby, the one you should pursue."

"Are you suggesting—surely you aren't suggesting I buy a circus!"

"Who said anything about buying one? I'm suggesting you indulge the boy in you, the boy that grew up too fast and never really had a childhood. I think you should run off and join a circus, live out your childhood fantasy, the dream that got away.''

He gave Wade a wry smile. ''You say you've often wondered what would've happened if that circus owner hadn't talked you into returning home? Well, it would have ended the same way, you know. Eventually you would have gone home on your own. Aside from your overgrown conscience, you have too much drive to settle for a marginal existence among a bunch of... well, not losers, but certainly not people in the mainstream of life. Now you can have it both ways. You can afford to indulge the boy in you. So go for it. I'm betting it will bring you out of your doldrums, if only because you'll get it out of your system.''

But Wade was already shaking his head. ''And your patients pay you a hundred-plus an hour for this kind of advice?''

''Most of my patients are just the opposite of you. I have to work hard to get them to accept responsibility. But you—that's the story of your life, isn't it? Meeting your obligations, doing your duty. And now your brothers no longer need you, and you're rich enough to do anything you like with the rest of your life. So do something completely wild and crazy and off the wall. When you get tired of it, then you can decide what comes next. One thing I'm sure of—idleness isn't the answer, and neither is hedonism.''

Before Wade could tell him he had no intention of doing anything so juvenile as running off with a circus, one of his guests stuck her beautifully coiffed head in the door and demanded that he rejoin his own party. During the next few hours as he laughed and joked and danced with the guests he'd invited, he knew no one would suspect that only half his mind was occupied with being a good host.

But after the last guest was gone, including Monica Clarkson, the senator's daughter, who had dropped several hints that she was willing to stay, Wade retreated to his den, leaving his houseman and a crew of caterers' helpers to clean up the mess. For a long time he stood in front of the circus-poster collection before he turned out the lights and went to bed.

In the morning, after he'd breakfasted on the omelet and bacon his live-out housekeeper had prepared for him, he picked up his phone, dialed long-distance information and got the number of the Showman's League in Tampa, Florida. A few minutes later he had the business address of the Peeples Circus—and their route list for the rest of the summer.

After all, he told himself as he jotted down the information, what did he have to lose except time, and for once in his life he had more of that than he needed.

CHAPTER TWO

IT WAS STILL DARK when Tanya Rhodin slipped out of her snug little trailer. Stretching out on all sides in orderly rows were the mobile homes of other circus employees, everything from thirty-six-foot luxury Winnebagos to tiny silver teardrops to converted vans and cab-over RVs. Circus people called this area, the living quarters of a circus lot, the "back-yard." For the next five days the backyard of the Peeples Circus would be located at the municipal fairgrounds in Topeka, Kansas.

Tanya was dressed warmly against the early-morning chill in well-worn jeans and a bulky sweater, her heavy mane of hair tucked under a Greek fisher-man's cap. For a moment she paused to take a long breath, as if testing the air. An instinct, a feeling that was as much a part of her as her chestnut brown hair, her tawny skin and amber eyes, stirred. Lately, some-thing was off kilter with the circus. Octavia Barna, the circus's fortune-teller, would have called it "a bad aura," and her friend Marshall, who had literary leanings and who claimed to be the world's only ti-tled midget, would have said that "a miasma of trou-ble hangs over the circus."

With an impatient shrug Tanya went on, deter-mined not to think of unpleasant things. After all, this was her favorite time of the day, this hour just before the circus began to stir around her. Other than the security guards and the cook's helpers, who would be making coffee for early risers in the cook-house, she was one of the few people up and about, and she savored the relative quiet of these few minutes, the only time of the day she seemed to have completely to herself.

Her step soundless on the hard, packed-down earth, she moved quickly toward the second largest of the menagerie tents, stopping once to rearrange the piece of plastic wrap she'd put around the bowl of food she was carrying. As a professional animal trainer—no circus person ever used the term animal *tamer*—she seldom indulged her big cats, experience telling her that respect between the big beasts and humans must be rigidly maintained. Leopold, the oldest of her cats, was that rare exception. If there were saints among lions, he was one. Even so, her circus friends would tease her unmercifully if they ever caught her bringing Leopold a bowl of his favorite food on the sly.

By the time she had reached the menagerie tent, the sky above the fairgrounds was streaked with color. Only one light, a naked bulb suspended from a pole, burned inside the tent as she slid through the canvas opening. An assortment of odors, sharp, pungent and ammoniac, assaulted her nostrils, but they were so familiar that they no longer registered. Leopold, in the first of the cages, was lying on his side in his favorite sleeping position, his head on one front paw and his rear legs braced against the bars. Although Tanya's step was as light as a cat's, he sensed her presence and raised his massive head to stare at her. A rumbling sound started up in his throat.

The largest of her seven lions, he was also the most majestic looking with his dark mane and long side whiskers, his broad nose and golden, black-fringed eyes. With a grumbling moan he rose lithely; his rose-colored tongue emerged from between ivory teeth to curl around the triangle of his nose in anticipation of the treat he knew would be forthcoming. When Tanya opened the cage door quietly and slipped inside, closing it behind her, he batted one paw against the floor of the cage, his throat vibrating with delight.

Tanya scolded him fondly as she unwrapped the bowl and set it before him. "What an old fraud you are! If the towners saw you slurping down strawberries and sour cream, they'd say you're getting a little long in the tooth. And they'd be right. Right now you're the leader of the pack, but someday the younger cats will find out you're just an overgrown pussycat, and then you'll be in big trouble."

She sat back on her haunches, watching as Leopold polished off the strawberries. By the time he was finished, his nose was covered with sour cream, and she wiped it off with a tissue, muttering affectionate insults about his sloppiness, his laziness, his general failings as a ferocious lion. Leopold yawned, then rolled to his side with a long complacent sigh. Tanya yawned, too, and settled down beside him, using his back as a headrest.

Her thoughts drifted. Lately she had felt... well, restless was the word that came to mind. Maybe it was the responsibilities that suddenly seemed to be crowding in on her these days, or maybe it was simply uneasiness about the two new tigers Pop Peeples had bought from a wild-animal broker and who were still such enigmas. Even though she'd been observing them for three days, she hadn't yet made up her mind about them. She'd be working the male for the first time today. After the first few minutes she'd know if the animal broker had been lying when he'd told Pop they were completely wild.

"Straight off the boat," he'd claimed.

But he'd been pretty vague about details, and the price had been much too low for two such prime animals. Tigers were extraordinarily expensive because they didn't breed well in captivity the way lions did, and so were much scarcer. If they were completely untrained, the circus had a bargain. Cats raised in the wild were still wary of humans, and the procedure for training them was much more simple. But if they had been domestically raised, the pampered pets of some so-called animal lover, they probably had learned contempt for humans, and that called for a more complicated method of training. No matter how long she worked with them, they would always be unpredictable and a source of special problems.

She would know soon after she faced the male in the training cage today. Certainly the price had been right—a factor that was becoming increasingly important to the circus these past few years.

Tanya frowned, remembering Pop's last session with the government auditors. The fine they'd levied for overdue taxes had taken a bite out of the profits last year. The circus was still holding on—but just barely. One disaster, such as a long rainy spell, and they would be in big trouble. Lately it had been obvious that Pop was deeply worried. Of course he always had a lot on his mind, but this was different, as if he was hiding something. For one thing, he was just a little too hearty, too talkative, and that was a sure sign he was covering up something he didn't want her to know.

Leopold lifted his head and gave his grumbling

cry, "Ooh-ah, ooh-ah," and she realized he was awake, watching her. She knuckled his broad brow affectionately, then settled her head against his back again.

It had always seemed to her that there was something magical about the sounds of a waking circus. This was her world, the only place she'd ever wanted to be. Even though she'd been born in a tent, she'd never yearned for distant horizons, never made half-serious jokes about "running away to join a home," as other circus people did. To outsiders circus life might seem stifling and narrow, but to Tanya it encompassed the whole world.

In a few hours the fairgrounds, the midway and concession stands would come alive, and then the Spec, short for Spectacular, the walkaround of the performers, the clowns and the animals that always began the Big Show, would start in the exhibition hall. No matter how many times she witnessed it and was a part of it, the excitement, the color and pageantry had never lost their magic for her.

She heard the clatter of footsteps, then men's voices and deep laughter. Someone called out a strident, "Cookie's flag is up!" and she knew that the day had officially begun. The unattached working men who lived in the dorm tents—roughies, or roughnecks, tent men, canvas handlers, electricians, laborers and mechanics—would be heading toward the cookhouse for their morning coffee, for pancakes and sweet rolls, grits and scrambled eggs, bacon and toast, as well as a little roughhousing and an exchange of good-natured insults.

Those who lived in the backyard in their trailers or who stayed in nearby motels would be stirring, too, getting ready for the day ahead, for the 101 chores involved in putting together the matinee and evening shows that would entertain and delight the circus's patrons.

Tanya stood and stretched, then bent to give Leopold's leonine head a final pat. He opened one eye, groaned, then closed it again.

"You're lazy—like all male lions. Letting the females do all the work. Shame on you!" she scolded.

She locked the cage door behind her and moved along the line of holding cages, pausing in front of each one to examine the cat inside with appraising eyes. Morris Vaughn, who was not only her head cageman but the menagerie boss, would be along soon to supervise the feeding of the big cats, making sure they got their daily ration of food, which included sixteen pounds of raw meat each. He would personally dispense cod-liver oil, lime water and worm medicine as needed, and afterward his two assistants, Moon and Charlie, would hose down the floor of the cages, which were kept immaculate because the big cats were subject to stomach disorders and infection.

Morris had been with the circus for twenty-five years. He knew as much about animal care as any veterinarian, and his two helpers were just as conscientious and reliable. Even so, Tanya was always very much aware that it was her life that was on the line every time she went into the Big Cage, so the health of the cats was something she took very seriously. A lioness with a toothache or a tiger with an ear canker was a very touchy animal and totally unpredictable. That she had so far escaped the scarring common to most lion trainers was because she had been taught since childhood to be wary of them, to be constantly vigilant and never, not even for a moment, take them for granted or let down her guard.

Except with Leopold, she thought, smiling to herself. *He breaks all the rules.*

She was standing in front of the cage that held one of the new tigers, a male, when Morris Vaughn joined her. He was past middle age and had a perpetual squint and long, lanky hair. He seldom smiled, nor did he waste time with idle chatter. For a while he sized up the male tiger, watching as it silently prowled back and forth behind the bars, its eyes reflecting the overhead light. "Whatta you think, Tanya?" he asked.

"I think Pop should've let you look them over before he bought them," she said bluntly. "They're supposed to be wild, right off the boat, but they didn't get sleek and fat like that hunting zebras in the bush. This one's left-pawed—watch this." She rattled the cage door and the great yellow tiger rushed toward it, swatting it with his left paw, his tail twitching angrily.

Morris nodded. "How about the female?"

"She's left-pawed, too. I think they're from the same litter—their markings are almost identical. Well, they're a pair of beauties. They'll add flash to the act."

"At least they ain't neither of them cross-eyed," Morris growled. "Lord deliver me from a cross-eyed cat."

Tanya laughed at his glum tone. "Or one with a kink in his tail?" she teased.

"You can laugh if you wantta, but I know what I know. There's some things you pick up when you've been with the business as long as I have. Take a long-nosed cat with a narrow head. That's a sign of inbreeding every time. Warped minds and no brains— and I don't like the way this tiger is so quiet, never making no fuss like the female does. Give me a noisy rebel every time. You know where you stand with that kind."

She nodded. "I'll keep a close eye on him," she promised.

"You want I should set up the Big Cage this morning?"

"The sooner the better. Have to take advantage of this layover date," she said, referring to the circus's relatively long engagement at the fairgrounds.

"Well, the layovers give the ladies a chance to do some laundry," he said sourly, "but they sure don't fill the money bags, not when they're sponsored by a civic organization. You ask me, there's been too many of that kind this tour. And it's about time we gave up the canvas and moved indoors all the time. Less fuss that way. The season can be longer, too, when we don't have to worry so much about the weather."

"I know you're right, but I'd miss the Big Top," Tanya said wistfully. "It doesn't seem the same without the smell of tanbark underfoot."

Morris grunted, a sound that could have meant anything. "So okay, Tanya," he said. "I'll round up Moon and a couple of roughies and get that cage up. You gonna keep the session closed?"

Tanya considered his words. Ordinarily it didn't matter to her if she had an audience, even when she was working with new animals. Her concentration when she was in the cage was total, so why was she nodding, agreeing that it would be best to keep spectators away when she faced the male for the first time? Was it because of the unusual intelligence in the tiger's eyes as he watched her, his ears flattened against his head?

"Good," Morris said. "Not that an audience ever seems to bother you, even when you're working on a new routine. I've never seen anyone who could concentrate like you do. When we had that thunderstorm in Missouri last week, you didn't even notice it until your act was over.''

"Oh, I noticed, all right. I kept praying the noise wouldn't spook the cats—and that the power wouldn't go off. And if you see Pop, keep any doubts you have about the tigers under your hat or he's sure to be fussing around like a nervous nellie.''

"You're his family, girl. He couldn't think no more of you if you was his own daughter,'' Morris said gruffly. "That's how all of us feel about you. We don't want nothing should happen to you.''

Unexpectedly Tanya felt like crying, an impulse so rare with her that she muttered something about getting dressed and rushed off toward her trailer. She changed into a rust-colored T-shirt, tucking it into her jeans so there wouldn't be any flapping tails to tempt a nervous tiger, and she pinned back her thick hair with a copper hair clip to keep it out of the way. As always when she was facing a new cat for the first time, she was exhilarated rather than nervous. It had been years since she'd felt any real fear of the cats, though this didn't prevent her from being careful.

Before she left her trailer, she paused for a moment in front of the framed photographs that were hanging on the wall near the door. In one, a radiantly beautiful blond woman with dark blue eyes was smiling into the camera. She was wearing a sequined white satin costume and she perched on the edge of a trapeze, looking as if she might launch herself into air at any moment. The other photograph was of a man. His hair was brown and his eyes were the same amber as Tanya's; he had a lithe athlete's body. Like the woman he was in costume—a red tunic with black jodhpurs—and he was carrying a whip and a stout hickory stick, the trademarks of a lion trainer.

Tanya felt a wave of sadness. Her father had died when she was three; her only tie to him was this picture and a scrapbook of clippings about his career as a lion trainer. Her mother, too, had died tragically young, and her death, from a fall while she was performing on the trapeze, had left Tanya without relatives.

A knock at the door interrupted her thoughts. She shook off her depression and went to answer it. The woman standing there was plump and undeniably plain, but her smile lent her face the illusion of beauty as she bustled in to give Tanya a hug. Alice Tolbert, the wife of Too Tall Tim, who was billed—untruthfully—as the world's tallest man, was the circus's wardrobe mistress. Not only was she a genius at devising new costumes for the artistes, as the performers preferred to call themselves, but she was also always available when someone needed repairs on a costume—or a sympathetic ear for troubles. Until she had saved enough to buy her own trailer, Tanya had lived with the Tolberts in their big custom-built motor home, and she still regarded them as family, just as she did most of the old-timers with the circus.

Alice stared at the pristine clean stove and sink in the trailer's tiny kitchen and gave an audible sniff. Tanya resigned herself to a familiar lecture, knowing how much Alice disapproved of her breakfast habits. "You're skipping meals again, I see," Alice scolded. "I swear, since you got your own trailer, you just don't eat right. Why don't I fix you a couple of eggs, or maybe some French toast?"

Tanya shook her head firmly, but she promised to eat a big lunch. She knew the reason for Alice's constant fussing over her. During those years following her mother's fatal fall, Alice had tried to be mother as well as friend to Tanya, as had so many others.

Sometimes while she was growing up, Tanya had had the feeling that everybody in the circus was her surrogate mother or father.

There was Marshall, the midget from England, who had an Oxford education and had taught her arithmetic and history and had made her understand the beauty of language. Then there was Octavia, who read tarot cards to clients in the fortune-teller's booth and who claimed to be a Gypsy but was really Hungarian with no Gypsy blood at all, and Too Tall Tim with his gentle humor and his loving heart. And Pop Peeples. The day after her mother's funeral, Pop had called a meeting and had brought up the question of what to do about Tanya. The circus people had voted unanimously to raise her as one of their own instead of turning her over to an institution, a decision she was eternally grateful for.

She must have sighed, because Alice's eyes sharpened. "What is it? You don't look well. Maybe you're coming down with something."

"I'm fine, Alice," Tanya said quickly. What she didn't want was one of Alice's evil-tasting home remedies. "I just feel... well, kind of restless lately."

Alice studied her carefully; unexpectedly her eyes grew a twinkle. "It's spring—and you're just the right age," she said mysteriously. "Lord, I was already married three years by the time I was twenty-one!"

"Uh-huh. Who do you have in mind for me—Acey Brenner, maybe?" Tanya was careful to keep a straight face.

"That Romeo! Why, he's a womanizer and twenty years older than you, to boot." Alice's voice held outrage. "You aren't interested in that poor excuse for a man, are you?"

"I've had a crush on Acey for ages," Tanya lied blandly. "He looks so handsome in his bandmaster's uniform—even if he is losing his hair and getting a paunch."

Alice gave another sniff and a reluctant smile. "Well, joke all you want about it, but eventually you'll fall for someone. I just hope he's good enough for you. You're so . . . well, you really don't know much about men, for all you've been raised on a circus lot."

"I'm not exactly an innocent," Tanya said dryly. "I know all about the birds and the bees."

"Knowing about something and experiencing it is something else. One of these days you're going to fall hard—and with your nature, it'll be all the way. I just hope—" She broke off.

"Hope what?"

"That he isn't some bum who will ruin your life. You should marry someone in the business, one of your own kind."

"You don't have to worry. I think I've already found the right man," Tanya said, unable to resist teasing her friend. "There was this man who was asking Pop for work yesterday. Bronze-colored hair and blue, blue eyes and a great build—"

She broke off abruptly, feeling uncomfortable. What had started out as an attempt to tease Alice had suddenly provoked a disturbing image in her mind of the man she'd seen talking to Pop Peeples the day before. The stranger had been tall and broad shouldered, with a self-assurance in the way he held his head that was unusual for a roughie, and yet he'd been asking Pop for a job. Although she'd slipped away unnoticed, she'd found herself thinking of him several times during the rest of the day, wondering if he'd been hired.

"A roughie?" Alice said. "You talking about a roughneck?"

"What's wrong with that? After all, he's in the business," Tanya pointed out. "That is, if Pop hired him."

"You should marry an artiste. That oldest Zorbi boy—he's from old circus stock and he's got a good future with his family's juggling act. Risley acts can always find work, and he's been mooning over you ever since they signed up last year."

"Not my type. He's all muscles and no brains."

"Well, don't you go falling for no roughie. They don't stay around long. Here today and off tomorrow with some forty-miler carnival," Alice said with the contempt most circus people hold for carnivals.

"Well, I guess I could always take up with some towner."

Alice snorted. "Towners—you'd go crazy living on the outside. Find yourself a circus man, someone decent and hardworking who will understand what you do and—" She stopped to give Tanya's expressionless face a closer look. "And that's not what I came here to talk to you about. It's Octavia. She's having one of her spells. Do you think you can fill in for her after the matinee? I think Tim and I can get her straightened out in time to catch the overflow from the evening performance."

They exchanged understanding looks. Octavia, when she was in one of her periodic depressions, found solace in a wine bottle. She was so good at what she did, telling fortunes with tarot cards, that the revenue loss when her tent was unmanned was very costly to the circus.

"Okay, although I'm not nearly as good as Octavia is," Tanya said, already making plans. Since the Big Cage was so difficult to set up and take down, her act was always the last one during matinees and the first at the evening performance. If she hurried, she could change her clothes and be in Octavia's booth a few minutes after the matinee show ended.

"I'll drop by Octavia's trailer and pick up one of her turbans and a costume. What set her off this time?"

"She was crying and carrying on like crazy, but it was in Hungarian. I think it has something to do with an anniversary."

Both women were silent. Although it wasn't the habit of circus people to ask personal questions, even of long-time friends, everybody knew that Octavia had escaped from Hungary with only the clothes on her back; the rest of her family hadn't been so lucky. It came to Tanya that Alice was looking unusually grave and worried. "What's wrong?" she asked. "Is something else bothering you?"

"It's—well, we lost another act to the Cookson Brothers Circus," Alice said, shaking her head.

"Which one?"

"The Auklanders."

Tanya groaned. Although the Auklander family was new this year and always kept to themselves, they were an agile, inventive acrobatic group. Their absence would leave a hole in the lineup, and they would be almost impossible to replace this late in the season.

"Well, maybe Pop can find someone to fill in," Tanya said, trying to sound optimistic. "Until he does, I can do a stall act. If I stretch out my time another five minutes, it will take up some of the slack, and the aerial-ballet girls can do some extra cloud-swings and turns on the webs. I'll hold Leopold back and do my face-in-the-lion's-mouth bit."

She winced. "Leopold detests it, you know. I think it insults his dignity, and I'm not exactly crazy about it either. His breath is enough to knock out an elephant."

Alice laughed at the face Tanya made. "Just keep smiling, and no one in the audience will ever know. The rest of the acts can extend their time, too, which will take care of it for now. But the audience expects a lot of variety, you know. I hate to think what could happen if we lost another star act."

"How did the Cookson brothers contact the Auklanders?"

"I don't know for sure. I did see a middle-aged guy—he was wearing a suit, looked like a towner—talking to Hans Auklander after the show in Kansas City. Maybe that's when the Cooksons made the offer."

Tanya nodded and finished dressing. She put on her leather gloves and found her whip and training stick, then strapped a blanking gun around her narrow waist. Although the gun didn't shoot bullets, the flash of the blanks was usually enough to repulse an attack, unless the big cat had been around long enough to lose his fear of man.

"So you're working one of the new tigers this morning," Alice said, eyeing the training stick with its fringe of noisy cans.

Tanya didn't find it strange that her friend expressed no concern about her safety. After all, this was her profession, the thing she knew best. Besides, circus people were superstitious, and Alice would have considered it unlucky to warn her to be careful.

"Are they domesticated or wild?" Alice asked.

"The broker claims they're just off the boat. The female seems man-shy, but the male...he's a little too quiet. If he shows any intelligence, I'll work him into the act as we go along, maybe teach him to do a rollover or, if he isn't afraid of fire, a hoop jump. But for a while, as soon as they're broken to the Big Cage, I'll just use them as seat warmers to pretty up the act." She dismissed the subject with a shrug and added, "Don't bother Pop about Octavia. I'll take over for her after the matinee. He won't even have to know about it."

"Okay, but it seems to me that everybody dumps on you these days, Tanya, even the head bullman. I saw you sitting up there on old Maisie during the Spec last week."

"Freddy was shorthanded, and my backside is still sore," Tanya said, making a face. "If there's anything that's got more bristles than an elephant's hide, I don't know what it is."

"Well, I have to go do some mending. I think the entire aerial ballet ripped their tights at last night's performance," Alice said with a sigh. But she lingered long enough to give Tanya a searching look. "Don't try to take on too much, hon," she advised. "Let Pop worry about the circus."

Unexpectedly Tanya's sight blurred and she looked away quickly, ashamed that she'd lost control of her emotions for the second time that day. "I owe you all so much, Alice," she said. "Pop could've turned me over to the Tampa social-service people when mom was killed, and he never could have raised me without the help of the rest of you. It's only natural I'm concerned about you all."

"That's plain silly. Sure, we're none of us as young as we used to be, but we're all still kicking, aren't we?" Alice's face saddened suddenly, and Tanya knew she was thinking of her husband, Too

Tall Tim. At forty-five he had already lived years longer than most people afflicted with the glandular disorder that caused giantism.

Aware that this was a constant worry in Alice's mind, Tanya put her arms around the older woman. "I'm the luckiest girl in the world to have friends like you and Tim. Everything I need is right here—in this circus."

Alice bristled, hiding her pleasure. "Get along with you! One of these days you'll meet a fellow and fall in love, and then you'll follow him wherever he wants to go. And that's the way it should be."

"He'd better be willing to stay with Peeples Circus," Tanya said firmly.

"You say that like you're kidding, but there's enough truth in it to worry me. You take too much on your shoulders, Tanya. Everybody's gotten into the habit of using you to help out and fill in, including me."

"I don't mind. It's one way I can pay you back."

"Take care you don't overdo it. Just live your own life and let that be enough."

Tanya didn't argue with Alice. Instead she turned the conversation to the latest rumor that was going around the circus. But after Alice had returned to her mending, Tanya thought about their conversation, wondering why it had left her feeling so uneasy. Was it Alice's advice, or was it something else? And why, she thought angrily, did she keep thinking about that blasted bronze-haired man? He was just another drifter—and the last man in the world she could ever become interested in.

CHAPTER THREE

IT WAS STILL EARLY AFTERNOON when Wade arrived at the Topeka Fairgrounds to ask for a job with the Peeples Circus. Even so, the midway was already bustling with activity. Although the big show had moved into the fairground's exhibition hall for this engagement, a collection of tents, looking like dusty brown mushrooms, was lined up in the grassy meadows on both sides of the midway, sharing space with gayly painted wooden booths and, at the lower half of the midway, a variety of mechanized rides.

From the banners above the largest tent, which housed the "ten-in-one" show, Wade saw that the circus's current collection of human oddities included a midget called Lord Marshall, who claimed to be a real English duke, Too Tall Tim, billed as the tallest man in the world, a bearded lady named Lydia, as well as the usual assortment of sword swallowers and fire eaters and snake charmers.

A sign on a small tent near the entrance of the exhibition building, tucked between a Bally game and a cotton-candy booth, announced that Madame Octavia, Gypsy fortune-teller extraordinaire, would reveal the past, the present and the future of anyone in need of advice and counsel.

Other tents and booths sheltered stand-up grab joints, where pronto pups and hamburgers, hot dogs and pizza and sundaes on a stick were dispensed, or

"hanky-panks," where the customers could pitch
pennies into baskets or shoot at plastic ducks to win
one of the small prizes called "slum," which probably
had cost the concessionaire only a few cents whole-
sale, or, much less likely, a "plush" prize such as a
stuffed animal.

Wade stood for a while, watching the joey clown at
the dunking booth needling a customer into investing
a dollar for the pure pleasure of dropping him into the
icy water of the tank. As Wade walked on, the sounds
of the midway rose and fell around him like the chorus
under the baton of a manic bandleader—the whistles
and groans of the brightly painted ferris wheel; the tin-
ny music of the carousel; the sharp ping of a wooden
block being hurled upward by some athlete who was
trying to ring the bell at the top of the High Striker; the
swish of compressed air as the Tip-Top whirled its
three-seated metal baskets around and around; the
shriek of a customer inside the Hall of Mirrors.

Rising above the other sounds were the cries of the
talkers, working hard to turn a tip and coax the customers into playing their games or buying their
wares.

"Come on, come on. Health by the gallon, pink
lemonade for your kiddies right here, ladies!" "You
dunk your doughnuts, don'tcha? So dunk a man. Hit
the trigger with a ball and see him drop in the water."
"Lady, lady, lady—you look like an Annie Oakley to
me—take a chance and hit the trick and win yourself
a nice prize." "Right this way. Bingo, bingo, bingo.
You win, we lose, but that's how it goes!" "Mister,
mister, your lady wants a souvenir. So step right in
and have your picture took. Your head on a giraffe
or an elephant or a hippo." "Souvenirs, souvenirs,
souvenirs! All prime quality, all top grade...."

And the odors.... Wade sniffed happily. As he inhaled the mingled odors of caramel corn and diesel fuel, the cloying sweetness of cotton candy and the pungency of roasting peanuts, the years rolled off him and he felt as if he were sixteen again.

As he walked on, he noted the subtle signs that told him that the Peeples Circus hadn't changed, that it was still a "Sunday school" operation, with no grifters or flatties or other con games welcome, thank you. It showed in the neat white shirts and black bow ties universally worn by the booth attendants, in the cleanliness of the midway, in the generous application of colored sawdust on any spot that might raise dust.

Many things in his own life had changed since he'd spent his sixteenth summer with Peeples Circus, but here time seemed to have stood still. Or was the air of prosperity an illusion, like the contorted and bewildering corridors of the Hall of Mirrors? How was the circus really faring? Was it merely surviving, as most of the country's small circuses were these days, or was it continuing to prosper in this era of cable TV and video recorders?

A few minutes later, the slightly sour but not unpleasant odor of elephants drew him toward the menagerie tents. During the weeks that he'd worked as an elephant handler, he had developed a fondness and a deep respect for the huge, intelligent beasts. His private name for the one in his charge had been Gray Lady, because in certain respects she had possessed a nobility of character.

As he approached the corner of the lot where a crudely painted sign had been nailed to a barrel and warned Keep Out—This Means You, he looked around with interest, noting that there were six ele-

phants, not the twelve that he remembered, lined up
beside the largest menagerie tent.

Each was chained by its left back and right front
legs to an iron stake, the chain hook inserted between
two links so that it would take both hands to unhook.
Wade smiled to himself, remembering that he'd
learned this particular lesson the hard way when the
supple trunk of his charge—what *had* her name
been? Mamie, no, Maisie, had deftly unhooked the
chain and loped off for half an hour's freedom in a
nearby field.

Just beyond the stake line was a large portable water
tank, flanking a small square tent that he knew must
be the menagerie's donniker—the portable sanitary
facilities. Wade had spent one ignoble day chasing all
over the circus and being passed from one circus hand
to another as he looked for the key to the donniker, a
joke he hadn't appreciated at the time. But ragging a
First-of-May guy, a newcomer, was part of the game.
If he was hired, he'd undoubtedly be the target of
more practical jokes, unless things had changed drastically in the past few years.

"Yeah? You looking for someone, cap?" a male
voice asked. The speaker was a small, pug-faced
man, stripped to the waist. He was standing in front
of a mirror that was hanging on a tent post, a straight
razor in his hand. Half his face was covered with
shaving lather. Two much younger men, little more
than boys, were lounging against a bale of straw,
watching Wade. Like all circus people in the presence
of strangers, they had fallen silent when they saw him
coming, which was why he hadn't noticed them until
now.

"I'm looking for a job—as a bull handler," Wade
said.

"You done it before?"

"A while back."

"Well, myself, I always hire boys for bullmen. They're lots more agile." He looked Wade over, taking in his faded jeans and denim jacket, the shadow of a beard he'd judiciously cultivated. "A husky fellow like you can always get a job as a roughie. Go see Pop Peeples. He owns this show. He's a damned good man to work for if you do your job and keep your nose clean."

Wade nodded. "I'll remember that."

The man, who introduced himself as Freddy, gave him terse directions for locating Peeples, and with one last look at the elephants, Wade went to find the man who had once had such an influence on his life. Did he owe Pop Peeples something for sending him home that summer sixteen years ago? It was more than probable, as Larry had pointed out, that he would have gone back on his own. Still, he was grateful to Peeples, if only because the circus owner had taken the time to try to straighten out a confused kid.

The business trailers, traditionally called silver wagons, were located in an out-of-the-way section of the fairgrounds. Two trailers, gleaming silver in the late June sunlight, sat at an angle, forming two sides of a triangle. Behind them was the ice trailer, where bags of crushed ice were constantly being manufactured and dispensed to the various booths, and also a maintenance truck, where everything from the tiniest screw to a complicated replacement part could be found.

One of the business trailers was outfitted with iron-grilled windows and a locked door. This was the bookkeeper's domain, where coins were exchanged for bills, and rolls of tickets, all carefully recorded, were dispensed. Pop Peeples both lived and held business meetings in the second trailer, which he used as a portable office and, when necessary, where he entertained local dignitaries and fairground officials.

A little to Wade's surprise, since it was midafternoon and Pop could be expected to be making his rounds of the midway, checking up on the quality of the crowd, he found Pop still in his office, poring over a stack of ledgers. For a moment, as Wade stood in the open door observing the older man, time again seemed to slip a clog and he was sixteen, back in his hometown, North Long Beach, California, trying to get up the courage to ask for a job.

Pop had the taut, wiry body of a bantam-weight boxer, which he'd once been. He looked much the same as he had sixteen years ago, except that his hairline had receded and his shoulders were a little more stooped. He had new lines in his face, too, or maybe they had always been there, Wade thought, and he just didn't remember.

Pop looked up then; his pale gray eyes sharpened, and for a moment Wade was sure he'd been recognized. Then Pop was beckoning for him to enter.

"Yeah?"

"I hear you might be hiring," Wade said.

Pop examined him for a long time, as if weighing him on some scale of his own. "You got any special skills?"

"I can handle simple carpentry, and I know my way around an engine," Wade said.

"Well, I've got plenty of carpenters and mechanics. But I could use another canvas man for when we raise the Big Top. If I sign you on the payroll, just do what you're told and we'll get along fine. This is a clean show. No grifters or flatties allowed—

and no going into business on your own, either. I control the concessions, fence to fence, except for the ones the locals arrange in advance for their private charities. Understood?''

"Understood, Mr. Peeples,'' Wade said.

"Call me Pop. So okay. Check in with Maude—that's my clerk—over in the silver wagon, and she'll give you a chit book. That'll get you a discount at any of the food-concession stands, or if you want, you can arrange to eat in the cookhouse. You got a car?''

"No, sir.''

"Well, tell Maude to assign you a bunk in the dorm tent for now. It's pretty crowded but it's dirt cheap. If you wanta stay in motels or make some arrangement to bunk down in a private trailer, that's up to you. If you've got a chauffeur's license and a clean record, you can earn some extra bread driving one of the rigs between stops. But I don't stand for no hot-rodding. Any traffic tickets come out of your pay, and any trouble with the law gets you fired. The hours are long, but you already know that if you've been with it before.''

"Understood,'' Wade said again.

Pop looked him over, a hint of puzzlement in his eyes. "You don't talk or look like the usual roughneck. Come down in the world a bit, have you? Well, nobody asks questions around a show. Just do your job and don't mess up and we'll get along okay. You understand?''

This time Wade only nodded, but Pop seemed satisfied.

"After you get squared away with Maude, report to Flat Iron Collins—he's the head canvas man. This time of day you'll probably find him over at the cookhouse, having a mug of coffee and a danish. He'll put you to work.''

With another nod Pop returned to the papers on his desk. Wade checked in with Pop's bookkeeper-clerk, then went in search of Flat Iron Collins, the man who would be his supervisor. He wasn't sure if he felt elated that it had been so easy to get a job or disgruntled because Pop hadn't recognized him.

It was past twelve that night when Wade finally rolled into the canvas bunk in the dorm tent he'd been assigned. As he tried to get comfortable on the narrow—and too short—cot, he thought of his own king-size bed in New York and groaned under his breath. As Pop Peeples had said, the tent was crowded. Tiers of bunks filled most of the space, leaving only narrow aisles between, and the air was stuffy, too warm, even though the June night outside was cool.

Despite his sore muscles from the unaccustomed exercise—he'd spent most of the day bagging ice—he felt an extraordinary sense of well-being. Was it because, for the first time in years, he was completely shut off from the stress of everyday life? No phones to bug him, no people he had to be polite to or even think about. He'd told his friends and acquaintances that he'd leased a yacht and would be taking a long cruise, that he'd be out of touch for a few months. He was sure there'd been speculations, but since he wasn't available for phone calls or invitations, he also knew that his absence would soon be relegated to yesterday's news.

Meanwhile, he was doing just what Larry had advised—reliving a boyhood dream. It wasn't something to which he could devote the rest of his life, of course. He knew his own competitive nature too well to fool himself about that. But for the time being the experience was so novel that he felt like a different man. He fell asleep to the sound of snores and coughs and someone muttering in his sleep, but he was so tired he tuned out the noise and didn't wake until the next morning.

His first duty of the day, he discovered after breakfast, was to help set up the Big Cage in the fairground's exhibition hall. The man he reported to was a cageman named Moon. He was a talkative man in his fifties, who was soon regaling Wade with stories of other circuses he'd been with in what he described as a long, checkered career. He had once been an animal trainer, specializing in a fight act, he bragged, but he'd lost his nerve. Now he took any job he could get, as long as it was with a circus.

"It gets in your blood, man," he said. "I'd rather clean out cages in a circus than work in an office for twice the bread. When I had my own act—I was with Vivona Brothers for almost four years—I did one of the star turns, a solo in the center ring. Then one day I got arena fever—you know, I lost my nerve and couldn't face the big cats anymore. It was rough, a real comedown for me, but it's been better since Pop Peeples took me on. He treats you like a man, no matter what your job—y'know what I mean? And it's a real pleasure working for Tanya Rhodin. This little ole gal is...well, I've seen them all, from Bobby McPherson to Chubby Gilfoyle to Mabel Stark, but Tanya is tops. Cool as ice when she's under fire—one of the best in the business."

"If she's that good, why doesn't she sign on with a bigger circus like Ringlings?" Wade asked as he helped the older man lift a section of steel bars and lock them into place in the large circular cage.

"She'd make more money than she does here, wouldn't she?"

Moon gave him a disgusted look. "You sure don't understand circus folks. Tanya grew up with this operation. She's like a daughter to half the old-timers here, including Pop. She's the main drawing card— fills the Big Top and takes up a lot of slack in the program, which is a little thin on talent these days."

An image suddenly slipped into Wade's mind. There had been a tiny pixie of a child with wistful eyes and a wild mane of sun-streaked brown hair who had pestered him no end the summer he'd been with the circus. She had played under the feet of the elephants, as unconcerned as if they were stuffed toys, and the big gray beasts had stepped around her with the delicacy of ballet dancers, letting her swing on their trunks and sometimes even sleep on their broad backs. She had tagged after him, following him like a shadow, even though he'd ignored her most of the time. Was it possible the woman Moon was talking about was the same girl? Hadn't her name been Tanya, or was his memory playing tricks on him?

"She's working a couple of new tigers, gonna start breaking one in this morning," Moon was saying. "Tricky business, putting a cat through its paces for the first time. We have to wait around and take the cage down as soon as she's done, so you'll get to see how she works. Stay close to me and don't get in the way."

Moon finished screwing the last section of steel bars into place and gave an okay sign to a tall, rail-thin man who was standing near the cage door, flanked by Pop Peeples and two burly roughies. One of the men held a water hose, while the other was fiddling with the gate mechanism of a canvas chute that was attached to the doors of a holding cage, a cage on wheels, one of two that had been pulled into the arena. In one, a massive lion watched the proceedings with somnolent eyes, while the tiger in the second cage prowled restlessly up and down, occasionally moaning low in his throat.

"Who's the thin guy with the squint?" Wade asked curiously.

"That's Morris Vaughn. He's the menagerie boss, and he also doubles as first-aid man for the whole outfit. He's better with the animals than any vet, even if he never got no degree. Been with Pop for more years than you been on this old earth—less'n you're older than you look." He lowered his voice to add, "Pop's like an old woman where Tanya's concerned. That's why he's turned up here today."

Wade started to ask Moon why Tanya was training new cats when the season was almost half over, but the question died on his lips. The woman who had just appeared on the ramp at the front of the arena had taken his breath away. As she walked toward them, her attention on Pop and the other men, she absently slapped the whip she was carrying against her thigh, and Wade recognized her as the girl on the poster in his den.

So she *was* real—and every bit as striking as her picture. In fact, the artist hadn't succeeded in conveying the grace of her slender body, with its tiny waist, high, firm breasts and slim hips. Nor had he done her justice in another area. Even in washed-out jeans and a cotton T-shirt, she had a sultry beauty that made Wade stare like a schoolboy. Her nose, small and straight and patrician, was an odd and intriguing contrast to a full-lipped mouth that looked as if it would respond with fire and passion to a man's kiss—but only to the kiss of a man of Tanya's own choosing, Wade thought.

With her high cheekbones, delicately arched eyebrows and almond-shaped eyes of amber smoke, she could have walked right off the fresco of some ancient Greek or Roman temple; the illusion of imperiousness was intensified a moment later when she looked up and saw Wade staring at her.

Her lips tightened to a straight line and her eyebrows came together in a frown. Wade braced himself, sure she meant to challenge his presence there. But Pop Peeples made some remark to her, diverting her attention. When she gave a husky laugh, something primitive and intensely male stirred deep inside Wade, and he felt deprived as she turned her back and circled the Big Cage, inspecting it carefully.

Satisfied finally, she made a sign to Moon, ignoring Wade. "That's Tanya," Moon said unnecessarily. "Ain't she something?"

"She's something, all right." Wade's voice sounded so hollow that he cleared his throat before he added, "What's next?"

"Well, Tanya's been studying them new tigers for several days, figuring them out and trying to decide whether she'll hafta use a collar and lunge rope on them or work them freewheeling style. So far they seem to be man-shy, which makes her pretty sure they were raised in the wild."

"Doesn't that make them more dangerous?"

"Naw, it makes them easier to train. You watch and you'll see. She won't do much today except maybe try to get the male up on one of the seat blocks." He pointed to the heavy cubes of wood they'd carried inside the cage earlier. "And she'll bring in old Leopold, too, to get the tiger used to being in the same cage with a lion, see? There ain't nothing a tiger hates more than a lion—and that's one reason you always want a mix. That way, the lions and tigers are so busy hating each other and trying to figure out how to tangle, they don't have time to go after the trainer.''

"And the gun on her hip? Would she kill the tiger if it gets out of control?"

Moon gave him a disgusted look. "Kill him! Why, tigers are almost worth their weight in gold. That's a blanking gun. It don't have no real bullets in it! It just makes a flash and a lot of noise. The big cats hate noise. That's why Tanya's got cans tied to the end of her training stick. She'll use the chair, too. The tiger'll be leery of tangling with them legs. Course this tiger is whatcha call an unknown quality. No telling how wised-up he is. Hell, the guy who sold them to Pop didn't even know if they'd been named. But they came cheap, and Tanya lost both her tigers to a virus just before we left winter quarters, so he hadta take a chance on them. If it turns out they're too dumb or unreliable to train, she'll use them as seat warmers.''

"Seat warmers?"

"You know, they just sit on their pedestal and look pretty, don't do no tricks. Some cats are so slow-witted you can't even teach them to roll over— and that's the easiest trick of all.''

Tanya slipped into the cage, the door clicking shut behind her. She studied the blocks of wood, changed their position slightly, then glanced toward the burly man who was manning the chute gate. "Let him in, Charlie," she said in a conversational tone.

Wade watched, his mouth dry, as she positioned the sturdy chair in front of her, her eyes fixed on the chute. A moment later, urged by the wooden prod of the cagemen and their cries of "Hi-yuh! Hi-yuh!" the tiger came out of the chute in a rush, his yellow eyes smoldering, his ears flattened against his head, his tail lashing angrily. When he spotted Tanya, he stopped, staring.

"What he does next is what counts," Moon said in a low voice. "If he takes his time, feeling Tanya out before he rushes her, then he's got some respect for humans. But if he figures her for easy meat and springs right off, then watch out. He either hates people like crazy or he's learned contempt for them, and then she'll always have trouble with that tiger."

Tanya, her eyes watchful, stood very still and straight with the training stick extended, the chair ready in her left hand. Her body language radiated confidence. Only the whiteness of her knuckles holding the stick and the slight, almost imperceptible rise and fall of her chest gave sign that she had any nerves at all.

The tiger, prowling back and forth, watched her in turn; it was a while before he decided to test her. With a rush so fast it took Wade by surprise, he sprang at her—and promptly got a piston-quick clout on his nose with the stick. With a snarl that showed an expanse of yellow teeth, he backed away, circled, then lunged again. Tanya stepped aside, her body moving as lithely as the big cat's, and this time she was the one who pounced, the chair extended toward the tiger, using the intimidating chair legs and the noisy cans on the end of her stick to force him, inch by painful inch, into the bars.

"Seat!" she commanded, her voice imperious. The tiger only crouched there, watching her with angry eyes.

She used several words that Wade recognized as the same command in other languages, but the cat didn't respond other than to edge along the bars, his eyes watchful.

"I'd swear the bloody cat's been trained, Morris," Tanya said finally, not taking her eyes off the tiger. "But he doesn't understand English, French, Swedish or even Zulu!"

"Try German," Morris called.

"Sitz!" Tanya said.

The tiger gave a plaintive cry, as if asking a question, before he crept toward her, his sinewy body tense.

"Sitz!" Tanya's voice rang out again. She didn't back away, but this time she gave the stick in her hand a shake, setting the cans to rattling.

The tiger snarled; his ears flat against his head, he stared at the stick with its troublesome and noisy cans. Tanya repeated the command in the same tone of voice, making the same downward gesture, and the tiger shook his head, as if trying to brush off a pesky fly. When, for the fourth time, she barked the command, he gave a final snarl and then, slowly and with obvious reluctance, sat back on his haunches.

Tanya laughed. "So you have had some training," she said. "And in German. But what's your name? And what else can you do? Let's see if we can get you up on that pedestal."

For the next few minutes it was a war of nerves, Tanya advancing, not allowing the tiger to escape her commands or her noisy cans. Only when the big cat finally stopped prowling and settled back on his haunches again did she rap the wooden block and rap out another command in German. Not to Wade's surprise, a few minutes later the tiger was sitting on one of the pedestals, looking anything but happy.

"So you know that much, but what did they name you?" Tanya said, her tone conversational. "Well, I'll call you Bennie since you're a Bengal. And it's time to see how you behave with a lion. Let Leopold in," she said, raising her voice.

A minute later the large lion Wade had noticed earlier sauntered into the cage through the chute gate. He looked bulky and muscular next to the lithe tiger as he surveyed the area with calm, golden eyes. When he saw the tiger his tail twitched, then twitched a second time. For a moment a fire seemed to smolder in his eyes, then he strolled unhurriedly across the cage and, at Tanya's command, took his place on the second pedestal. The tiger growled low in his throat, crouching as if he meant to spring, but Tanya's voice stopped him.

"*Sitz*, Bennie!" she commanded, and he settled back with a final snarl.

The lion surveyed him with lofty indifference. His teeth flashed ivory as he yawned, then gave a coughing "Ooh—ah" as if expressing his opinion of tigers, especially one who didn't know enough to show respect for his superiors.

Wade found himself smiling. "A real clown," he said.

"Maybe—but in a showdown between the two of them, I'd bet on old Leopold," Moon said. "Tigers, they're sneaky and unstable and you can't never trust one, but in a battle between a lion and a tiger, the lion's got a couple of advantages. For one thing, he's got that thick mane. The way the tiger attacks, in a rush, he's apt as not to get his claws tangled in all that hair. A lion, he can take more punishment, too, and he can stop a tiger with one crunch of them big teeth because he always hits the back of the neck or the spine. Course, the tiger's got it all over him for speed, and he uses both paws, while the lion only uses one."

"I'd say you favor lions over tigers," Wade observed.

"Yeah. They got some human traits a tiger don't. The male'll help raise his cubs, for one thing. And a lioness will protect her young no matter what, but a tigress—they've been known to kill their own litter. Not that you can trust any of them. All big cats are treacherous. You can't ever make them pets. Tanya knows that, which is why she's never been clawed."

Wade was only half listening now as Moon went on to tell him that Tanya did a picture act, specializing in tableaux in the European manner, and that she seemed to have some special rapport with her big cats. As Tanya put the lion through a few simple tricks, Wade noticed that her attention never strayed from the tiger, who perched uneasily on his pedestal, watching the lion's every movement. Once, when he crouched as if to spring, Tanya kept him there by the force of her voice and the cracking of the whip, which had replaced the training stick in her hand.

When she finally sent the lion back to his pedestal and nodded to the cageman to rattle the chute gate, a signal to the tiger to return to his cage, Wade breathed an unconscious sigh of relief. Moon heard the sound and grinned at him.

"She got to you, right? Well, you're a good-looking dude, but she ain't for the likes of you. She's what you call circus aristocracy and off limits to a common roughie."

Wade, who was watching Tanya, didn't answer.

She called out the tiger's name and snapped the whip over his head, and although the big cat moved with obvious reluctance, he sprang to the floor and soon disappeared down the chute.

Wade expected her to send the lion down the chute next, but she turned her back on the cat and bent to pick up the discarded chair. The big lion moved—so quickly that Wade's breath exploded into a shout. Tanya turned scornful eyes on him as the lion bounded up to her and began licking her hand with his rough tongue. As he nuzzled her leg, she gave him an affectionate swat on his sleek flanks.

Wade knew his face was flushed as he turned to the cageman, who was making no attempt to hide his amusement. "I thought you said you couldn't make a pet out of a lion or tiger," he said.

"Oh, I forgot to tell you there's a few exceptions, and old Leopold is one of them. He's the only cat I ever saw who doesn't have an ounce of meanness in him, at least where Tanya's concerned. But I wouldn't advise you to stick *your* hand in his mouth."

His grin widened. "She can really freeze you with that look, can't she? I saw her face down a couple of big towners once, both of them drunk and coming on strong. She had them apologizing like crazy before she got finished with them. That look of hers—it kinda reminds me of old Leopold. Both of them can be real friendly, but you don't dare go past a certain point. If you're a ladies' man, I advise you to forget it. You can get tossed off this lot faster than you can blink that way. She ain't available, y'know what I mean?"

Wade shrugged, hiding his discomfort. Was his interest in Tanya Rhodin so apparent? Hell, he wasn't sure himself what it was that he felt. Was it the attraction of an undeniably beautiful woman, or was it something more—the admiration of one scrapper for another? Whatever the case, he hadn't come here to indulge in any sexual adventures with a circus woman. What he wanted was a change of scene, a hiatus from stress. What he didn't need was an involvement with a woman, even one as special as Tanya Rhodin....

TANYA WAS ANNOYED WITH HERSELF—and with the man who was the cause of it. Although she hadn't relaxed her guard for a second, all the time she'd been working the new tiger, she'd been aware with some part of her mind of the roughie's presence. What was there about him that disturbed her so? Okay, any woman would be intrigued with his looks, that bronze hair and brown skin and those devastatingly blue eyes, and she had no doubt that he would set the aerial-ballet women, most of whom were unattached, on their collective ear. But that didn't explain why she, who didn't go in for that sort of thing, was so...so disturbed by him.

She tossed her head, angry with her own thoughts. Maybe it was the way he watched her, as if she were some kind of strange animal he'd never seen before. Had there been disapproval in that stare? Was he one of those people who believed that circus animals were mistreated and starved and beaten into submission? If so, he'd had an education that morning and discovered it was the other way around; the one who took all the risks was the trainer.

Resolutely she put the man—she didn't even know his name, for heaven's sake—out of her thoughts and went to dress for the Spec, the parade around the arena that started the big show and in which all the performers and most of the animals participated.

Although it would be several weeks before she could hope to include the new tigers in her act, she knew the other cats would be restless at having the new ones around. They wouldn't be easy to handle today, yet she had to stretch out her act to fill in some of the dead time left in the program by the desertion of the Auklander family.

In the end she cut out the "bounce," the rehearsed charge of several of the lions, which was the most dangerous part of her act, even though she was in control of the cats every minute. Instead she substituted a flashy trick that always pleased the customers, the animal pyramid, and wasn't nearly as dangerous as it looked.

She also stretched out her act by including the trick that involved putting her face in Leopold's open mouth, a trick she detested and seldom used. For one thing, it seemed to rob Leopold of dignity and brand him as a pussycat. For another, there was the matter of his breath. She wondered what the audience would think if they knew that though lions had little or no body odor, the breath of even the healthiest one was enough to knock you down.

It was some consolation that when she left the arena after the matinee, the roar of applause and shouts of approval were still ringing in her ears.

Once she had inspected the cats, something she never neglected to do after a performance, she hurried toward the fortune-teller's tent, which was located near the exhibition hall where it could draw the spillover from the big show. Earlier, when she'd dropped by Octavia's trailer to borrow one of her costumes, Octavia, looking forlorn and ashamed and even older than her sixty-plus years, had promised she'd make an appearance at the evening performance. When the fortune-teller added, her dark eyes tearful, that this was the last time she'd even look at a bottle of wine, Tanya nodded as if she believed her, and as if she hadn't heard the same promise a dozen times before.

She changed into one of Octavia's flowing caftans now, wrapping the fortune-teller's gold lamé turban around her head to hide her hair, then, using a blue makeup pencil and lots of white powder, she aged her appearance, knowing that the heavy makeup would pass in the dark tent, where only two red-tinted lamps were kept burning. She put on extra petticoats, too, to give her figure a matronly look, then took the deck of tarot cards kept for her use from the wooden box where the superstitious woman always stored them.

Although Octavia had taught her the meaning of the tarot cards when she was still a youngster, Tanya didn't really believe in them. Which was why, she was sure, she wasn't nearly as effective with the customers as her friend, who thought the ancient fortune-telling cards held the key to just about any question. For the most part, Tanya relied on her observations and a shrewd assessment of the people who paid to have their fortunes told, and she was very careful never to give anything other than general advice, the kind a good friend might offer. Even so, she dreaded the next couple of hours and wished someone else would substitute for Octavia.

She was spreading a black velvet cloth over the round table in the center of the tent when a deep voice spoke from the doorway. "Excuse us, ma'am. We were told you're having some trouble with a lamp that keeps flickering?"

Even before she turned to face the two men standing there, Tanya knew the speaker was the new roughie. He was holding a toolbox in one hand, and as he nodded respectfully, an idea came to her. It was born from both her love of mischief and something more obscure, her resentment that this man could be so disturbing to her that even now the sight of him had set her pulse racing.

"You're new here, aren't you?" she said, careful to pitch her usually husky voice to a high and quavery level. The other man, a roughie named O'Brien, eyed her with surprise, and she gave him a warning look.

"Yes, ma'am."

"You got a name, young man?"

"Wade—Wade Broderick."

"You're a good-looking fellow. I'll bet you're quite a hand with the ladies," she said.

Behind Wade, O'Brien snickered. When Tanya frowned at him, he turned the laugh into a cough. "Why don't you sit down and let me tell your cards," she cooed.

"That isn't necessary—"

"Oh, go ahead, Wade. I'll fix the lamp," O'Brien said. "You don't want to pass up a chance like this. Octavia'll give you a real earful, that's for sure."

With a shrug Wade sat down in the chair. Under the small table his long legs brushed Tanya's knee, and she was aware of a feeling of excitement, an almost painful intensity, before she quickly moved her leg away.

She told Wade to shuffle the tarot deck, and watched as he handled the colorful pieces of cardboard with a deftness that suggested he had some skill with cards. His hands were large but well formed, with broad palms and surprisingly graceful fingers. For a moment she felt stifled, as if something was constricting her breath, and her voice was thin as she told him to lay them out in three piles of three cards each.

"This is your past," she intoned, tapping one pile with her forefinger. "This is your present, and your future," she added, touching the other piles in turn.

She flipped the first three cards over, pretending to study them carefully. "I see...yes, I can see that you've led a very exciting life. There's some mystery here, some kind of deception in your past. Well, we won't bother with that. Most circus people have secrets they don't want to talk about, but be careful. The past has a way of catching up with you when you least expect it."

She turned the next three cards over, the Fool, the Hanged Man and the Empress, and despite herself she felt a stir of interest. "Ah, what have we here? A man at the crossroads of his life, trying to decide what path to take next. There's plenty of trouble up ahead. Someone is making a fool out of you, and will make a bigger fool of you in the future. You do seem to draw trouble—what was your name again? Wade? Beware of a woman, Wade. She seems to have taken a dislike to you and means to teach you a lesson."

"A woman? Is she young?"

"Oh, yes. Very young. And very pretty, too."

The other man snickered. Tanya let her eyes rest on him reflectively, and he ducked his head and returned to his task.

"Is she dark-haired or blond?"

"Her hair is dark...brown, I'd say. And I wouldn't advise you to tangle with her. She looks like she can lick her weight in wildcats, as the old expression goes.''

This time a strangled laugh escaped O'Brien's throat. Tanya ignored him and turned over the remaining three cards. Her breath caught sharply as she stared down at them.

"What is it?" Wade said, sounding amused.

Tanya felt a flush rising to her cheeks; she was grateful for the dim light. She swept the cards into a pile and said briskly, "Sometimes the cards don't make much sense, especially when the subject is skeptical."

Wade rose, looking relieved. "Thank you for the reading, Madame Octavia," he said politely.

O'Brien clicked the lamp on and off and told her it was working now. He winked at her behind Wade's back as they went out. When she could no longer hear their voices, Tanya turned the cards over again, staring down at them.

"The Lovers," she said aloud, touching the card where two lovers were entwined. "His own true love...and the Tower card means lots of trouble heading his way. Well, that much figures. He looks like a troublemaker. But what is the Queen of Wands, *my* card, doing in Wade Broderick's future?"

CHAPTER FOUR

THE GRINDING OF A TRUCK ENGINE just outside the dorm tent awakened Wade. Even before he rolled off his bunk he was aware of a feeling of anticipation. Was it because, for the next few weeks, he would be immersed in an atmosphere that was totally different from his own familiar world of sales meetings and production figures and stock ratings? Or was it simply that he had been given the chance so few men have of reliving a truly happy time from his boyhood?

Whatever the reason, he was sure of one thing. The day ahead would be exciting, packed with new experiences as well as hard physical labor. He might even learn something—if not of monetary value, then at least about human nature. He'd been convinced that he knew a lot about circus life from his own brief experience and from reading about the subject in books, but he was discovering that reality was much different from the nostalgic memoirs of old circus hands.

There was the earthy language, for instance, which included the kind of creative oaths that would arouse the envy of a sailor. And the jargon.... So often these past few days he'd felt as if he was trying to learn a foreign language. Some of it had come back to him, but other expressions had passed right over his head.

Circus language was a fascinating phenomenon, and it had a very practical purpose because it kept outsiders in ignorance of what was going on. There had

been a time when ruffians had made life miserable
and very dangerous for traveling shows. Circus jargon, like most patois, had developed from the necessity of having a shorthand language for people who
often spoke different languages but who needed to be
able to warn one another of dangers, without at the
same time spelling out the same information to outsiders who might be hostile.

To most circus people there was nothing particularly glamorous about their jobs, but there was a
camaraderie within a show that was irresistible to
people who so often could find it nowhere else. And,
as Wade himself knew so well, there was nothing
quite like the feeling—circus fever, one writer had
called it—when the lights were up in the Big Top and
the opening Spec started rolling forward, full of
pageantry and excitement.

But there was another side of circus life. The gruel-
ing work of setting up and tearing down two dozen
booths and tents for every new engagement, the day-
to-day tedium of feeding and caring for the animals,
everything from ring stock—the high-school and
rosinback horses for the equestrian acts, plus trained
dogs and bears and chimps—to the big cats in the
lion trainer's act. Then there were the elephants, who
both appeared in the show and worked as beasts of
burden, unloading the trucks and helping to put up
canvas.

There was also the sheer volume of planning needed to bed and feed so many people, to transport them
and their gear from one engagement to the next. The
logistics involved in ordering supplies, making scheduling changes, keeping tax and other government
records up to date, plus coping with the inevitable
emergencies that constantly beset the circus, kept

Pop Peeples and his bookkeeper-clerk tied to their desks in the silver wagon several hours every day.

And then there were the smaller, everyday problems involved with living on the run—laundry and car repairs, and even such irritants as getting a haircut. No wonder circus people welcomed a still date so much.

Well, he *was* enjoying himself—so far. When his new life palled on him, then he would go back to New York. But for the present it was intriguing and stimulating.

Moving quietly so he wouldn't disturb the few off-duty men who were still sleeping in their bunks, he got clean jeans and a long-sleeved cotton jersey pullover from his canvas tote bag, dressed quickly and started for the cookhouse. Already, even after only four days, he had fallen into a routine and felt as if he belonged here—though he was probably the only one who thought so.

A few of the men, including Moon, were friendly enough, but the rest still eyed him with a wariness that seemed to say, "Prove yourself to us, you Johnny-come-lately!" and he was well aware that they were reserving their judgment on whether he would fit in.

The fact that he was willing to tackle any job that was assigned him without complaint helped, of course, and the men he'd worked with directly had already relaxed their guard. But the others were still wary, and who could blame them? Roughies—what outsiders called roustabouts—came and went. So many of them were drifters. Why bother to invest friendship in someone who might collect his pay one day and move on the next?

When he came into the cookhouse, Wade saw

Moon sitting with a group of men on the long side of
the tent where the workmen ate. Moon waved a hos-
pitable hand at him, and after Wade had filled his
tray with a mug of coffee, a stack of soggy pancakes,
three limp pieces of bacon and a couple of runny
scrambled eggs, he joined them, smiling easily at
their cool nods of acknowledgment.

One of Wade's fellow canvasmen, a narrow-faced
man named Murphy who had a habit of talking out
of the side of his mouth, gave him a sidelong glance.
"I heard old Octavia told your fortune yesterday,"
he said.

Another man choked on a bite of toast. There was
a flurry of excitement as someone slapped him enthu-
siastically on the back and someone else advised him
to wash it down with coffee. The man, a large Swede
with yellow hair and outsize biceps who worked as a
shanty, an electrician, took the advice. When he
could talk he said, "I sure hope you took them cards
seriously. That Hungarian woman really knows her
tarot. What'd she tell you anyway?"

"Nothing special. Just the usual stuff."

"That ain't the way I heard it. Didn't she say
something about some female who was out to get you
in trouble?"

Wade sent a contemplative look at O'Brien, who
gave him a sly grin and a shrug. "Oh, that. Well, I'll be
careful," Wade said. He applied himself to his food.

The Swede looked as if he wanted to persist, but
Moon changed the subject, and the men were soon
arguing about a family act of acrobats who had quit
the show to join a rival circus. Wade listened silently,
not voicing any opinions, and Moon went on to tell
about a run-in Tanya Rhodin had had with the same
agent who had hired away the Auklanders.

"You shoulda seen Tanya run that dude off," Moon said admiringly. "He's one of those big bruisers with eyes that look like agates, but when he said something she didn't like about her wasting her time with a fourth-rate circus and a loser like Pop Peeples, she lifted that whip of hers and took out after him. You shoulda seen him run! Legs pumping up and down—I like to busted my gut laughing. He cleared out of here like the devil hisself was chasing him."

"Tanya's got a temper, but she's a real trouper and easy to work for as long as you don't mess up," Murph said. "Wish I could say the same about everybody around here. That German guy who does the trampoline and bar act—he really chewed me out yesterday just because I dropped a bench while he was practicing."

"You have to keep the star acts happy," the Swede cautioned. "If we lose any more, it could go bad for the circus. Might even mean some cancellations."

"Don't you worry none about that!" Moon's voice was sharp. "Pop always lands on his feet. He'll keep it all together. I sure don't want to go back to working in a carnival. The other circuses won't hire an old-timer like me."

"Maybe that's what's wrong with this one," O'Brien said, giving Moon a sly look. "Too many old-timers. Even the catcher in the aerial act is over the hill these days."

"Hold on there, O'Brien," Moon snapped. "It's the old-timers the customers come to see. Sure, they spend their money at the booths and on the rides once they get here, but it's the show in the Big Top that draws them in. And don't be so quick to put Bruno out to pasture. He still catches as good as he ever did, even if he is past forty."

"Mebbe so, but I heard one of the flyers complaining. Not naming names, you understand, but he said the old guy's timing is off—"

O'Brien broke off as two female acrobats, wearing practice leotards and tights with sweatbands tied around their foreheads, passed the table on their way to the coffee urns. "Knock it off," Moon said in low voice. "You know that kinda talk just causes trouble."

After he left the cookhouse, Wade reported to Flat Iron Collins and spent the rest of the morning hauling supplies from town to stock the refrigeration truck. Early that afternoon he was drinking coffee at one of the grab joints, listening while the talker at the fishtank booth did his "bally," trying to entice the sparse early-afternoon crowd to pay a dollar to dangle a hook in a running stream of water on the chance that they would hook one of the elusive fish that would award them a plush prize, such as a stuffed animal or camera.

Wade had just finished draining his mug when Pop Peeples spotted him and beckoned impatiently. "I want you should hustle over to Clown Alley," he said without preamble. "Jeep Simmons—he's props boss—is short a hand in the Big Tent during the matinee. Report in to Gogo first—he's the head joey. He'll fix you up with a costume and tell you what needs to be done. You'll be hauling off props after the joeys are finished with them, and don't mess up or those clowns will skin you alive."

Although he nodded silently and hurried off, Wade was wary of the assignment. From his own experience he knew that newcomers could expect at least one variation of the donniker stunt that had been pulled on him as a youngster, and he was way overdue to be the butt of the circus's version of hazing the newcomer. It occurred to him that this might be it, though Pop didn't strike him as being the kind to indulge in practical jokes.

As he bent his head and ducked under the rolled-up canvas above the opening to the clowns' tent, the odor of greasepaint assaulted his nostrils. The tent was full of men in various stages of dress and undress. The air was hot and stuffy, redolent not only of greasepaint but of the putty used for the bulbous noses of the clowns, of cheap talcum powder and the acridness of cigars left smoldering in tuna-fish-can ashtrays.

There was a din of raised voices, the loud wail of a radio tuned to a rock station, which everybody seemed to ignore. One clown, who sported an enormous bow under his grotesquely madeup face, sang a snatch of a rock-and-roll song to the accompaniment of jeers and threats until someone silenced him by tossing a filled powder puff across the room, catching him in the mouth and drenching him in white powder.

But the wrangling was mainly good-natured, and Wade stood there, feeling like the new kid on the block, a fascinated and silent witness to the organized chaos. His attention was caught by a gaunt-faced man wearing full makeup. He was dressed in the tatters and rags of a tramp clown and was absorbed in the tricky job of drawing a black tear-shaped line under each of his sorrowful eyes. A painted-on mouth, outlined in red, stretched from ear to ear across his face. The pinkish color of his face indicated that he was an auguste, a clown who specialized in being the butt of other clown's jokes. Wade gave an involuntary smile when he recognized the man.

During his brief stay with the circus he had been fascinated by the clowns. Whenever he got the chance he had hung around their tent, called Clown Alley, even though he'd been the recipient of numerous practical jokes. Gogo had been a young clown then, a graduate of one of the clown-training schools around Sarasota, Florida. He had lived strutting around in front of the younger boy, bragging about his accomplishments. Now he was Pop's head clown, Wade thought with amusement, and maybe with a tinge of jealousy, as he went up to the man.

"I was told to report to you, Gogo," he said politely.

"You know me?"

"I've caught your act a couple of times. You do a Diogenes routine, don't you?" he said, sure of his ground because a clown seldom changed his basic act once it had been established.

"Yeah, that's my speciality, but only when we're working under canvas. Solo acts get lost in the indoor arenas, so we mostly do group productions these days." Gogo paused to brush a speck of loose powder off his tattered sleeve before he added, "Did the old man send you over?"

"Right. He said you need someone to pick up props after the walkarounds."

"Yeah, well, we lost both our prop men last night, so you'll really have to hop. One of them got into a donnybrook with Wee Willie and took off, and the other one picked up some towner Jane and never made it back to the lot last night. You'll have to be quick out there. Soon as you get the prop boss's signal, dash out, pick up the props and bring them to the rear. No loitering or gawking at the show. You ain't no paying customer, so keep your eyes on the joeys. You understand?"

Wade nodded, though privately he intended to see as much of the show as possible.

Gogo tossed him a pair of outsize trousers, a bright orange shirt big enough to cover two men and a large bow tie. "Here, wear these duds and you won't stand out so much."

Wade couldn't help grinning at this amazing statement, and the clown gave him a hard look. "Keep your head down, don't stare at the audience and get right to business. Take the props out through the back door—that's the performers' entrance, in case you don't know—and bring them here to Clown Alley. You can stash them away in those boxes over there." He pointed to several packing crates in the rear of the tent. "If the regular gofers don't turn up soon, you can give us a hand again at the evening performance."

He gave Wade a few more instructions in a rapid-fire voice, then bustled off, leaving Wade to change into his costume. Since no one was paying any attention to him, he took his time, enjoying the exchange of insults, the tart comments, the sometimes rough horseplay. He was so absorbed, in fact, that at first he didn't realize someone was tugging at his shirttail. When he did and looked down, he couldn't help a start of surprise. A diminutive man—he couldn't have been more than three feet tall—was standing there, staring up at him. From the expression on his face, he was in a testy mood.

The midget was wearing evening clothes that had the impeccable look of English tailoring. When he spoke, his accent matched his clothing—it was pure British. "What happened to Oscar?" the man said in a surprisingly deep voice.

Wade was so bemused that he didn't answer, and the man snapped, "What are you staring at, man? Haven't you ever seen anyone wearing evening clothes before?"

Again Wade had to hide a grin. "Sorry. Your accent startled me. You're British, I presume."

"That's right. Any objections?"

"Just a friendly comment."

The man looked Wade over carefully. "I'm Marshall," he said abruptly, putting out his hand.

Wade shook it gravely and discovered that Marshall's grip was almost uncomfortably strong. "My name is Wade—Wade Broderick."

"I've heard about you. Green as grass, and full of brass."

"I don't know about the brass part, but I'm certainly new at all this." Wade gestured toward the clamorous clowns.

"Well, I'm not usually involved with the joeys, but I'm helping out today as a personal favor to Pop. Gogo's cooked up a turn to stretch the first walk-around time. He needs someone to dress up like a baby. Usually I do my own thing in the ten-in-one tent. I'm billed as Lord Marshall. It's just a gimmick, of course—you know, that I'm the son of a duke."

"You could fool me. That *is* an Oxford accent, isn't it?"

The man gave him a long, considering stare. "I have to get into makeup. I don't have time for chit-chat," he said gruffly, and marched away, leaving Wade to wonder why he was so sensitive about having an accent that indicated he'd gone to Oxford.

Later, while he was waiting on the sidelines for the clowns to start their second walkaround, Wade watched the aerial-ballet women working the web, the vertical ropes that are suspended from ceiling girders to the floor. There were three women—one blonde, one brunette and one very flamboyant red-head. Although they turned and twisted in unison, the blond woman's timing seemed to be slightly off. Even under her elaborate makeup her skin was pale, and he wondered if she was ill.

It wasn't only this that captured his attention. Despite her petiteness, her figure was spectacular. Her costume, red satin with spangles and sequins that flashed and glittered in the spotlight, hugged her high, round breasts, her slender waist and trim hips as she whirled, doing a maneuver that he vaguely remembered was called a one-arm flange.

He was still watching her when she did her final whirl and started a swift descent down the rope toward the web-sitter, who was holding her line taut. It was only after she and the other women had finished taking their bows and the blond woman was running toward him that he realized she'd noticed his staring—and wasn't pleased about it.

He was startled when she stopped in front of him with a smile that could only be described as provocative, and it was all the more surprising because he could have sworn he'd seen anger in her heavily madeup eyes only a few seconds earlier.

"Hello, there." Her voice was a sultry purr. "You're new, aren't you?"

"You could say that—at least I'm new to the circus."

"I saw you watching me. Do you like blondes?"

"*And* brunettes *and* redheads," he said, suddenly amused. "I'm a great admirer of female beauty."

"Oh, aren't you smooth! I just love smooth men."

"Uh-huh. Well, you don't have any rough spots yourself, miss," he said, and wondered what some of his friends would say at this corny dialogue.

"Call me Maisie—it sounds more friendly. I do like a friendly man, even if he is a First-of-May guy."

Despite the slight sting in her words, her smile was broad, and her teeth were very white and even. "You must be sick of cookhouse food by now. How would you like a nice home-cooked meal, say, tomorrow evening after the matinee? My trailer is parked in the backyard. You won't have any trouble finding it."

Wade hesitated, then gave a mental shrug. After all, why not? A home-cooked meal was not to be sneezed at. Cookie's skill as a cook had deteriorated drastically since the days when a much younger Wade had believed that Cookie's cookhouse stew was the best food in the world. Or maybe he'd just grown older and more critical.

As for the "friendly" part, what it implied, he'd make sure nothing came of that. One thing he didn't need was to get involved with a circus woman, especially one who was so indiscriminately friendly. On the other hand, he didn't want to get the reputation for being *unfriendly*, did he? Besides, he was curious. There was something off-key about this little lady and her generous invitation.

More amused than truly interested, he nodded his acceptance. "I'll be there. What kind of trailer do you have?"

"Brown—a large brown one. Just ask anyone where Maisie lives and they'll point it out." Her smile flashed again, and this time he was sure it was genuine. "There's only one Maisie in the show."

She tripped off toward the performers' dressing-room tent. Wade was so bemused by the exaggerated swing of her slim hips that he almost missed the prop boss's signal.

The next day, immediately after he'd put away the props, Wade stripped off his work clothes, took a shower in the men's wash house and put on clean jeans and a knit T-shirt before he strolled unhurriedly through the lot toward the backyard. The first person he saw was a matronly looking woman who was sweeping the sand off the side steps of her trailer.

"Maisie? You say her name was Maisie?" she said in answer to his query. "I don't think I know anyone by that name. Could be you got it wrong."

"No, I'm sure she said Maisie. She's an aerialist, one of the ballet women, a blonde. She told me anyone could point out where she lives because there's only one Maisie with the show."

The woman was silent for a moment. "Well, you'd better ask...uh, ask someone else." She turned away and began furiously brushing at the steps with her broom.

Half an hour later, after he'd been passed along to "someone else" three more times, Wade finally recognized the pattern and knew he was getting the runaround. Either the circus people suspected his motives and were protecting the blond woman, or he was the victim of a practical joke. He opted for the latter and gave up his search. That night in the cookhouse he found out the whole circus was in on the joke.

"Hey, Wade, I hear you had a hard time running down Maisie this afternoon," O'Brien said. "Why didn't you ask me? I coulda told you where to go."

"No problem," Wade said. "It wasn't important."

"Now that ain't the right attitude. A lady like Maisie is always important. I'll bet she's pining away, wondering what happened to you."

"I doubt that," Wade said dryly.

"You don't want to drop it. After all, it ain't every day Maisie takes a shine to someone, leastways a roughie. Why that lady is famous all over the circuit for...uh, being hard to get. And she's about as pretty as they come. Them big eyes and that cute figure...and she's got just about the prettiest nose I ever did see."

Someone snickered and Wade shrugged, feigning indifference. "No big thing. There are plenty of other women around."

"Oh, but not like Maisie. You're making a big mistake if you let her get away. She's got the best disposition of any female in the circus. A cheap date, too, I hear. It only costs peanuts to feed her 'cause all she eats is cereal and veggies and fruit. Lots of fruit. And the only thing she'll drink is water, though I did hear a rumor that she'll accept a beer now and then. Like I say, a cheap date."

Wade was trying to think how to change the subject when something clicked in his mind. Maisie...of course! That was the name of the elephant he'd called Gray Lady because of her docile disposition....

It took a great effort, but he managed to hide his chagrin. He'd really fallen for an oldie, but maybe he could still turn the tables on the jokester, whoever she might be.

"Well, the lady is a real charmer," he said aloud. "Her nose is a little big, but did you notice her ears? Really spectacular. And her teeth are great, too. Both of them."

Moon gave a hoot of laughter. "Guess he's way ahead of you, O'Brien. How long did it take you to catch on, Wade? Guess you ain't as green as she thought."

"As who thought?" Wade said easily.

"Uh-uh. You'll have to figure that out for yourself."

"Why don't you give him a clue, Moon?" O'Brien's smile was tinged with malice. "Go ask Octavia to do your tarot cards again, Wade. That old gal's got all the answers."

Amused glances were exchanged, but Wade pretended not to see them. His mind slipped back to the fortune-teller's tent—that very dark tent. The Hungarian woman had looked old in the reddish light, but that could have been makeup. Her voice had been strangely young and strong, and her accent had slipped a little at the end, too. The odds were that the same woman had made him the butt of her joke twice, and he didn't intend there to be a third time.

"I would say that Octavia and Maisie are two of a kind. Both full of tricks, and about the same age, too."

The men laughed uproariously, especially Moon. "No moss on you, is there, Wade?" he said, slapping him on the shoulder.

Wade grinned good-naturedly, knowing he'd played his cards right, but he made a mental note to find out the name of the woman who'd gone out of her way to play tricks on him so he could put a stop to it. He hadn't handled recalcitrant union organizers and officious government men, weathered stockholders' rebellions and takeovers and successfully fought off internal company conspiracies just to be twitted on the nose by some circus woman.

The conversation turned to other matters, mainly to the rotten state of cookhouse food. This was a favorite topic with the working men of the circus, as long as it was out of Cookie's hearing. It was going to be a long day, since this was a teardown night. The next engagement was in Wichita, a long haul for the big rigs. No one would get much sleep until they had pulled into the lot in Wichita.

Cots and hammocks would be set up in the men's dorm rig for those not needed for driving, but since the show was short on help, Wade had been pressed into service and would sit up front in the truck cab to spell one of the drivers. Even though he knew he'd get little sleep, he found himself looking forward to the long drive through the night. There was something magical about tires singing on concrete, the velvet darkness that made the truck a small, microcosmic world, the easy conversation with the other man, the feeling of rootlessness, of lack of responsibility. . . .

Moon stopped him as he was leaving the cookhouse. "We'll be loading the cats into the animal rigs as soon as Tanya's act is over, and we could use an extra hand. Better talk to Flat Iron and get his permission, though. Could be he's got other plans for you. If he says it's okay, go to the menagerie tent as soon as you finish picking up the joeys' props after the finale."

Wade got Flat Iron's okay, but when he went to Clown Alley he found that both the regular prop men had returned and he wouldn't be needed. Since it was a little late to get a work assignment elsewhere, he decided to go to the menagerie tent early, sure he could find something to keep him busy until it was time to move the big cats.

As he lowered his head and slipped between the canvas flaps of the menagerie tent, he caught a flicker of movement in front of a cage. Before he could call out, he heard a husky voice saying, "Oh, you want another scratch, do you? Well, how about this? Right behind your ear."

Wade moved in closer, walking on the balls of his feet. A boyish figure was standing in front of one of the cages, an outsize cap pulled down low on his forehead. From his size, he appeared to be just a kid—a very stupid kid. He had both arms inside the cage of the big lion they called Leopold.

Wade leaped forward, grabbed the boy by the shoulders and yanked him back, only to find himself fighting a scratching, writhing whirlwind. He finally stopped the struggle by pinning the boy's hands to his side with one arm and muffling his angry yells by holding his face up against his chest with the other.

"You little fool, that lion could snap your arm off in one bite. Don't you have any more sense than to tease a big cat?"

The boy sputtered something, but since his face was buried in Wade's sweater, the words were undecipherable. Wade suspected it was a curse. Since he was finding it increasingly difficult to hold on to the squirming body, he tightened his trip. The boy cursed again as Wade felt a hard kick on his shins, pain arching up his leg. He had almost decided to give the boy a good shake and then let him go when abruptly the struggling stopped.

"Hey, mister," the boy whined, his voice high and thin. "I was just petting that lion. I didn't do nothing wrong. You ain't gonna report me to that lady tamer, are you?"

Wade was silent. While they had struggled, he had felt a warm body against his, and it hadn't been a boy's body. No, this was a female, very much so. He was pretty sure it was Tanya Rhodin, and he was also sure that she was the woman who had made him the butt of two practical jokes. From that last little speech, she was trying for a third.

"No, I won't report you to Ms Rhodin," he said grimly. "But I think you deserve a good lesson. Maybe then you won't try any more practical jokes on your betters."

He hooked his leg behind Tanya's knee and gave her a push. They both tumbled onto a mound of straw in front of the cage, but Wade didn't give her a chance to squirm away. With the weight of his body pinning her down, he captured both her hands in one of his and kissed her, hard and relentlessly. With his free hand he explored the parts of her wriggling body that he could reach—her breasts, her narrow waist, her firm round hips.

Later he couldn't have said just when the lesson he'd been administrating had become something much more personal. Maybe it was the frantic struggling of her body against his, or the incredible softness of her ripe full lips, or the scent, musky and pure female, of her heated skin that aroused all his male instincts. When he felt a building of tension, a throbbing and stirring of his own body that warned him he was in danger of losing his head, he released Tanya immediately and rolled away, only to stop again to stare down at her small, triangular-shaped face.

Why had she stopped struggling even before he'd released her? And how was he to interpret the expression in her eyes as she touched her swollen lips with her fingertips? It wasn't fear—no, this little lady was not that easily frightened. It was bewilderment and surprise, as if she'd just had a shock.

Then she was on her feet, hands on hips, her eyes blazing. "I'll tell Pop to fire you," she stormed. "I'll have you thrown off the lot!"

"I don't think so, Tanya," he said softly. "You wouldn't want the whole circus to know that you got some of your own medicine back, would you? And I have a hunch you're fair enough to admit that you deserved it. You've been ragging a First-of-May guy who turned the tables on you, and the only thing that got hurt is your pride. You were never in any danger from me and you know it. In fact—'' his eyes dropped to her mouth, still moist from his kiss "—I have a hunch you enjoyed it. So let's call it quits, okay?''

"You haven't heard the last of this," she said, her face flaming. "If I had my whip, I'd give you what you deserve, you...you Johnny-come-lately!''

Wade grinned at this choice circus insult. "Uh-huh. And you're upsetting your cats, or don't you care?''

She gave the row of cages a startled look, and he knew she was just now realizing that the cats were in an uproar. She muttered a word under her breath that he pretended not to hear, but her eyes were still flashing fire as she whirled on him again. "Where's Moon, and the other cagemen?'' she demanded arrogantly.

"Moon told me to meet him here to help out with the teardown, but I'm a little early. I think I hear someone coming now," he said.

She gave him a hostile look, her eyes hot with anger, but when Moon and Charlie arrived a few seconds later she put them to work immediately without any mention of the incident. It intrigued Wade that, though there was no question of who was boss, she worked right along with the men, setting up the flexible chutes and loading the big cats into their traveling cages, cleaning out and hosing down the larger holding cages, then disassembling them and the tent and packing everything away in one of the big rigs, all of which was hard physical labor.

By the time everything was ready for the move, Wade felt a deep respect for Tanya, despite her unrelenting hostility toward him, which she manifested by ignoring him completely except when she gave him an order. She might be as touchy as one of her own cats, with a volatile temper, but she carried her share of the load. In fact, she carried other people's loads, as well. Since she'd been in costume in the fortune-teller's tent, she must have been substituting for Octavia that day, and she had been filling in for one of the aerial-ballet women, too, in addition to her own strenuous act. No wonder she had looked so pale under her makeup in the spotlight.

Tanya Rhodin was something of a paradox. She was responsible where her cats were concerned, and obviously respected and well loved by the rough circus men, who seemed proud of her spunkiness, yet she was addicted to practical jokes, too.

And why was he so sure that the jokes directed at him stemmed from some personal antagonism? He had sensed it the day he'd watched her training her new tiger, when he'd been the recipient of her cold looks.

She wouldn't be playing any more practical jokes on him in the future. And that kiss—he had liked that kiss a little too much. In fact he'd had an almost overwhelming physical reaction to it, which could be explained away as the normal feelings of a man for an attractive woman. But the part that puzzled him was the desire he'd also felt to comfort her, to protect her. That was alarming—and very dangerous.

What he didn't need at this point of his life were complications, and he had a hunch that Tanya Rhodin could make a hash out of his peace of mind if he didn't stay away from her.

CHAPTER FIVE

As SHE OFTEN DID when she was troubled or upset, Tanya sought out her old friend, Marshall. He was one of the "little people," as he preferred to be called, but his size didn't begin to reflect his sharpness of wit. He had been her teacher, mentor and watchdog, guiding her education with an iron hand. Although he had concentrated most of his attention on teaching her English and literature, history and math, he had also included what he called "the rudiments of culture." She privately thought of this as a waste of time. Knowing how to order a meal in a French restaurant and studying ancient Greek seemed to have nothing to do with her real life, which centered on the circus, but she was careful to keep these reservations to herself.

Although she had often chafed at Marshall's decree—which was backed by Pop—that her lessons came first, she was grateful for his heroic efforts to educate her. She was well aware that the English she spoke was grammatically correct, unlike that of so many of the circus people. It might set her apart in some subtle way, but it also earned her a certain automatic respect. Although circus people had nothing but scorn for anyone who tried to put on airs, they also had a deep desire for learning, and most tried to see that their own children received a good education, even if it meant sacrifices on their part.

It was because of Marshall's insistence that Tanya take advantage of the multinational backgrounds of other circus people that she had learned several languages, enough to converse in them freely. In addition, Marshall had taught her to speak French, calling it "the only civilized language," and because it had been the tongue of her French father, she had applied herself diligently to her lessons. Being a perfectionist, Marshall made sure that her accent was impeccable.

Bruno Reuter, the catcher for the circus's star aerial act, had supervised her lessons in German, which she spoke with what he insisted was a proper Berliner accent. From Octavia she had learned more than a smattering of Hungarian and Russian. The Rodriguez family, one of the show's equestrian troupes, spoke only rudimentary English even after twenty years in the country, and they had taught her their own version of Spanish. Although Marshall called it "bastard Spanish," Tanya could make herself understood to almost any Spanish-speaking person. Her skill with languages often came in handy when Pop needed a translator. Not only was he hopelessly inept with any language other than his own, but he firmly believed that if he only shouted loud enough—and other people would listen better—he would be understood, even by a foreigner.

Under Marshall's tutelage, Tanya had also achieved a wider view of literature and world events than was common in the closed world of the circus. Although he was secretive about his own past and was noted for his irascible nature, he had shown Tanya only kindness, and his wry humor had influenced her own way of looking at the people she dealt with every day.

So whenever she was bewildered by her own conflicting emotions, it was natural that she would take her problem to Marshall.

Today she found him in his motor home, fixing lunch. As always, Marshall's home reminded Tanya of a doll house, and when she went inside at Marshall's invitation, she was glad that she was small herself. Every item of furniture, from the velvet-covered sofa to the wood-trimmed club chair, had been custom built to accommodate Marshall's size. The only items that weren't reduced were the books that lined one wall, each row tucked snugly behind a wooden rack to keep them from jarring loose during travel, and kitchen appliances such as the toaster and coffeepot. Even the TV set was small, and in the tiny kitchen the range had been lowered to match Marshall's height, as had the counters and cupboards.

Marshall was standing at the range, a butcher's apron around his trim waist and a pancake turner in his hand, when Tanya came in. "Would you like a Reuben sandwich?" he asked briskly.

"Sounds great. I haven't eaten lunch yet."

Something in her voice must have alerted him, because he gave her a sharp look. "Is anything wrong, cupcake?"

"Not really. I just wanted to talk to you about... about a small problem," she said.

Since Marshall took his food seriously and was something of a gourmet cook, she wasn't surprised when he said, "You can tell me about it after we've had lunch."

Lunch consisted of the grilled Reubens, rye bread spread thickly with corned beef and melted swiss cheese, with a layer of sauerkraut and Marshall's own special Thousand Island dressing. A spicy mustard sauce accompanied the salad of mushrooms, tomatoes and endive, another of her favorites, but Tanya, who usually had a hearty appetite, only picked at her food, earning her a disapproving frown from Marshall.

After he had cleared the table, refusing her offer of help, he settled himself in his easy chair and said briskly, "Let's have it, dear girl. What's this problem that's been giving you trouble?"

"It's... well, it's a man," she said, hesitating over the choice of words. "I don't know how to handle his... his attitude toward me. He stares at me as if I'm some kind of strange creature who just crawled out from under a rock."

"Uh-huh. Well, you should be used to being stared at. You're an exceptionally lovely young woman, just like your mother," Marshall said with a sigh.

"Mother was beautiful, and I'm not."

"You don't have her fair skin and blond hair, no, but you're every bit as beautiful. You have a very earthy beauty, Tanya. It's no wonder this man—and you haven't said who he is yet—keeps watching you."

"I have the feeling that he doesn't like me. He treats me as if I'm some kind of child."

"And of course there's no earthly reason for this? You haven't done a thing to cause it, have you? Such as one of your little practical jokes?"

Tanya knew she was flushing. "We had a misunderstanding... I did lose my temper," she confessed. "But that doesn't give him any reason to—" She broke off, chewing on her lower lip.

Marshall eyed her thoughtfully. "To what?"

"To... to treat me like that."

"What exactly did he do?"

"Well, for one thing, he was very... very rude. Who does he think he is, anyway?"

"I have no idea. Who exactly is he?"

"Oh...you probably don't know him. Pop hired him a few days ago as a roughie. His name is Wade Broderick."

Marshall's eyes sharpened. "Yes, I do know him. And if I can believe the gossip going around, you've been making life miserable for the poor man ever since he signed on. Something about a tarot-card reading and a date he was conned into making with a lady called Maisie, right? Which brings up another question. You can be a royal pain in the neck sometimes with your teasing and your tricks, but you usually don't pick on newcomers, only on your dearest and nearest friends. So why this vendetta against a First-of-May guy? He seemed like a rather nice chap to me."

Tanya gave him a sulky look. "Well, I don't like him. He's rude and overbearing and he doesn't have any respect for...people."

"And I think the lady doth protest too much. What form did his rudeness take, by the way?"

"Okay...he kissed me."

"You've been kissed before—quite a few times when you were going through your experimental stage. If I remember correctly, you didn't much care for it, and you decided to give it up until you were older. So what's the problem—" He stopped, and his small body seemed to swell. "This man...he didn't force himself upon you, did he?"

Tanya shook her head quickly. "No. No, it wasn't like that. It's just that I wasn't expecting it, and he took me by surprise or I would've slapped his blasted face."

"And now we get to the crux of the matter. Is it possible that you not only weren't expecting it but liked it? Could this be what's really bothering you?''

Tanya shook her head violently, repudiating his words. "I hated it! And I hate him! He's just a common roughie, and yet he acts so...so superior!''

"Calm down now. It's all over, and I'm sure you blasted him as only you can when he kissed you. In fact, he probably thought a cyclone struck him when you told him off, right?''

Tanya was silent. What if she told Marshall that she'd been so stunned by her own response to Wade's kiss that she hadn't said anything at all for a long time, and that even then she'd had to pump anger into her voice? And what if she told him that rather than being relieved, she had felt deprived when Wade had finally released her? Which, as Marshall had said, was the real crux of the matter. She had felt so quivery and excited when this stranger had kissed her that she hadn't been able to stop thinking about it since.

Wade wasn't the first man to kiss her, of course. She had a normal interest in sex, and she had gone through an experimental period when she'd thought she was in love with half a dozen boys. But when she'd allowed them to kiss her, she had felt only curiosity and a vague disappointment because there hadn't been any fireworks—none at all. But Wade's kiss had stirred up something inside her that both frightened and fascinated her. How was it possible that she could feel this strongly for a man she didn't even like?

She was glad when Marshall changed the subject and started telling her about a new recipe he'd discovered for bolognese sauce. In fact, she was already sorry she'd told Marshall about Wade's kiss, and that in itself was strange. She had always confided her fears, her problems, her innermost thoughts and even her daydreams to Marshall. Although she thought of Alice as her surrogate mother, Alice was too prone to worry about her. Marshall, on the other hand, was never surprised or upset or critical, no matter what she said to him or what secrets she revealed.

So why, all of a sudden, did she feel reluctant to talk to one of her oldest and dearest friends about Wade Broderick?

THE FIRST DAY of the three-day run in Wichita went smoothly. The Kansas city had the reputation among circus people for being a "good town," and the audience was enthusiastic even with the rather slim array of acts in the Big Top. Owing to the stretching of the acts, the two-hour show went off without a hitch and without having to be shortened. Ordinarily after she had returned to her trailer, Tanya would have stretched out for a few minutes' relaxation, but today she was summoned to the silver wagon to help with a crisis, a shortage in the cash box. The missing amount was a rather substantial sum, kept on hand for small purchases those times when local merchants were reluctant to take checks or extend credit to a traveling show.

As usual the culprit was Pop, who had forgotten to drop in the receipts for several cash purchases he'd made, and although there wasn't a shortage after all, it took almost two hours of searching to track down the problem. By the time they were finished, both Tanya and Maude were exhausted, and Tanya was in a pensive mood as she started back to her trailer.

Some impulse, probably a simple feeling of loneliness, made her change her mind about taking a nap.

She hadn't given Leopold any special attention since they'd left Topeka, so she decided to make up for it by taking him a dish of strawberries, his favorite treat. She thawed a package of the frozen fruit, which she kept in the freezer compartment of her small butane refrigerator, then dumped a glob of sour cream over the top. Not wanting to advertise what she was doing and lay herself open to teasing, she slid the bowl into a brown paper sack.

When she got to the menagerie tent, she realized that someone was already there. She heard a man's voice coming from the area of Leopold's cage, and she hurried down the line of cages, ignoring the "ooo-ahs" of Chub, one of the male lions, and the mocking snarl of the tigers.

Her breath caught with outrage when she saw that the man, who was standing with his back to her, was poking a stick through the bars of Leopold's cage. With one swift movement she reached around him and snatched the stick out of his hand. Only when he swung around to face her did she realize she was staring into Wade Broderick's startled face.

Her temper exploded into words. "You...you bastard! Tormenting a helpless animal—you should be horsewhipped!"

Wade started to say something, but her voice overrode his. "Get out of here and don't ever let me catch you around my cats again. I don't want you near them!"

"Wait a moment. Let me explain—"

"What's going on here, Tanya? I could hear you yelling all the way out to the parking lot." It was Moon, accompanied by his assistant, Charlie.

"This...this psycho was poking Leopold with a stick," she said angrily. "Get him out of here before I forget I'm a lady and turn Leopold loose on him.''

Wade's face went blank and cold. He crossed his arms over his chest and stared at her. ''Don't you think you should give me a chance to explain?'' he said quietly.

''I wouldn't believe you if you swore on the Bible. Now clear out, you hear?''

''I hear. The whole circus can hear you. And since I can't stomach women who act like spoiled brats, I'll leave, but before I go, I think I'd better warn you about the broken bottle in your lion's cage. If someone doesn't get it out of there soon, he's liable to be hurt.''

He swung around, ignoring the two men, and stalked away. Tanya turned to look into the cage and saw the shards of glass lying close to Leopold, who was sprawled out, watching them with sleepy eyes.

''What the hell—how did *that* get in there?'' Moon said.

Tanya shook her head, too stunned to speak. Wade had only been trying to save Leopold from being cut by the broken bottle. She had jumped to conclusions and made a fool of herself just because she didn't like the man. What had happened to her judgment lately? Usually she bent over backward to give other people a chance. If it had been anyone else except Wade, she would have listened to an explanation.

Her lips set, she opened the cage door and cleared out the broken glass that Leopold was much too sensible to step on. For once indifferent to an audience, she took the container of strawberries and cream from the sack and set it down in front of the lion. Although she recognized the reason for the diplomatic silence of the two cagemen, she resented it, too, especially because she knew they were both having a hard time keeping from laughing. When the bowl was empty, she picked it up and hurried away, her face stony.

Later, after she'd agonized over the incident for hours, she finally came to the only decision possible. She had wronged Wade, insulted him and chewed him out in front of witnesses. By now half the circus would know that she'd called him a bastard and a psycho. She owed him an apology, and it had to be in front of witnesses. That was only fair.

She waited until the next morning before she sought Wade out. As she came into the cookhouse, she was aware of covert glances, a few amused smiles, but she ignored them and stalked to the long side, where Wade sat with several other roughies and canvasmen. Although she winced inwardly when she saw that one of the men was O'Brien, who was known to be a trouble-maker and to have a foul mouth, she didn't hesitate. When she was standing beside Wade, he raised wary eyes to her face, a forkful of flapjacks suspended above his plate; it was obvious he wasn't going to make it easy for her.

"I owe you an apology," she said, her voice loud enough to be heard all the way over to the short side of the cookhouse, where the artistes and the show bosses sat. "I'm sorry that...that I jumped to conclusions. I should have given you a chance to explain that you were only trying to get a broken bottle out of Leopold's cage."

Although he only nodded and didn't smile, she was sure Wade was enjoying her discomfiture, and also that he was quite aware what her public apology was costing her pride. "It's okay," he said easily. "You have to be careful about your cats. I'm sure you've had experience with people tormenting them."

"But it isn't okay. I made a mistake and I want to make it up to you," she said, gritting her teeth. "I'd like you to have supper with me tomorrow night." She hesitated, then added, "I've invited Pop and Marshall, too."

For a moment, as he surveyed her with amused eyes and took his time answering her, she was convinced he would refuse the invitation. But no, he was nodding, smiling. "I'd like that. What time?"

She hesitated, a little nonplussed. She had been so sure he would make some excuse that she hadn't really considered details. "After the evening show," she said, making up her mind.

"Man, I wish she was sore at *me*," O'Brien told Wade with an ugly laugh. "Tanya's one of them gourmet cooks, or so they say."

Tanya ignored him. With another nod she turned and walked away, her head high. She'd done the right thing; she had swallowed her pride and apologized, but after this evening she meant to stay as far away from Wade as possible. After all, what did one more roughie mean to her?

THE NEXT AFTERNOON, Tanya shopped for food supplies at a supermarket in a nearby plaza where the circus people did most of their shopping when they were in Wichita. Unlike some circus people, Tanya never felt ill at ease away from her own kind. She suspected this was because she looked much like a towner. So many of the circus women were conspicuous away from the lot because they felt naked without heavy makeup and wore it most of the time, even to go shopping or while traveling. Since Tanya seldom wore makeup when she wasn't working, she knew she could pass for a young suburban wife shopping for her family in her jeans and tunic top, or even as a high-school girl, shopping for her mother.

As she was putting tomato sauce in her cart, she overheard two women talking further along the aisle. Although their voices were loud, she didn't pay any attention to their conversation until one of them made a slighting remark about Caroline, the show's tattooed woman, who was also at the supermarket. Tanya's face flushed with anger. If she hadn't known that it would embarrass Caroline, she would have ticked the woman off in no uncertain terms.

As it was, she relieved some of her ire by giving the offender a long hard look before she turned her back and hurried to the check-out stand to pay for her groceries.

After considerable thought she had decided to serve Pop's favorite dish, Cincinnati-style chili. Not only would she please her friend, but she would also be making a statement to Wade. She wanted to make it very clear to him that she hadn't gone to any special trouble just because he had been invited for supper.

Even so, before the evening performance she prepared the chili with more than usual care, cooking the beans from scratch rather than using canned ones, letting the chili simmer long and slowly. Before she went to dress, she chopped onions, grated yellow cheese and set a large pot of water on her small propane stove, ready to start the spaghetti when she returned.

After the show it took her a while to decide what to wear. She was tempted to settle for her usual jeans and one of her jersey tops, only to change her mind and choose an embroidered blouse, one of several she'd bought in Mexico during last year's tour, and a flounced, calf-length black felt skirt. She arranged her hair with more than usual care, telling herself that she wanted to look nice for Pop and Marshall. Only when she found herself applying lipstick with a lavish hand did she stop, wipe it off and give herself a lecture about acting like a fool.

Marshall was the first to arrive. After he'd told her she looked like a butterfly in her yellow blouse, he sniffed hungrily and added that she might be unorthodox in her cooking methods, but she had all the instincts of a fine chef.

"Who but you could make a gourmet dish out of a simple dinner of chili and spaghetti," he said, shaking his head. "And the way you mix national foods is amazing—but then you're something of a duke's mixture yourself, of course. Russian and French and possibly a few other nationalities, too."

"Not like you, you snobbish son of an English duke," she teased.

"Ah, that's just my gimmick," he said lightly.

"Uh-huh. Well, I know your secret, and if I ever need money badly enough, I just might blackmail you. Think how the guys would love to hear about that coat of arms I saw on one of the letters you got from your—"

"That's enough, Tanya," he said sharply.

Tanya was instantly contrite. "I'm sorry. My teasing gets out of hand sometimes. And you know I'd never discuss your personal business with anyone, although I don't know why you act as if your background is some kind of crime. After all, you do call yourself Lord Marshall."

"That's my little 'in' joke. The difference is that

everybody believes it's a gimmick. But if it got out that it was true, that would be a different story.''

"I see,'' she said, though she really didn't. ''It sure is a strange world,'' she added, sighing.

"Strange, yes,'' Marshall said, his face tight. ''What's strange is being born into a family that is so ashamed of you that they keep you tucked away in a separate wing of the house until you finally rebel and...and then only consent to send you to university if you promise to use another name. That's what's strange.''

"Your mother—did she go along with all this?''

"My mother is so afraid that I'll do something to disgrace my precious brothers and sisters that she pretends I don't exist. The only time I hear from any of them is when they want me to sign some papers concerning the family trust. Since I'm the oldest son, it seems I'm legally the heir. Which is why I took myself off to another country, as far away as possible from the lot of them. I found acceptance here among strangers that I never found with my own flesh and blood.''

"And I found the same acceptance,'' she said huskily. ''I could have been raised in an institution somewhere or in a whole series of foster homes.''

"So that makes us two very lucky people.'' Marshall studied her, his face somber. Not for the first time she thought how well formed and perfectly proportioned he was. Although some of the towners called him a dwarf, circus people referred to him correctly as a midget. ''Don't be too grateful, Tanya. We—all of us who took on the job of raising you— got more out of it than you did. You're the family Pop and Alice and some of the rest of us never had. So be grateful, yes, but don't think you have to devote your whole life to making it up to us.''

"I seem to hear an echo in the room," Tanya said with a half laugh. "That's almost exactly what Alice told me last week."

"She's a very wise lady. Maybe we both see something in you that bothers us. It's possible to be too loyal, you know."

"Well, I don't agree—"

There was a sound at the open door. She turned and saw Wade standing there, looking in. Although he was smiling, the smile didn't reach his eyes. How long had he been there, listening to them, she wondered. Somehow, even though she resented the man, she was sure he wouldn't deliberately eavesdrop. But just what was there about him that made her so sure of this? Why was he so different from the other men she knew?

Of course he was extremely attractive in a rugged, masculine way. She didn't doubt he'd had a lot of success with women. Already every single woman— and some not single—in the circus was twittering about him, each going out of her way to attract his attention. But other men were just as good-looking. Other men had lithe, well-built bodies and crisp, thick hair and eyes that seemed to hold just a tinge of aloofness, even when he was smiling as he was now....

Tanya realized that she was still staring at Wade, and that his polite smile had changed into a genuine grin. Feeling embarrassed and awkward, emotions rare to her, she opened the screen door and invited him inside. Because she was irritated over the effect he had on her, her voice was a little sharp when she said, "Marshall tells me you two have already met."

Wade nodded to Marshall. "In Clown Alley," he said. "Marshall gave me some pointers about the art of clowning."

"How did you like the new act Gogo cooked up?" Marshall asked.

"It was good. Sort of a takeoff on one George L. Fox made famous, isn't it?"

"Fancy you knowing that."

"Oh, I'm something of a clown buff."

"And what else are you?" Marshall said, his eyes narrowing.

"I don't understand—"

"You don't speak or act like a roughneck—or look like one, either. So I asked, what else are you? You wouldn't happen to be an agent, say, for the Cookson Brothers Circus, would you?

Tanya was too stunned to move. Asking personal questions just wasn't done around the circus, and Marshall, for all his natural testiness, was never deliberately rude unless provoked. As for accusing Wade of being an agent for the Cookson Brothers Circus—that wasn't logical. She'd chased the Cookson agent off the lot a week ago. Of course they could have sent two agents, but why would they go to so much trouble and expense to recruit from a small circus like this one?

Marshall knew all this, so why his sudden hostility toward Wade? She might have a good reason to resent Wade, but Marshall didn't. He'd always been very protective toward her, but he was well aware that she could take care of herself around men. Even so, he was eyeing Wade with the bellicosity of a father meeting his daughter's unsuitable suitor for the first time.

Wade smiled at Marshall; the glint in his eyes revealed he was more amused than offended. "I'm not an agent for anybody. I'm a working stiff, and a roughie's job in a traveling show is perfect for someone who has wanderlust. I have no ambitions for anything else.''

There was a ring of truth in his voice, and after a pause Marshall nodded. But he sounded testy as he commented, ''This is a good show for a man who doesn't step out of line. It doesn't pay as much as others and the work is hard, but Pop is always willing to give a man a chance.''

''That's all I want—a chance to earn my pay.''

To Tanya's relief, Pop arrived before Marshall could answer. As she finished dinner preparations in her tiny kitchen, she kept glancing through the latticework partition that acted as a room divider, thinking what a contrast the three men made.

And yet they had one thing in common. Each was very masculine in his own individual way. Pop, with his fringe of gray hair, his tough boxer's body, his unconscious air of authority. Marshall, who was all man despite his size. And Wade. How to describe Wade Broderick? He was obviously a man who had no doubts about either his own masculinity or his own worth. So why was he content to be a roughneck, a common laborer?

And why did he keep watching her, as if he were trying to make up his mind about her? Although she was careful not to show it, she felt as if her nerves had all been exposed and were supersensitive to every gesture, every word he spoke. He seemed to throw her off balance so that she overreacted to everything he did—she who could face down wild tigers, lions and drunken towners without turning a hair!

She served the meal outside on a small portable picnic table in the shade of the trailer. As they ate she was silent, letting the men talk without offering any comments, not even on subjects about which she had strong opinions. The chili, a rich mixture of spices and meat, was lavishly praised, even by Marshall, who professed scorn for most American favorites.

"What spices did you use?" Wade asked as he accepted another helping of chili. "It's different from any I've ever eaten—or is it a secret?"

"No secret. Cumin seed and cinnamon and bay leaves, among others. It's Cincinnati chili, Pop's favorite."

"Well, it's very good."

"Tanya can cook just about anything," Pop said. "When she was twelve, she decided cookhouse food was giving me stomach trouble, so she got the women to teach her how to cook. Being Tanya, she usually mixes them all up together—Spanish and German and Italian and Romanian—but somehow it all comes out right. I didn't want her to bother, but Tanya is one stubborn gal, as you'll find out if you stay around here very long."

"I'm sure she is." Although Wade's words were noncommittal, Tanya was sure she read amusement in his voice. "She has one hell of a temper, too."

"Indeed she has, right along with the world's softest heart for anyone or any animal in trouble. I hear you got the worst of it yesterday," Pop said, grinning.

"It was like being attacked by a tigress," Wade replied.

"Well, she may be quick to fly up sometimes, but she always says she's sorry afterward, if it's needed."

"Would you two please stop talking about me as if I'm not here?" Tanya said crossly.

"Oh, princesses have to expect that," Wade said.

"Yes, Tanya is that, a princess in the narrow world of the circus," Marshall said, his voice heavy. "The thing is, what would she be in the outside world?"

The two younger men exchanged glances, and again Tanya wondered what was going on between them. Marshall seemed antagonistic toward the newcomer, and yet they also seemed to share some secret that excluded her and made her feel like an outsider.

Pop yawned and stretched. "Well, me for bed," he said. "Tomorrow's another breakdown day, and it's a longish stretch to Claremore. You'd better get some rest, hon," he added pointedly, looking at Tanya.

Taking the hint, Wade rose. "And if I don't want to be late in the morning and get Flat Iron down on me, I'd better get in some sack time, too."

"Yeah. Well, keep your nose clean and you won't have no trouble with Flat Iron. He says you're a good worker, and that kind is hard to find these days."

When the men were gone, Tanya cleared the table, then did the dishes and put them away. She got ready for bed, but she didn't fall asleep right away as she usually did. Instead she lay awake, thinking about Wade and the evening's conversation, which had seemed to have so many undercurrents. What had Wade and Marshall meant with all that talk about a princess? And why should she care, when it was obvious that Wade had no personal interest in her, that she was only an object of amusement to him? Why did that hurt so? Why did she keep wishing that things were different, and that she hadn't started off by antagonizing him?

CHAPTER SIX

DURING THE NEXT FEW DAYS, as the circus moved from Kansas into Oklahoma, Tanya seemed to see Wade every time she looked up. She caught glimpses of his tall, muscular body as she went about her duties, taking care of her cats, helping out where needed. And every time she saw him, she was reminded of those few minutes in the menagerie tent when he'd kissed her, a kiss that had haunted her ever since.

Although reason told her that in such small, tight quarters she was bound to see every person in the circus at least once or twice a day, she suddenly seemed sensitized to Wade, to know instinctively when he was in the crowd walking by the ten-in-one tent where she was substituting for one of the cashiers, or when he was passing the open door of the silver wagon as she helped Maude, Pop's clerk, work on Pop's mangled books.

Although he always nodded and smiled, he never stopped to talk to her, and this, too, was a source of grievance, more because of her own disappointment than anything else. She, who had never run after any man, who had developed a prickly shell that discouraged unwanted male attention, began taking extra care of her appearance, wearing her most becoming clothes even when she was working with the cats.

Although she had never been vain, she found herself staring into the mirror with indecent regularity, wondering what *he* thought of sun-streaked chestnut brown hair, of amber-colored eyes. Probably he preferred blondes. He had certainly stared at her the time she'd worn a blond wig and taken Shirley's place on the web. Once when she saw Wade talking and laughing with Karen Owens, one of the aerial-ballet women, who had a fantastic body and thick, dark red hair, she writhed with jealousy, and it was this more than anything else that alerted her to something she had been trying to deny. She was no longer angry with Wade. In fact, she would have given anything to be his friend, to be the object of his attention, to laugh with him—and maybe even more.

It wasn't until a week later, when they were working a county fair in an Oklahoma City suburb, that she finally got a chance to talk to Wade again.

She was cleaning out one of the animal cages, a job the cagemen usually took care of, but Moon was down with a virus, and Charlie had hurt his back. She had just turned off the hose and was trying to coax Moana, who like all lions hated to get her feet wet, to leave the corner where she was crouching so it could be hosed down, too.

"You do just about every job around the show, don't you?" Wade said from behind her. "A real Jill-of-all-trades."

To her embarrassment, Tanya felt her heart give a convulsive leap and then begin pounding very fast. "We're pretty shorthanded lately," she said, relieved that her voice sounded cool and impersonal. "It keeps us hopping."

"Not everybody. I haven't noticed the other performers putting out any extra effort."

"Well, I like variety," she said quickly.

"A little better organization and planning on the part of management might help," he said almost to himself, and she bristled, instantly defensive of what she took as criticism of Pop.

"This is one of the best shows in the country, and Pop is the best manager," she said tartly.

"And you, my friend, have the fastest temper and the quickest loyalties this side of the Pecos," he said, his lips twitching.

"I don't like to hear anyone criticize Pop. He's been like a father to me ever since my mother died."

"And the other old-timers around here? Are you just as defensive of them, too?"

"They're good people."

"But even good people have to retire eventually. You must have noticed that some of them can't handle the load any longer. It would take three of you to do it for all of them. When was the last time you had a whole day off?"

"I don't need any time off. I get plenty of that during the winter," she said evasively. "I like being busy, and besides, I'm still young. Work doesn't bother me."

"You obviously thrive on it." His eyes moved over her, and she felt a blush staining her cheeks as his gaze lingered on her mouth. "You have to be the loveliest—" He broke off, and she had the impression he was annoyed with himself. His voice was brusque when he added, "Morris Vaughn asked me to help you out since your cagemen are both sick. What do you want me to do first?"

For the next hour they worked together in companionable silence, broken only when Tanya explained some chore to Wade. She noted that she only had to tell him once. He immediately seemed to grasp the mechanics of the squeeze cage she used when she had to examine a sore paw that was making Romulus limp, and to administer worm medicine to the tigress, Bathsheba, who had been showing ominous signs of infestation.

Wade was also quick to learn the simple process of herding the animals from one side of the cage to the other while he and Tanya washed it out with a pressure hose. After they had finished feeding the cats, he stood beside Tanya, laughing at the antics of Moana, the youngest of the lionesses, who was rubbing up against the bars, her tawny eyes fixed on Leopold. The aging lion, who obviously took her attention as his due, returned her stare, his yellow eyes languid.

"The old boy still has a way with the ladies," Wade commented.

"Oh, male lions remain active sexually until they're very old. Leopold is the equivalent of an eighty-year-old man, but he fathered at least two litters in winter quarters last year. Lars Larson—he's the man who taught me how to train cats—runs a jungle farm near Sarasota where I keep Leopold part of the winter now that he doesn't need any more training. He gets along fine with the other lions at the reserve, even the males, which is rare. He always manages to gather together a small harem, too. We don't allow the cats to mate on the road. It makes for fights in the Big Cage."

Wade studied the male tiger as he paced up and down, staring at them through the bars with his yellow-flecked eyes. "Poor beast. I wonder if he knows what he's missing, being penned up in a cage like that and being made to perform tricks for his supper."

"I'm sure he's quite content," Tanya retorted.

"Why would he miss droughts and disease and starvation and injuries, which is what he could expect in the wild? You should see some of them when they're first captured—full of mange and skin infections, their ribs sticking out. Here they get good food, warmth when it's cold, better medical care than most people get. And in winter quarters they have even more freedom. They're even allowed to...you know..."

Wade raised an eyebrow. "You know? What's that?"

She tossed her head, realizing he was teasing her. "Sex—they're allowed to breed."

"I'd prefer my freedom, thank you. I'd be willing to take a chance on the rest of it."

"But you aren't a lion. They're really very indolent creatures. In the wild, the lionesses do the hunting and bring the food back to their mates."

"Now *that* I thoroughly approve of," he said.

"I'm not surprised. I'm sure you'd just love to have some woman waiting on you hand and foot!"

"Well, I have to admit that the idea of a young thing in my lonely—" Again he broke off. "And I think this conversation is heading for trouble. Tell me about the new tigers. Any trouble with them now?"

Personally Tanya agreed that the conversation had been getting out of hand, though she resented the fact that Wade was the one who had changed the subject. Her voice cool, she told him that the tigers had been integrated into the act without undue trouble; the female was already doing simple tricks and the male was gradually adjusting to discipline.

"Bennie is unusually bright. Since he isn't afraid of fire, I plan to train him for the flaming-hoop trick during the winter. I expect by next spring that he'll be doing his share. He's really such a beautiful animal—very large for a tiger."

She hesitated briefly, staring at Wade, then succumbed to temptation and asked. "What do you plan to do this winter?"

"I don't know. It's too early to decide. Anything can happen between now and then."

"Do you have a family somewhere?"

The small lines beside his eyes deepened, although he didn't smile. "Are you asking if I'm married, Tanya?"

"Of course not. It's none of my business whether you're married." She hesitated, then added, "Since you did bring it up—*are* you married?"

"No, and I don't have any plans for matrimony in the foreseeable future. I'm basically a loner, which doesn't make me very good husband material. And I thought circus people didn't ask personal questions."

Tanya knew she was flushing again, but she couldn't seem to look away from his quizzical stare. "It wasn't all that personal. And besides, I thought we'd agreed to. . .to bury the hatchet and be friends, so naturally I want to know a little more about you. You did bring it up, you know," she added, not entirely truthfully. "And I did apologize for being rude to you."

Despite her best intentions there was more than a hint of arrogance in her voice, so she was a little surprised when he said softly, "I'd like to be your friend, Tanya. The only thing is, it could be very dangerous to both of us."

"I don't understand what you mean."

"You really don't, do you? And yet you must feel

this...this chemistry between us. I wasn't sure at first, but now I'm convinced that you don't have any idea what you do to a man with that smile, that skin, that lovely mane of hair.''

He reached out to fondle a strand of hair that had escaped her cap. When she tried to tuck it out of sight again, he stopped her. "No, don't hide that beautiful hair. I've been wanting to lose myself in it ever since the first time I saw you.''

Fascinated by the huskiness in his voice and the warmth in his eyes, Tanya stared up at him. He slid the cap off her head, and when her hair tumbled around her shoulders, he buried his hands in it, doing it so naturally that she felt no threat.

"Your hair is so thick I thought it would be coarse to the touch, but it's very fine—like silk.'' He took her face between his palms and bent his head down so he could stare directly into her eyes. "So prickly and independent and tough on the outside, and yet so soft and yielding to the touch. Which is the real Tanya? Or are there two Tanyas inside that beautiful head?''

She couldn't find her voice, or the strength to pull away. With a groan he grasped her shoulders tightly and pulled her up against his hard body. His mouth closed over hers in a deep kiss, and still she didn't pull away. At some point, as his lips throbbed against hers and his tongue probed the softness of her mouth, she lost her breath and had to cling to him to keep from falling. As the kiss went on, his arms, holding her so tightly, were like a vise—a vise made of muscles and warm, hard flesh.

She wanted him to stop. Paradoxically, she wanted him never to stop. Even though the emotions his kiss aroused were frightening to her because they were so strange and new, they also seemed familiar, as if she'd felt this excitement, this wanting to yield, before.

Maybe in my dreams, she thought, only half coherently. She became aware of another pressure against her soft thigh. When she realized that Wade was becoming sexually aroused, she felt a surge of panic, mingled with a sense of power that both thrilled and frightened her.

But it was Wade who broke away first. The eyes that she'd thought were so cool burned with a blue fire, and his hands, still holding her shoulders lightly, were unsteady now.

"God, you do things to me, and I don't want that—it wouldn't be fair to you. Nothing can come of it but trouble. I can't make any commitments, Tanya, not even for the rest of the summer. Remember when you told my cards and the Hanging Man turned up? Well, that's what I am right now. And a man in transit travels best alone. I don't want to end up making you unhappy, and that's why I think we should cool this. . .this business before it gets started. I want to make love to you, but it wouldn't be fair. You're too vulnerable, and you have too intense a nature, too much loyalty to those you care about to become involved in a casual affair, a summer fling. If things were different—if you were older, more experienced—maybe I would take a chance, but as it is, I think this had better be the last time I kiss you."

He kissed her again, this time a gentle, friendly kiss that had nothing of passion in it. And then he was gone, leaving her standing there, her body throbbing and her thoughts in turmoil.

It was later that fury replaced disappointment and frustration. She felt humiliated, shamed—and angrier than she'd ever been before in her life. There

were so many things she should have said instead of
standing there in silence, watching that insufferable
egomaniac walk away. Why hadn't she said them?
She was fast enough with her tongue at other times
and could hold her own with everyone from too-
amorous roughies to hecklers in the audience who
had had too much to drink and wanted to help her
with her act. So why had she let Wade get away with
his condescending little speech? And how could she
get even and save her pride?

The answer came to her after a restless night. It
was such a good plan that it immediately restored her
good humor and soothed a little of her hurt pride.
When she saw Wade again, she behaved as if the episode in the menagerie top had never happened. Although he was obviously suspicious at first, her
friendly smile must have fooled him, because when
she told him, her tone casual, that she was cooking
for Pop and Marshall again after the evening show
and that he was welcome to come, too, he hesitated
only a moment before he accepted her invitation.

"Oh, and could you bring some wine? I'm fixing
Italian food and we need a good red to go with it.
Nothing fancy. A California mountain red would be
fine," she added, her smile demure.

ALTHOUGH WADE'S FIRST IMPULSE had been to refuse
Tanya's invitation, he knew that she would consider it
a rebuff. Since she seemed to have taken his little
speech to heart and had been friendly but also very impersonal when they'd met, he should be feeling
pleased. Instead he found himself looking for her
everywhere he went for the rest of the day, hoping to
catch a glimpse of her, and finally stealing into the Big
Top during the evening performance to watch her act.

In the Big Cage, in her forest green tunic and tight-fitting jodhpurs, she was a different person from the hard-working woman he saw around the midway. There was an authority in her voice, a sureness in her every movement that made it plain she was totally in control. That she also looked incredibly fragile in contrast with the great cats added to her mystique. Wade wasn't surprised that the audience ate it up. They applauded long after she had taken her bow and left the center ring, and he felt a queer surge of pride, a desire to yell out, "Hey, I know that woman—she's my friend."

Since heroine-worship was totally out of character for him, he told himself this only proved he'd done the right thing by cooling their relationship before it went any further. If it meant that she would treat him with a casual indifference from now on, so be it. At least they were still friends, or so her invitation indicated.

But it was strange how eagerly he showered and dressed that evening, even while he laughed at himself for behaving like a schoolboy. After all, he had escorted—and bedded—some of the most beautiful women in New York and California in his time. So why did he feel as if he were about to embark on a very festive occasion, even though he knew how simple the meal would probably be, since Pop was coming.

When he reached Tanya's trailer, carrying the bottle of wine he'd talked Cookie out of for a hefty fee, he paused, wondering why there was no sound of voices inside. Then he realized he was a few minutes early, and knew he must be the first of the guests to arrive. As he knocked on the door, he noted that a radio or tape deck inside was playing Chopin. A strange choice for a circus woman, he thought, and then winced at his own unconscious snobbishness.

A few seconds later, Tanya opened the door. She was wearing a long skirt made from some kind of silky material and a white off-the-shoulder Mexican blouse. Her smile was so warm that he felt a little dazed. Chatting animatedly, she got him settled on a small sofa, as gracious, he thought with amusement, as any hostess he'd ever encountered. He felt just as if he were being entertained in a Beverly Hills mansion instead of a twenty-by-fifteen-foot trailer.

It wasn't until she had already opened the wine he'd brought and had poured him a glass that she told him casually, "I'm afraid you'll just have my company tonight. Pop came down with that virus that's been going around, and Marshall had to go into Oklahoma City to see an old friend who is in the hospital. He sent his regrets, and I promised to have him to lunch tomorrow to eat some reheated pasta."

She gave him a winsome smile. "I hope you don't mind. I didn't want to call it off, especially since I had so much food already prepared."

Wade hesitated. Weren't her eyes just a bit too ingenuous? No, he was judging her by other, far more sophisticated women he'd known. Besides, he had no intention of doing anything rash, even if at the moment he found it almost impossible not to kiss those dark pink lips again. . . .

"All the more for me," he said aloud. "Italian's my favorite food."

Half an hour later, as he pushed back his plate with a groan, he had to make an adjustment in his thinking. He had expected the usual pasta with meat sauce, bread sticks and possibly some antipasto. What he had just eaten was gourmet food—stuffed breast of veal, an antipasto of diced tomatoes, egg-plant, celery and peppers mixed with olives and caponata, a pasta salad of zucchini, green fettucine and bits of parmesan and hot red peppers, and for dessert, cheesecake made with fresh lemon, orange peel and rum.

"You're a wonderful cook, Tanya," he told her expansively. "This meal makes Cookie's food look like prison fare."

"It *is* pretty awful lately, especially his stew," she said, laughing. "I don't know what's happening. Cookie used to be the greatest cook in the circuit."

She poured a little more wine in his glass. It occurred to him that although she had been sipping hers quite regularly, it seemed to stay at the same level. Before the thought had time to jell, Tanya was proposing a toast to Pop, and he politely drained his glass. After all, he thought a bit hazily, it was only wine. Even if he drank a whole bottle, which he didn't intend to do, it took more than a little California red to get him tipsy. . . .

They talked about a dozen different subjects. He had never thought of Tanya as a chatterbox, but tonight she seemed to have an opinion on everything. Not even to himself would he admit his stab of disappointment when she confided that although the whole circus thought of her as some kind of angel, she was not the innocent they believed.

"I have to admit that I wasn't too impressed by the boys I, you know, experimented with," she said breezily. "After all, what do boys know about sex? Maybe it's time I changed to older, more experienced men."

There was something wrong with that statement, something that didn't ring true, but he was diverted by her nearness. At some point during the past few minutes she had moved from the easy chair where she'd been perched to the sofa and was sitting so close that he could touch her and smell the sweet, sensual scent of her perfume.

"Your eyes remind me of those polished stones people in the West call Apache tears," he told her. "Another name for them is cat's eyes."

"Better watch out," she said softly. "Cats can scratch." She leaned closer, so close that he felt her breath on his cheek, and peered into his eyes. "Your eyes are the color of the sky over the Florida Keys on a sunny afternoon."

She didn't move away; as her gaze dropped to his mouth, her lips parted slightly, and she moistened them with her pink tongue, as if they were dry. He thought how sweetly the lower lip curved, how enchanting the deep indentation of her upper lip was. It seemed so natural to lean toward her, to taste the honey of those lips. As his mouth closed over hers, he sank into softness, moistness, and he felt exhilarated, as if he had just been handed a prize that he'd coveted for a long time.

The kiss deepened; she was close but not close enough to suit him. He put his arms around her and drew her up against his chest, and he could feel the warmth of her soft breasts through the thin material of her blouse as she pressed against him, sending a hot thrill coursing through his veins. Her arms, incredibly soft, slid around his neck, and her fingers found the hair at the nape and stroked it gently. He was so bemused that it was a while before he realized what was happening to him. What had started as a casual kiss had become something more. As he became aware of the pressure of her thigh against his, he knew he wanted her, that he must have her. Nothing, he thought, was going to stop him now—and he couldn't know that Tanya, snug in his arms, was thinking the same thing, and that she was afraid of the reaction to her own traitorous body.

ALL EVENING, as she had cozened up to Wade, Tanya had taken a secret satisfaction in how easily she'd disarmed him. It was obvious he had no suspicions that she hadn't asked Pop and Marshall to dinner, nor was she worried that Wade might eventually find out she'd lied about this. By the time he did, it would be too late. She would have had her revenge. . . no, not that. It wasn't revenge she wanted, just the chance to show him how insulting his rejection had been, his speech about how dangerous it was for *her* if he ever kissed her again. By the time she got finished with Wade Broderick, he'd know for sure that he was the one in danger, not her.

So she smiled sweetly into Wade's eyes while she continued to refill his glass. That she had replaced the gradually emptied wine bottle he'd brought with a full one halfway through dinner, he couldn't have suspected since she had used a little sleight of hand to make the switch. After all, she'd learned how to play the old carney game, three-card monte, practically in the cradle, and switching bottles was a snap next to that.

When Wade's strong face took on a flush and his eyes began to glaze slightly, she eased onto the sofa beside him and let him get a good whiff of her perfume, bought especially for the occasion. She seldom wore perfume because her cats were sensitive to floral scents and found perfume irritating. The tiny bottle she'd bought had been French and astonishingly expensive, but if it worked, it was worth it.

And it did seem to be working. When Wade leaned
forward, almost casually, to kiss her, she slid along
the cushion toward him, making it easy for him to
put his arms around her. She felt his hard thigh
against her softer one and knew that he was becoming aroused. It was time for her to pull way, toss his
words back in his face—but maybe not just yet. For
one thing, she felt a little dizzy. Maybe the glass of
wine she'd sipped so carefully all evening was affect-
ing her, too. After all, she seldom touched any kind
of alcohol. Well, there was no hurry. It wouldn't
hurt to wait a bit and ensnare him even more. It felt
so comfortable here in the circle of Wade's arms, and
after all, so far he was only kissing her. . . .

The kiss deepened, and Wade's tongue tantalized
the sensitive flesh inside her mouth, arousing erotic
feelings that were new to her. A warmth started up
inside her chest, and there was a delicious tingling
along her inner thighs as if her legs had gone to sleep
and the circulation had just been restored.

Wade's hands had been holding her face so he
could kiss her; now they touched her throat, stroking
the soft flesh there, then moved downward to cup her
shoulders. Without conscious thought, she arched
her torso, giving him easier access to her body, an invitation that he took advantage of by lowering his
head and burying his face in the deep hollow between
her breasts.

The coolness of air against her bare skin was her
first intimation that he had slipped down the gathered neck of her blouse, taking her bra straps with it.
He pushed aside the lacy strip that was her bra and
touched her breasts with his fingertips, then with his
lips, and a rush of pleasure moved through her, so
strong that she moaned softly. She was aware that

the core of heat was expanding, and then, as if it had burst inside her, she felt a sweetness, a recklessness, an obliviousness to anything except the sensations sweeping her.

Wade's fingers, which she knew to be so strong, were gentle now as they caressed the hollow between her breasts, then circled her nipples, tantalizing, promising more delights to come, and she wanted him to go on, to do other things...things she was vague about but which she knew would lift her to heaven. She slid her arms around his neck, pulling his face down for a kiss that left both of them straining for breath.

His hands trembled as he slid her blouse over her head, then fumbled with the waistband of her skirt. There was something so poignant about this strong man's loss of control that she felt a wave of tenderness as she whispered, "Wait—I'll do it, Wade."

Quickly she slipped out of her skirt and slip; now there was only a wisp of lace between his burning eyes and her ultimate secrets. When his eyes darkened she felt a deep pride because she knew that what he saw pleased him, moved him, aroused him. As he slowly slid her last defense over her hips and knew her with his eyes, she was sure she would burst into flame. The ache was almost unbearable as his hand caressed the soft swell of her stomach, then slipped down to touch the moist valley below, caressing, stroking, exploring until she shuddered with desire.

Wanting to feel his naked flesh against hers, she helped him undress. When he stood before her, she felt no embarrassment, only a wonderment as she stared at his hard maleness with hungry eyes. When she reached out tentatively and touched him with a fingertip, he groaned and told her, his voice, hoarse, "You're killing me, Tanya—killing me!"

He knelt on the floor in front of her and gathered her pliant body in his arms, his face buried in her softness. She caressed his dark hair, and then slid down until she was kneeling, too, pressed tightly against him: breast to breast, hips to hips. The strength and power of his body excited her, threw her into a frenzy, and she rubbed against him, instinctively seeking closer intimacy. He parted her thighs with his knee, and when he pressed himself between them, a sensation of pleasure so intense it was nearly unbearable swept through her.

He touched her hair, then stroked her shoulders, her back, the indentation of her waist, the soft mounds of her buttocks, as if memorizing them.

"I want you, Tanya," he murmured, his breath stirring the fine hairs over her ear. "I've dreamed of you every night since the first time I saw you facing that tiger in the Big Cage."

"And I want you, too," she said, her breath catching. "I want you right now."

He laughed deep in his throat and ran his hands over her breasts, her flaring rib cage and narrow waist. "I think you must be a witch," he said, stroking the dimpled flesh behind her knees. "A man could go crazy just thinking about touching you like this. Do you have any idea what you do to me?"

"And you to me," she whispered. She slid her hands between their bodies, wanting to feel all of him, to explore him as he was exploring her. He groaned again, and his body moved convulsively against her hand. As she felt the pulsation that revealed his excitement, she was sure that she was melting, that the core of heat inside her would consume

her. A stray thought came to her, a bewilderment
that what had started out as a plan to teach Wade a
lesson had turned out to be her own entrapment. But
oh, she did want him—wanted all of him, wanted to
feel him inside her, to finally come into her own as a
woman. Most of all she wanted to bring him pleasure, to satisfy the torment that burned in his
eyes....

Wade kissed her again, his tongue plunging deep
into her willing, eager mouth, and then he was kissing her throat, her breasts, the soft curve of her
stomach, and then, finally, the yielding flesh below
that throbbed to his touch and ached to receive him.
The world around her dissolved, and there was nothing that mattered except this burning sensation, this
arching hunger.

And still he caressed her, bringing her ever closer
to the heaven she wanted so desperately. When she
was sure she could wait no longer, she moved against
his stroking hand, mutely asking him to take her, and
he laughed softly, then lowered her to the floor. As
he parted her thighs with hands that trembled, a moment of uncertainty, a fear that she wouldn't be able
to satisfy him, touched her, and she murmured,
"You'll tell me what to do, won't you?"

At first she thought he hadn't heard her, and then
she realized that his body, poised above hers, was
still. "Are you a virgin, Tanya?"

The sudden harshness in his voice startled her.
"I...does it matter?" she stammered.

"Does it matter...?" He pulled away and ran his
fingers through his hair, a distraught gesture that
sent a cold chill through her. "What the devil do you
think I am? A seducer of virgins? Why did you...
what was all that talk about your experimenting with

boys? Did you decide it was time to give up your virginity and I happened to be convenient? I could cheerfully throttle you. Do you have any idea what could have happened to you if you'd chosen the wrong man for your...your experiments?''

She looked into his burning eyes and realized he was furious. She wanted to plead with him, to tell him that he was the one she wanted to be not only her first lover, but her last.

But her pride, the pride that was so much a part of her, stirred, and suddenly she was shaking with anger. With all the dignity she could muster, she pulled away from him and rose to her feet. Silently, her back turned to him, she threw on her clothes. He didn't move, or at least she didn't sense any movement behind her as she slipped her feet into her sandals. Still not looking at him, she went into the small kitchen and began making coffee.

Only when she was sure that her voice wouldn't betray her hurt did she say, ''It seems that you were the one who should have been careful. And I don't know what all the fuss is about. After all, a little making out never hurt anyone, did it? Don't make such a big thing about it.''

She expected him to retaliate with his own scornful words. What she didn't expect was the kindness in his voice as he said, ''I'm sorry, Tanya. You're disappointed and it's all my fault. I should have bowed out when I realized Marshall and Pop wouldn't be here. I knew it was dangerous to be alone with you, and all that talk about you experimenting with sex didn't ring right. I should have known it was just that... talk. I hurt your feelings the other day and you tried to get back at me by leading me on, but don't you realize that you can't fool around with something as powerful as sex? If you hadn't asked me to tell you what to do, it would be too late by now."

For a moment she was silent; her anger had evaporated as quickly as it had come, leaving her without defenses. She turned her head to look at him, even though she knew that her vulnerability must have been written on her face for him to see, and discovered he was fully dressed. "Would that be so terrible, Wade?" she asked quietly.

"No, it would be heaven, but can't you see that I couldn't do that to you? Your heart is too close to the surface. You have no defenses against . . . strong emotions. I'm so much older than you—"

"Surely no more than a few years."

"Ten years, and there's more than just the age difference. You've lived in a cocoon all your life, Tanya. All you know is the circus. Tomorrow or next week or next month, I'll be gone. How can I be the spoiler that might leave you discontented with this life?"

"Maybe . . . maybe it's already too late," she said.

"I don't think so. You'll forget this happened in a few days, but if we had gone all the way, then I would always be the first one. I've been called ruthless in my day, but I can't do that to you. Your first lover should be someone close to your own age, someone who doesn't have such a cynical view of the world."

"But I don't want a lover my own age. I want someone who can teach me how to be a woman, who will set me on fire and let me love him, take care of him—"

"I'm not that man, Tanya. Maybe you're willing to take a chance, but I'm not. I don't want you on my conscience—or in my head for the rest of my life."

He didn't kiss her when he left. As if he were afraid that he might weaken, he left her with only one last long look and a brief smile. After he was gone, she collapsed on the sofa, leaving the glasses still sitting on the table, the dishes and pots still piled in the sink, while she cried her heart out with only her old stuffed lion, the last remnant of her childhood, clutched tightly in her arms to comfort her.

CHAPTER SEVEN

TANYA SAT at one of the long, narrow plank tables in the cookhouse, a mug of Cookie's potent coffee in her hand, listening to the hubbub of voices around her. She felt strangely detached, as if a high wall separated her from her friends. It was Pop's sixty-fifth birthday, and it had been the unanimous opinion of the circus, of everybody from the lowest josser to the highest star act, that it couldn't be allowed to go uncelebrated, even though they were in the midst of a run of short engagements.

Pop had seemed properly stunned when he'd been lured into the cookhouse on some pretense and found one-third of the circus personnel, those who could get away from their duties for a while, waiting for him, ready to yell "Happy birthday, Pop!" Even if there was a twinkle in his eyes, no one could be sure he really wasn't as surprised as he let on.

Cookie had prepared a monumentally large cake, heavy with green and blue decorations, which Tanya thought made it look like a giant gum ball. He'd also fixed a couple of crocks full of his mysterious nonalcoholic punch, which was red, fruity and tasted of cinnamon, his favorite spice. The celebration was in full swing now with people coming and going, taking turns at wishing Pop well, because someone had to man the booths, the rides, the grab joints for the afternoon crowds.

In another half hour or so the party would break up, and the performers would return to their dressing tents or trailers to start preparing for the evening performance. Why, Tanya wondered, did she keep wishing so fervently that it would end and she could get away from the noise, the risqué jokes, the constant necessity to smile and nod and pretend she was having a good time? What was wrong with her, anyway? These were her friends and she loved them, even though they could be difficult at times.

And why, why did she keep watching the door, looking for a tall, well-built man with eyes the color of the morning sky? Even if he came, Wade probably wouldn't pay any attention to her—not that she had given him much of a chance to talk to her lately. Ever since that humiliating scene in her trailer she had avoided him. The few times he'd tried to speak to her, she'd cut him off, ignoring him so pointedly that he couldn't mistake her message. And she meant to continue to ignore him, too, even though she knew that the whole circus was gossiping about the bad blood between them and putting their own interpretations on its cause.

Next to her, Alice made a comment, and Tanya smiled automatically, even though she hadn't heard a word of her friend's conversation for the past few minutes. She was sitting between Alice and Too Tall Tim, who was listening with his usual courtesy to one of Pop's long-winded tales about his boxing days. Marshall, perched on several stadium cushions so he could reach the table, was in his element as he argued hotly with Cookie about the proper way to put together a slumgullion stew. Cookie, who claimed to have hoboed around the country as a youth, swore that it was okay to add anything found growing in a farmer's field, including squash, pumpkins or even melons, while Marshall was of the opinion, loudly expressed, that since it was a British dish, which had been originated by British traveling tinners, it was criminal to use anything but the traditional ingredients—chicken or beef, carrots, onions and potatoes.

At a table in one corner of the tent, several roughies were swapping jokes. Although most of the jokes were decidedly risqué, Tanya wasn't offended. She'd heard raw language and imaginative curses all her life, though she herself seldom used anything stronger than an occasional "damn" or "hell." When she was a youngster she would have earned a mouthful of soap from any one of her surrogate parents if she'd dared say a swear word. The habit persisted, though there were times when she thought a good curse would have relieved her anger or frustration and cleared the air.

At a table behind them, two circus families, the Rodriguezes and the Zorbis, were comparing notes about their younger children, who had been left behind in Florida to go to school, about shows they'd played in the past, and about the retirement homes they both had purchased in Gib'town, Florida, where so many of the circus people lived during the winter months. Although neither couple spoke the other's language, they all had a smattering of English, which they complemented by gestures, winks and what the Spanish call "the language of the eyes."

Several times Tanya looked up to catch a languishing stare from the Zorbis' unmarried son, but each time she looked away, pretending not to notice. Just a few weeks ago she had been flattered by his crush on her; he was a good-looking man two years her senior, with snapping black eyes and a flashing smile.

Now she was completely indifferent to him. And how was it that nothing or no one seemed to matter to her lately except an egotistical roughie who had such a good opinion of himself that he'd actually told her he felt he had to protect her from herself when he was around?

"You worried about something, hon?" It was Too Tall Tim. His wide shoulders, stooped from so many years of leaning down to talk to shorter men, were several feet above her, even though he was sitting down. Most people found his height intimidating, but she never had, not even when she was a tiny girl. She had taken her first tumble off a rosinback horse while Tim was giving her a riding lesson. He had caught her before she reached the ground, and then let her ride on his shoulder while she screamed with excitement. Even then she had known that this giant of a man, holding her so carefully that she couldn't slip off his shoulder, would always be there to pick her up should she fall.

"I'm just a little tired," she told Tim, smiling at him. "It's been a hectic tour."

"Yeah. We haven't been drawing horse's feed at the box office, either," he said gloomily. "Georgie Green hasn't been able to turn a tip an hour at the ten-in-one tent these last few stops, and all those municipal dates don't do much for the pocketbook. You can't depend on lodges and chambers of commerce to sell tickets. Those fellows think it's enough if they give you a permit and put their name on the bill as sponsors. And it'll be more of the same for the rest of the week, too, with that three-day still date just after we play Fort Worth. I sure wish we could've arranged for a gig in Houston that weekend. That town is always good to us."

"But we did," she said, puzzled. "We're booked in Houston next Friday, replacing the Martinez Circus because they had that fire. The contract went out a couple of weeks ago."

"Well, it must've been cancelled. The route list hasn't been changed. I was looking at it this morning in the silver wagon."

"But I saw the contract—" Before she could question him further, Pop stood up and rapped a spoon on his coffee mug to get their attention. After he'd given a short, rather embarrassed thank-you speech, there was a series of accolades, some humorous, some ribald and some so heartfelt that they brought tears to Pop's eyes, though his dour expression never changed.

Tanya was listening to the current woes of Octavia, who was wearing a flowing caftan that made her look like a ship under full sail, when Wade finally made an appearance. Although she'd been watching the door, waiting for him, Tanya immediately launched into an animated and rather incoherent conversation with Octavia, who looked a little bewildered.

A few moments later she felt strong fingers pressing into her shoulder and caught a whiff of aftershave lotion. She didn't have to look up to know who was bending over her.

"I have to talk to you, Tanya," he murmured so low that no one else could have heard him. "Meet me out back in five minutes."

He was gone before she could tell him that she'd rather meet King Kong on top of the Empire State Building. A minute later he was sitting with a group of roughies and canvas men, looking so at ease that she felt like throwing one of Cookie's stainless-steel napkin holders at him.

"No way, she thought grimly. *No way am I going to jump to your tune, Wade Broderick. . . .*

Which was why it was so strange that, a few minutes later, she found herself rising, murmuring something to Octavia and Alice about taking a shower before she changed her clothes.

There was still bright sunshine outside the tent, even though it was past six o'clock. In a few minutes the party would break up so everybody could get ready for the evening performance. For a moment, Too Tall Tim's misunderstanding about the show date in Houston crossed Tanya's mind, then was gone as she saw a tall, broad-shouldered man coming around the corner of the tent.

As casually as if it really were an unplanned meeting, Wade stopped in front of her, his smile warm. She didn't return it. Already she was sorry she had come—and also not sure why she had. Simple curiosity, she told herself. And maybe this was her chance to show him just how indifferent she was to him. Yes, *that's* why she'd come. To show him how little he meant to her.

Her manner aloof, she asked, "Well? What is it?"

Wade shook his head, looking exasperated. "This has to stop, Tanya. I'm not your enemy. I didn't mean to hurt you."

"Hurt me?" she said, raising her eyebrows. "Whatever do you mean?"

"Look, let's not play games. Any minute now, the rest of them will come piling out of the cookhouse. There isn't time for sparring. I want to apologize and tell you how sorry I am that I didn't handle things right the other night. I really messed up and I take the blame for that. But there's no reason for hurt feelings. This business of pretending I don't exist is childish. I do exist, and what almost happened isn't something that can be brushed aside. It was a mistake, but we're both adults. We can still be friends, can't we?''

Tanya's first impulse was to slap his patronizing face. Her second was to burst into tears. But she did neither of these things. It took every bit of gumption she had, but somehow she managed to come up with a cool smile.

"I have no idea what you're talking about unless...surely, you don't mean that little...uh, session we had? Why on earth would you think it meant anything special to me? You have a big ego, you know."

"Then I'm wrong, aren't I? And that means there's no reason why we still can't be friends. So I must have been imagining that you've been avoiding me all week."

Since she'd been neatly trapped by her own words, Tanya was forced to shrug, a gesture Wade obviously took as agreement, because he looked relieved. Before he had a chance to say anything more, she nodded stiffly and walked away, holding her head high. Although her legs felt a little weak, she didn't waver—until she was out of Wade's sight behind the transformer truck. If she was a little pale at the evening performance, no one commented on it, and if she cried herself to sleep that night, who was to know?

Although she was sure that she never wanted to face Wade again, the tension between them eased after that. Whenever she saw him around the lot, it was possible to stop and talk, to exchange a few impersonal words, as if he really were a casual acquaintance. So Wade's instincts about clearing the air between them had been right, but that didn't make her feel any better.

All this was wiped out of her mind on the following Friday when they arrived at the Houston fairgrounds in the middle of the night to find that not only weren't they expected, the fairgrounds had no record of a booking for the Peeples Circus that weekend.

It took a while to untangle all the details, but eventually it became clear that someone had made a mistake. The signed contract along with the deposit check, which would have held the fairgrounds for them, had never arrived. Since Jerome, the advance man, had already flooded the Houston area with posters and even arranged a few interviews for the performers with local newspapers and radio talk shows, he was naturally incensed, as was Pop.

It didn't take Tanya long to realize that Pop was to blame. She herself had prepared the contract for his signature when they'd learned about the cancellation at the Houston fairgrounds, which corresponded with one of their still dates, and he had promised to mail the letter that afternoon. When she found it, still in the pocket of his Windbreaker, it was obvious that he had forgotten to drop it into the mailbox, and that he hadn't been alerted when a confirmation didn't arrive from the fairground officials.

Rather than confront him with the proof of his culpability, Tanya took the blame. When he bawled her out royally in front of Jerome, the advance man, and Maude, she took his tongue-lashing with a rare meekness. Although part of her decision to cover up for him was to save Pop's pride, there was a more practical reason. Adding fuel to the rumors already circulating that Pop was getting a little senile could only hurt the circus. The old-timers would remain loyal, no matter what Pop did, but it was different with the newer ones. They had no particular ties to Pop, and it was important that they continue to think of him as always being in control.

No, it was better that she accept the blame, even though his sharp words and his disappointment in her were hard to take. When she apologized for one last time and then started back to her trailer, her nerves felt so raw that she wanted only to be alone for a while to lick her wounds.

She was sitting at the trailer's tiny breakfast counter, a mug of lukewarm coffee between her elbows, when a knock sounded at the door. When she opened it, Wade was standing there, smiling at her, and in her surprise she rushed into his arms, pressing her face against his chest. He stroked her hair, his hand so gentle that it could have been Alice comforting her.

"I heard what happened," he said quietly. "I thought you might need a friend."

"I do," she said, her laugh shaky. "Pop just about took the skin off me. I feel as if I've been through a meat grinder."

"If that's all he did, you got off easy," he said. "If I'd been running things, I'm afraid I would have docked your pay to cover the losses. So count your blessings—it could be worse."

As the meaning of his words sank in, Tanya felt a rush of anger. With an outraged cry she pushed him away. "I might have known. Look who's talking! How dare you criticize me, you...you loser! After all, what have you done with your life? How much responsibility have you taken on?" Wade's lips tightened, but she rushed on, uncaring. "I don't know

why you came here, but you can just clear out. And
stay away from me in the future. I don't need your
kind of fair-weather friendship.''

Wade was silent for a long moment. "I'm sorry
that you misunderstood me, which is something you
do quite often, Tanya. And I shouldn't have bothered to come," he said stiffly. "It's obvious you
don't need my help."

Then he was gone, leaving her feeling deflated and
still angry, because once again she had overreacted to
Wade—and because, in her heart, she knew she had
been wrong.

AFTER WADE LEFT TANYA'S TRAILER he took a long
walk to cool off, cutting across the meadows that
surrounded the lot where the circus personnel had
parked their trailers and rigs temporarily. The morning wind, fresh off the Texas plains, cooled his face,
but it did little to cool his temper. He had left
Tanya's trailer so abruptly instead of having it out
with her because he'd had an insane desire to shake
her for being so unreasonable and touchy, an urge so
foreign to his usually well-controlled temperament
that it alarmed him. What was just as unnerving, he
had wanted to pull her down on the sofa and make
love to her for the rest of the day.

The past week had been hard on his peace of
mind—and a little humiliating, too. In his whole life
he had never wanted a woman as badly as he wanted
this fiery-tempered little temptress, who had all the
weapons of womanhood and who used them so effec-
tively and, he knew in his heart, so unconsciously.

Seeing her walk across the midway, her legs swing-
ing so freely, her chin in the air, was enough to keep
him unsettled for hours. And to come face-to-face

with her, to see her eyes darken and know that she wanted him as badly as he wanted her, that if he hadn't suddenly developed scruples, they would already be lovers—it was unendurable! He had always appreciated women, loved the subtle way they thought, their softness and their toughness, their mystery and their promise, but never before had he been so enthralled by one that he couldn't walk away with his heart still intact, affected as little by their response as by, much more rarely, their indifference.

But Tanya had walked right into his heart, taken it over as if she belonged there. It was almost enough to make him believe there was such a thing as love at first sight—and this from a man who was a cynic about love in any form. And why this particular woman? What was there about Tanya, of all people, that made her so important to his well-being? A serious relationship between them was impossible. He could make love to Tanya and have a summer affair with her, but then what? After he had made himself that much more important to her, it was inevitable that he would walk out of her life—and leave scars behind. He, who had so many scars of his own, couldn't do that, not to someone like Tanya with her spirit, her fine high pride, her loyalty and compassion.

No matter how strong the sexual pull between them, he couldn't, in good faith, make her any promises. Eventually he would return to his own world. Although it had been an adventure he wouldn't have missed, circus life was not something he could stay with forever. He didn't mind hard physical labor and was not too proud to take orders, but it wasn't his nature to stand back and let others take command. Already he was chafing at the waste, the incompetence he saw on every side. And something else had changed. After a few weeks away from responsibility, he was eager to take charge of a business of his own again. This was one thing the summer had accomplished, just as Larry had promised.

In the fall he would return to New York to take up his old life—with a few changes, of course. No more...what had Larry called it? Hedonism? He would renew old friendships, those that were important to him, and even though these particular friends were not snobs, Tanya would still be an oddity, an outsider, among them. She could never fit in. New York would be as alien to her as the circus was to outsiders. Here she was somebody, a princess. Away from the circus she would be lost, out of place. To use her simply because of this passion he had to possess her would be criminal, and he wasn't about to compound the damage he'd already done by letting his sexual drive get out of hand.

But God, how he'd wanted her a few minutes ago! If he hadn't turned and walked away, he would have kissed those sweetly curved lips, touched those ripe breasts, made passionate love to her—and then the damage would have been done. As it was, even if her feelings for him were deeper than the crush of a younger woman for an older man, she would forget him in fast order. Another man would taste her sweetness, not Wade Broderick....

He turned and started back toward the lot where the company trucks were parked. Since the date had been cancelled, there was no activity anywhere. Most of the circus personnel were in their trailers and vans, catching up on their sleep and, he suspected, wondering what the foul-up in the schedule would mean in practical terms.

As Wade passed the silver wagon, he caught a glimpse of Pop's gray head bent over his desk. At the sound of feet on the gravel outside the door, Pop looked up. When he saw Wade, his mouth tightened to a thin, straight line.

There was a glower on his face as he got to his feet and came to the door. "I've been looking for you, Broderick," he snapped. "I expected better from you."

"I don't understand. What's wrong?"

"Don't bother to put on no act. I know you've been giving Tanya a hard time. I found her crying in her trailer a while ago, just after you left there. When I asked her if you'd done something to hurt her feelings, she said she hated you and never wanted to see you again. Then she ran into the bathroom and wouldn't come out. I've already figured out what I owe you, so take your bloody money and clear out. We don't want troublemakers like you in the show. You have half an hour to get off the lot before I have some of the boys throw you off. That should give you time to pack your bag."

"I guess it wouldn't do any good to tell you that you're wrong? That I'd never do anything to hurt Tanya?"

"I seen what I seen. Tanya hardly ever cries, and never about nothing important. I don't want you going near that girl again. She's worth a dozen of you. So get out of here fast or I'm liable to toss you out myself. I'm real disappointed in you. I been hearing some rumors about you coming on to Tanya, but I didn't want to believe them. Fact is, I thought you were square, on the up-and-up. And all the time you've been sneaking around, trying to get at Tanya. You ain't nothing but another grifter, the worse kind."

The disgust in Pop's voice made Wade wince. He started to defend himself, but instead he remained silent. What could he say? That he *hadn't* made Tanya cry? He had, of course, but how could he say that the trouble between them had started when he'd refused to make love to her? And even if he skipped that part, could he truthfully say that he hadn't kissed her, that he didn't want her?

Maybe the solution to the whole problem was simply to accept Pop's edict and leave. He would chalk up the past weeks to an experiment that had failed. After all, he had intended to quit when the show returned to winter quarters. Now the decision had been taken out of his hands.

He turned, ignoring the pay envelope Pop had so contemptuously tossed on the desk, and was already out of earshot before Pop had time to speak again. Ten minutes later he was walking down the highway near the fairgrounds, heading for the nearest bus stop—and New York.

CHAPTER EIGHT

ALTHOUGH SHE HAD NAMED the new male tiger Bennie because he was a Bengal, Tanya had quickly discovered that the friendly name didn't suit his personality. From the first time she'd faced him inside the Big Cage, she had found him difficult to train, though unusually intelligent. His sister—if indeed she was his sister—was quite different, a docile, lazy cat who, after endless hours of coaxing and training, had finally learned to do a few simple tricks. When Pop, always so pragmatic, asked her why she had named the tigress Bathsheba, she laughed and told him she had chosen the name because she didn't have a tiger called Bathsheba, a bit of nonsense that earned her one of his rare smiles.

Early in her career as an animal trainer she had realized that it was almost impossible not to have favorites among the big cats, and she soon became very fond of the sloe-eyed tigress with her languishing glances and kittenish ways.

It was different with Bennie, who aroused her admiration but also her wariness. Ever since they'd returned to winter quarters near Sarasota, she had been working with him, trying to perfect the fire-loop drill. It was a spectacular trick, something that always evoked the applause of an audience, especially when done by a tiger. After she'd discovered that Bennie wasn't intimidated by fire, she'd been very patient, first getting him used to jumping through the hoop before gradually goading and coaxing him until he would hurl his orange-and-black body through the flames on command.

She taught him other tricks, too, one of which involved positioning him on top of a pyramid of lions. It was a difficult trick but also particularly crowd pleasing, and she hoped to liven up her act with it. Since he seemed to have an unusual hatred for lions, teaching him was a laborious process and took a large portion of her work hours during the four months the circus was in winter quarters.

For some reason, probably because he was unusually competitive, Bennie seemed determined to challenge Leopold for dominance of the other males. Leopold, with the loftiness of one who knows his own worth, had so far ignored the Tiger's challenging snarls, possibly because Tanya was careful to always keep them widely separated in the Big Cage. It didn't help that Bathsheba was one of those female tigers who came into season several times a year, and it was Leopold who drew her provocative glances.

"Ah, the perversity of females," Marshall said. He was standing with Tanya outside Bathsheba's cage, watching her antics. The tigress's yellow eyes were fixed on Leopold, who had just returned from his winter sojourn at the jungle farm, and she was rubbing her whiskers against the bars of the cage, making small mewling sounds in her throat. "They always go for the most unlikely and unsuitable male around."

"Oh, come now! What about that long-legged waitress at the truck stop down the highway who's been coming on to you like crazy lately? Are you saying she chose the most unlikely and unsuitable male around?"

Marshall's eyelids twitched, a sure sign that he was pleased by her teasing. He was amazingly successful in his amorous adventures, something that always surprised other men, but not the kind of women who recognized a real man when they saw one, no matter what size package he came in.

"Oh, a few of them have the good sense not to judge a man by his height," he said complacently. "But what about a tigress who has a yen for an aging lion who's losing his teeth? And what about a beautiful lion trainer who mopes around, looking as though she just lost her last friend, over a roughie who walked out on her?"

Tanya looked away from Marshall's too-observant eyes. She wasn't really surprised that he had guessed her secret, though she hadn't confided her desolation even to Alice after Wade had left the circus without one word of goodbye. Her own angry words still haunted her. Had they offended him so much that they'd driven him away? After all, he'd warned her that he was a man in transit. In either case, she would never see him again, and the knowledge was ruining her sleep and her usual zest for life.

"I don't want to talk about Wade Broderick," she told Marshall. "There was nothing between us— nothing at all."

"Nothing except the fact that you were crazy about him, and he gave every indication that he was just as crazy about you. And before you tell me to mind my own business, I'll drop the subject. I might also add that if you need someone to talk to, I'm always available. I have broad shoulders—well, not so broad, maybe, but they're always there when you need a pair to cry on."

Tanya gave him a tremulous smile. "You also have

a big heart. How did such a small man get such a big heart, Marshall?''

Marshall bristled at the compliment, as she knew he would. "That's a lot of nonsense. There's nothing soft about my heart. I'm as tough as they come. And don't give me any garbage about overcompensation. I got enough of that while I was growing up. My old man was always sending me to some London psychiatrist or another to find out why I was so belligerent. They usually trotted out that old bromide about overcompensation. The truth is that I would be competitive even if I were the size of Too Tall Tim. Too much adrenaline in my blood, I suspect.''

"Which made you a real slave driver of a teacher. What other circus kid has to learn how to read Greek and memorize the meanings of words like 'ubiquitous' and 'polymorphous'?''

"Uh-huh. Which reminds me. Did you read that book I lent you last week? I intend to quiz you on it, you know.''

She groaned. "Give me a break! School's been out for three years—not that you seem to notice.''

"If you don't use it, you lose it. Nobody should stop learning, not even when they're in their nineties.''

"Okay, okay. I did read the book and I enjoyed it—well, moderately, though I'm not really into philosophy. So fire away with your questions.''

For the next few minutes, as they walked across the weed-filled compound that surrounded the large weather-beaten barn the circus used for a practice arena, they chatted companionably about books. Although she wasn't much interested in some of Marshall's favorite subjects, Tanya indulged him as much as possible, knowing the satisfaction he derived from "educating" her. In a fairer world, one that didn't judge a man's intelligence by his size, he would have been in his element as a teacher. Since this outlet had been denied him, it seemed a small thing to let him continue to direct her reading.

They had reached the stables next to the training barn when a voice hailed them. Turning, they saw it was Flat Iron Collins. The canvas boss's broad forehead was wrinkled with worry lines as he asked, "Hey, Pop's called a general meeting for tonight. You know anything about it, Tanya?"

"He didn't say anything to me about a meeting. In fact, I haven't seen him for the past week. He said he had some business to attend to in Tampa. I hope nothing's wrong."

"Well, we'll find out soon. He wants us in the training barn at eight. I just set up the benches and now I'm getting ready to call around and see how many people I can reach. Could be somebody's got a special beef. It's about time we had a grievance meeting, I guess. Hell, I've got a couple of my own, like when are we going to get some new canvas? I can't put up a decent-looking Big Top until I get rid of that patched-up old pile of junk that should've been tossed out last year."

Tanya nodded agreement. The canvas tent that housed the Big Show took such a beating from wind gusts and rain and the general wear and tear of being raised and torn down so often that it usually was replaced every winter. This year there hadn't been enough money for even major repairs, much less the considerable expense of new canvas. As for the meeting, it was time for a session when grievances could be aired, before they festered and burst into flame. The meetings were also helpful for settling controver-

sies over programming and billings, always a sore
subject with circus people. The simple act of being
able to speak up and present an opinion about the
running of the circus was a good way to let off
steam.

Since she had been the recipient of an unusual
number of complaints lately, Tanya was aware that
several things were brewing. Pop must have realized
it, too, and decided to call the circus people all together. But why such short notice? Usually the meetings were posted at least a week in advance so as
many as possible could make it. It would be difficult
to reach everybody in just a few hours. Most of the
circus people had scattered to their winter homes all
over the Tampa area, and quite a few of them had
taken winter jobs, too.

Shrugging off the problem, she left Marshall at the
edge of the parking lot and returned to her trailer,
which was parked for the winter in a fenced-off area
near the stock barns so she could be near her cats.
She was making herself a sandwich for lunch when
the Anderson twins, who were the fliers in the circus's star aerial act, rapped on her screen door.

"Expecting company—or do you have time to
rap?" Jim, the male twin, asked. Like his female
counterpart, he was blond and slender, with an open,
friendly face and a sunny disposition. At the moment
he looked glum, and more than a little sheepish, too,
Tanya decided.

Although she was two years younger than the
twins, she sometimes felt as if she were their older
sister; she had seen both of them through innumer-
able affairs of the heart and other personal and
financial crises.

"Come on in. You know I always have time for

you two," she said warmly. "I'll fix you a sandwich.
We can talk over lunch."

A few minutes later, as they munched on baloney-
and-cheese sandwiches washed down with Cokes,
Sally said, "We've got a little problem. We thought
you might give us some advice."

"If I can help you, you know I will."

"It's about Bruno. His timing is off lately. We
want to give up the net, but we're a little nervous
about it. You got any ideas?"

Tanya's heart sank. Bruno was one of the people
who had voted to let her stay with the circus when
she'd been orphaned. He was in his forties, yes, but
some catchers worked until they were older than that.
Was it true that his timing was off?

Suddenly, despite the Florida sun outside, the trailer seemed very cold and she shivered as her mind
slipped back to the day of her mother's fatal fall.
Even before then she had harbored a secret fear of
heights, and although her mother had been training
her on the trapeze, Tanya had coaxed Lars Larsen to
let her help with his cats. She had told him she wanted to help because she loved animals so much. Even
though she still worked out sometimes with the aerialists because she was ashamed to admit her fear to
her friends, she always had to fight the old sickness
the moment she started climbing the rope ladder, and
she dreaded the times when she was asked to substitute for one of the aerial-ballet troupe.

She tried to remember if she'd noticed anything
wrong the last time she'd watched Bruno and the An-
dersons perform. Of course, there *had* been that incident in Shreveport last year when one of the twins
had taken a bad fall into the end of the net. Later,
when she'd asked Jim what had happened, he'd

shrugged and said he'd had an "off" day. Had the fall been Bruno's fault? Had he missed the lock on Jim's wrist?

"What do you want me to do?" she asked aloud.

"We thought you might feel Bruno out about... uh, switching jobs," Jim told her. "Maybe he could do riggings or training or something."

"What about a replacement? Do you have anyone in mind?"

"There's this guy we met at the Showman's League banquet who wants to make a change. He's one of the catchers for the Delo group, but he doesn't get along with the leader too well. A conflict of ideas, that sorta thing. We felt him out and he's willing to take less salary to join Pop's show. He's good, too— he's got some great ideas for adding class to the act. The thing is, we don't want to hurt Bruno's feelings. After all, he broke us in, took us on with just a little high-school acrobatics behind us."

Tanya took a deep breath. "Are you sure you really want to replace Bruno? Has he ever made any serious mistakes?"

The twins exchanged looks. "Not really," Jim said. "It's just this feeling we have that...well, sometimes he cuts it awful close. I guess the whole thing could be in our minds. Fliers do get a little paranoid at times."

Sally sighed deeply. "Maybe we'd better let it ride for a while, Jim. I'd sure hate to upset Bruno."

After the twins had finished eating and were gone, Tanya found she was too restless to take a nap, as she'd planned. She changed into shorts and a halter and went to see Octavia, who was full of stories about her winter job, reading palms for a Tampa tearoom. Octavia was wearing a spectacular purple muumuu that clashed with her dyed hair, at present an attention-getting orange red.

She soon had Tanya laughing as she related an anecdote about the advice she'd given a matron to stop complaining about her husband's philandering and keep his bed warm if she wanted him to stay home nights. To please Octavia, Tanya allowed her cards to be read, although she suspected that Octavia's remarkable knack for uncovering her customers' secret fears and worries came more from an intuitive sizing up of their facial expressions and body language than it did with the supernatural.

"You have a lot of trouble up ahead," Octavia told her, after she'd studied the cards for a while. "There's love here, too—a to-the-death kind of love. But there are obstacles—lot of obstacles. Watch your pride, Tanya. Having too much pride to say you're wrong can cause you a lot of heartache. Just follow your heart. Forget everything else and do what your heart tells you and you can't go wrong."

"You don't happen to see any money in my cards, do you?" Tanya said, trying for a light touch. "One-third pay doesn't stretch very far during the winter months. I'd get a job except that I have to work on the new act and take care of the cats."

Octavia gestured for her to reshuffle the cards again, then laid them out, turning them over three at a time. Her breath caught and her heavily madeup eyes widened as she studied them. "Money—so much money! You're going to meet someone who is very wealthy—but there's trouble here, too." Her eyes held worry as she looked at Tanya. "Storm clouds up ahead for you, Tanya. Better watch your step or you could lose all you hold dear. And beware of your pride. You have much too much of that, you know."

Tanya wouldn't admit to the small chill that Octavia's words produced. She smiled and promised to be careful, and was grateful when the conversation turned to other things.

At eight that evening in the training barn, a crowd of circus people assembled, settling themselves on plank benches, the overflow sitting on the tanbark that covered the hard-packed earth floor where the equestrian acts practiced. There were the usual jokes and exchange of gossip, the shoptalk and catching up on news about one another or mutual friends.

Not to Tanya's surprise, Pop timed his own entrance for eight o'clock sharp—too late to be button-holed by anyone who wanted to air a private grievance in advance. The expression on his face was unusually glum, and to Tanya, who knew him so well, he looked worried, a little hangdog. Whatever he had to announce, she was sure it wouldn't be good news, and she felt a wave of apprehension as she watched him raise his hands to get the attention of the others.

But to her surprise and relief, Pop started the meeting off as usual by asking if anyone had a grievance. Monty Valeski, the concessionaire who held the contract for the show's grab joints, a red-faced man with a thin, high-pitched voice, was the first to jump to his feet. As he droned on, listing the midway placement changes he wanted to make for the coming season, Tanya's eyes wandered back to Pop. Although he seemed to be giving Monty his full attention, it was obvious to her he was only half-listening. His eyes kept straying toward the door, making her wonder whom he was expecting. Whatever was bothering him, it was serious. Twice, when she caught his glance and smiled, he looked away quickly as if ashamed to meet her gaze.

The second item was a disagreement between Freddy, the head bullman, and Morris Vaughn, the menagerie boss, a long running controversy that erupted into open warfare at least once every season. Both were hot-tempered men who were jealous of each other's authority. This time the disagreement was over the feeding budget, both of them demanding a larger cut for their own particular animal charges. As Pop soothed their ruffled feathers, he continued to look distracted, and again Tanya wondered what was up. Had there been more trouble with the tax people, or was it simply preseason nerves, something that affected all of them to some degree this time of year?

Since all her attention was focused on Pop, she was startled when, without asking for further grievances, he glanced toward the door and then announced, "You all know that the circus has been having financial troubles. With falling receipts and inflation, we're almost bankrupt, which is why I was forced to sell fifty-one percent of my stock."

He paused, waiting for the wave of consternated voices to subside, before he added, "Most of you know my new partner. He's just come in, and I'm sure he has some things he wants to say to you now."

Automatically, Tanya turned her eyes toward the door. A shock ran through her when she realized the man Pop had introduced as his new partner was Wade Broderick.

He was wearing casual clothes, but they bore little resemblance to the jeans and knit T-shirts he'd worn before. His jacket was a rich brown suede, well cut, his slacks tailored to fit his strong, muscular body. His smile was quizzical, yet it held another element that Tanya couldn't define. As he made his unhurried way toward Pop, he looked perfectly at ease, not at all ruffled by Pop's abrupt and less-than-friendly introduction.

It was all Tanya could do to keep her face expressionless. So much was suddenly clear, including the fact that Wade had never seemed like a roughie. Had he been spying on them, posing as a working man while all the time planning to take over the circus? She remembered his comment about the circus needing better management, and her blood ran cold. Was he here to push Pop out and send in his own replacement? If so, he had a war on his hands. She—all of them—would fight him tooth and nail.

Although Wade didn't look in her direction, she knew, every fiber of her being knew, that he was very much aware of her, and that he was giving her time to recover from the shock before he made eye contact with her. She wanted to leave, to march right out the door, but she had too much pride. If he expected her to show surprise or excitement or even anger, she didn't intend to indulge him. Her expression indifferent, she allowed her eyes to rest on him as if he were a stranger, and when he finally glanced in her direction, she had the satisfaction of seeing him frown slightly before his expression smoothed out again.

"Most of you know me, and no, I didn't take a job with the circus with the intention of spying on you. I had no idea I'd be buying into the show when I came to work here. I had just sold my computer business and I needed a vacation. A friend of mine suggested I get a job at a circus because I've been a buff all my life. He meant it as a joke, but the more I thought about it, the more appealing it sounded. Then after I got the job, I caught circus fever—it got into my blood. After I went back to New York, I missed the life. Since I'd been looking around for a business to invest in, I made inquiries, discovered Pop was willing to sell some of his stock, and here I am. I don't intend to be an absentee partner. I'll be around. But Pop will still be manager and all questions should go to him as always. And that's about it, unless someone has a question?''

"I have two questions for you." Marshall seemed to be seething with some strong emotion. Tanya suspected it was anger. "And I think I'm speaking for all of us. What changes are you planning to make, and what does your takeover mean to us?''

"Fair questions. First of all, it isn't a takeover. I don't intend to make any changes—not at first. Things will go on as always, but there'll be money now to buy new rigs, which you all know are badly needed, and replacements for several of the older rides. To bring the equipment up to par, there'll be canvas for a new Big Top, plus other tents, material for new booths and new costumes, too. We'll also be hiring additional personnel and performers so there'll be no need for doubling up in the future. You'll be responsible for your own act or job, and that means you can devote all your time to doing the best work possible.''

A ragged cheer went up. Tanya gritted her teeth, fighting resentment. Had the last remark been directed at her? Several times Wade had commented—and not always kindly—about her helping other people out when needed. Had he been saying not so subtly that he felt her own job had suffered? Even more than that, she begrudged the cheer that had gone up. As she looked at Wade, it occurred to her that he was used to maneuvering people, putting them in his pocket with just the right words and gesture.

Already he had them eating out of his hand with his promises to hire more help and to buy new rigs and equipment. Time would tell whether it was just that—promises. As for her, she wasn't as gullible as some of them. In the future she meant to stay out of Wade's way, to ignore him as much as she could. And when that wasn't possible? Then she'd treat him as if he were just a casual acquaintance—one she didn't particularly like.

CHAPTER NINE

AFTER A SLEEPLESS NIGHT during which she had run the gamut of emotions from disbelief to rage, Tanya discovered that her primary feeling was shame—shame that she'd been taken in so easily by Wade. She writhed inside when she remembered that she'd called him a loser. How he must have laughed to himself at that, especially when she'd shown so clearly that not only was she willing to let a man she considered a loser make love to her, but she'd also wanted it desperately!

And why hadn't he taken advantage of her willingness? Despite her lack of personal experience, she was no innocent. Among circus people there was a descriptive phrase—summer marriages—for those relationships that lasted only during the summer circuit, and no one raised around a circus could be ignorant of sex. She was very much aware that Wade had been deeply aroused by their lovemaking. Had he stopped because he *did* have a conscience of sorts?

It was obvious now that he'd cultivated her for the purpose of learning all he could about Pop and the financial troubles of the circus. Was it possible he'd been ashamed to use her sexually because he'd been there under false pretenses, or had he simply lost interest because she'd been too willing to fall into bed with him? One thing she was certain about—he was lying when he said he'd had no intentions of buying into the circus at the time he'd asked Pop for a job. Why else would a wealthy businessman work as a common laborer, the lowest-rated job in a circus, unless he had some monetary motive?

Tired of questions for which there were no answers, Tanya dressed and fixed herself coffee and even forced down a few bites of toast before she abandoned breakfast to take a walk. She was coming around the corner of the cookhouse when she heard loud voices. She started to turn aside, not wanting to be drawn into any discussions about Wade, who must be the main topic of conversation this morning, only to find herself in the midst of a crowd of men. Most of the men, including Wade, she recognized, but several of them were strangers.

Wade, his face stony and eyes cold, was the focus of attention. Tanya took in the cameras slung over the shoulders of three of the men and realized what was happening. The press had descended on the circus, but that wasn't so unusual. Circus life was often the target of feature writers, but why so many—and why were they all harassing Wade?

"Come on, Mr. Broderick, give!" one of the men said, shoving a small black microphone into Wade's face. "What would possess a man like you, a computer genius, to buy a circus?"

"Yeah, what's cooking here?" The speaker was a brash-looking redhead with sharp eyes. "You're a multimillionaire—if we can believe those rumors about your deal with General Electronics. So why a circus? Is this some kind of tax shelter?"

"It's simply a business deal," Wade replied sharply. "I invested in a business. That's all."

"Yeah? So why are you involving yourself in the running of the circus? You have the reputation for being a financial shark, always taking advantage of the big chance to pull in the multibucks. Why would you be interested in the operation of a small-time business like this?''

''I take all my investments seriously.'' Wade snapped off the words. ''And the circus is a good investment. By the end of the season it will be one of the most profitable shows in the country.''

There was another rash of questions, but this time Wade only scowled, swung around and quickly disappeared into the cookhouse. Tanya turned, too, but not soon enough.

''Hey, that's Tanya Rhodin, the female lion tamer,'' someone shouted, and a moment later Tanya was surrounded by reporters. ''How about a statement? What do you think about having an electronics whiz for your boss?''

Tanya tried to push past them, but the redheaded man wouldn't budge. Confused by the rapid-fire questions, she could only shake her head. Then a firm hard hand was cupping her elbow, pulling her away. Wade, his face grim, called out a sharp, ''Clear them out of here!'' to the circus men standing nearby, and a few minutes later the newsmen were being escorted, not so politely, toward the parking lot.

''You okay?'' Wade asked.

''I didn't need your help,'' she said angrily. ''I've managed on my own for quite a while now.''

''True—so why do I get the impression sometimes that you never really grew up? I saw that look on your face yesterday at the meeting. You looked as if you would have loved to shoot me. And how did it happen that I've suddenly become the villain of this piece? You heard Pop admit that the circus was almost bankrupt. There were no other offers. If I hadn't bought in, it would have closed down and the majority of your old friends would be out of jobs right now. Most of the circus people are willing to reserve their judgment and maybe even show a little gratitude because I saved their jobs. So why are you so hostile?''

Tanya's pride came to her rescue; she gave him a cool smile. "You overestimate your importance to me. I'd be completely indifferent to you except that I'm not convinced you're good for the circus. In fact, the only reason I've decided to turn down an offer I had from Cookson Brothers is because I want to make very sure my friends get a fair shake from you. I could change my mind and leave—at any minute," she added, giving his hand, which still cupped her elbow, a pointed look.

Wade's hand tightened briefly, then dropped. "And leave your cats behind? Oh, I doubt that. You do remember that the animals belong to the circus, don't you?''

Tanya stiffened under a new rush of outrage. She started to remind Wade that when she began her act at seventeen, she'd been too young to sign a purchase contract, so she'd made an agreement with Pop to take half pay, and in return the circus would buy the cats she needed. Although they'd never bothered to change that arrangement when she'd come of age, it was understood that the cats did belong to her. But a sudden thought held her silent. Was it possible that Pop hadn't told Wade about their arrangement? Maybe the considerable value of the big cats had affected the price Pop had received for his circus shares. If this were so, she didn't dare let Wade know the true story. . . .

"Pop will tell you that I've put quite a bit of my own wages back into the act to pay for supplemental food for the cats," she said in a controlled voice.

"I only know what I see on paper," Wade said, shrugging. "My investment included half of all properties owned by the circus, and that means the cats and other animals. Any private deal you have with Pop is your own affair." There was a tinge of satisfaction in his eyes as he studied her stiff face. "I suggest you forget about quitting. I know you don't want to be parted from your cats, especially that lazy old lion, Leopold. Who else would spoil him with strawberries and sour cream?"

"How did you—" Tanya stopped, biting her lower lip.

"I'm a very observant man." Wade's voice softened suddenly. "Tanya, why don't you give a little? You know you'd never be happy anywhere else except here. So relax and give me a chance. You might discover that things will improve."

In answer she turned abruptly and stalked off, sure that if she stayed there even one moment longer, she would start tossing angry words at him—or even slap his arrogant face.

It was inevitable that she would end up going to see Leopold, the one friend she had who wouldn't speculate endlessly about Wade Broderick and what he might or might not do for the circus—or give her advice about being nicer to Pop's new partner. The great cat's rumbling purr soothed her as she sat cross-legged on the floor of the cage beside him, brushing his long mane and whispering some of her confused feelings into his ear.

She was angry with Wade for his unfair use of blackmail to keep her with the circus, but she was

also bitterly disappointed that the circus people,
usually so wary of outsiders until they had proved
themselves more than once, had obviously let down
their guard with Wade. Most of all, though, she was
angry with herself. Even during their quarrel she had
been so aware of him as a man, so affected by the
weight of his hand on her arm, by his warm breath stirring the hair at the side of her face, that she'd had to
fight against the desire to reach out and touch him
back. . . .

During the next few days Tanya often felt totally
alienated from her friends. Although she didn't express
her feelings out loud, she observed with resentment
how quickly their original cautious attitude toward
Wade changed to open approval when he made funds
available for improvements and repairs. To her fiercely
partisan heart, it seemed disloyal to Pop that they
should be so enthusiastic about the changes.

It didn't help that Pop obviously felt the same and,
after an initial wariness, now consulted Wade about
circus affairs and more often than not took his advice. In fact, a friendship developed between the two
men as the days passed. But then she shouldn't have
been surprised. Pop was a tolerant man, who, for all
his gruff manner, seldom saw the worst in anyone
and was always willing to give others a chance. And
Wade was a very persuasive man—as Tanya knew, to
her sorrow.

Determined not to join the ranks of Wade's admirers, Tanya harbored her resentment. Even when the
menagerie food budget was increased to allow for the
purchase of the special—and expensive—food sup-
plements she usually paid for out of her own pocket,
she didn't waver. She was sure this was Wade's subtle
way of pointing out his ownership of the cats.

On the occasions when their paths crossed, Tanya retained her aloofness, never looking at Wade if she could help it, and speaking only when it was necessary to answer a direct question. When he joined any group she was with, she always left as soon as possible, even if it meant leaving behind an untouched cup of coffee or a cookhouse meal. Although she had always been an enthusiastic attendee at the business meetings Pop held every week, now she stayed away. As a result, she felt more and more isolated from the rest of the circus as the day of departure for their first engagement of the summer circuit approached.

True to his word, Wade had arranged for new canvas for all the tops and had purchased new equipment, including several more of the huge vans that hauled the circus around the circuit. Most of the rides had been rejuvenated or replaced, and there were new portable booths, shiny with bright paint, to gladden the hearts of the concessionaires.

He had also arranged for the hiring of new personnel, including three acts, all top quality. The Chungs were a Chinese family who did a Risley tumbling act and would replace the deserting Auklanders. The Lester Moran Troupe, an equestrian group, was sorely needed to flesh out the Big Top show, and the Wanamakers, a married couple, did a lively, innovative act on the high wire.

The men's dorm was refurbished with comfortable bunks and mattresses, a gesture that won over the roughies, who had originally adopted a "wait and see" attitude toward their former co-worker. Since money was made available for new costumes, the artistes succumbed next, especially the aerial-ballet women, who preened themselves in the prettiest costumes they'd had in a long time. Even Octavia, who

loved flashy clothes, was delighted with her exotic
new caftans, which made her look, Tanya thought,
like an Oriental dowager.

Marshall, who had a taste for elegant clothes, was
pleased with the additions to his wardrobe, which included a new top hat, though he told Tanya dryly
that he hoped this didn't mean he'd be expected to do
a song-and-dance routine on the top of a piano, à la
Fred Astaire.

Of all the circus people, he alone reserved his judgment of Wade, but Tanya could see that he was
weakening, and she resented this most of all.

It was at the next grievance meeting, traditionally
held just before departure on the year's circuit, that
she clashed openly with Wade for the first time.

She had gone reluctantly, and only because Alice,
for once firm, had insisted. "This sulking has got to
stop, hon," she said. "Everybody's noticed it, and
you don't want to start no trouble, now do you? So
come along like a good girl, and maybe be a little
nicer to Mr. Broderick."

"Mr. Broderick! When did you start calling him
that?"

"Well, it only seems proper. He *is* the boss now—"

"Pop's the boss."

Alice looked uncomfortable. "Of course Pop is
still manager, but Mr. Broderick is...he does own
the majority of the stock. It only seems right to call
him Mr. Broderick."

"Well, I never will—no, come to think of it, that's
just what I will call him! That should put him in his
place." And she knew from Alice's sigh that she
sounded like the spoiled child Wade had accused her
of being.

During the first few minutes of the meeting, while

reports were presented by various department heads, Tanya listened silently, expressing no opinions during the lively debates that followed, usually over budget shares.

"And you, Tanya?" Wade said finally, looking at her. "Do you need any new equipment or suplies."

Tanya turned her eyes away. "I've already given Pop my list, Mr. Broderick."

"I see. Well, since Pop asked me to take over this meeting because he had a last-minute emergency in scheduling, do you think you could give me a short version of what you told him?" His voice was mild, but there was a hint of steel beneath the politeness.

"I could—but I won't. It would only be a waste of time," she said, meeting his hard glance head-on.

Wade hesitated, then nodded. "Okay. Then let's hear from you, Morris. Any problems with the menagerie as a whole?"

During the rest of the meeting, Tanya was aware that the others were avoiding her glances, a realization that only increased her anger. She was the first to rise when Wade ended the meeting, and she was out the barn door before anyone else. Later, in her trailer, she sat brooding over the fact that she was the only one in the whole circus who didn't trust Wade. The others had all sold out to his bribes, but not her. She would never give in—never!

The next day the first run-through of the Big Show was staged, mainly to make adjustments in the length of the acts so that the show would be exactly two hours long. The bandmaster, Acey Brenner, was an officious, testy man. One of his few redeeming qualities was an uncanny knack for timing the dozens of song cues needed to run the two-hour show smoothly. As usual, he clashed with the equestrian director almost immediately. The two of them were arguing loudly, neither listening to what the other was saying, when Wade, who had been silently watching from the sidelines, intervened.

With a few quiet words he settled the argument and soon had the men laughing , doing it so adroitly that Tanya had a sudden picture of him presiding over a corporate boardroom, dominating a directors' meeting with his strong personality and undeniable presence.

Swallowing her resentment, she took her place in Ring Two, the center ring, and walked through her act without her cats so the bandmaster could set his musical cues. As she was going through the moves of the new drill she'd been working on that winter, tersely describing how the four male lions and the two tigers would do a "bounce" act, seeming to rush her in a group, Wade motioned for the timing clock to be stopped.

"What's this about including the tigers in the bounce part of your act?" he asked Tanya, frowning.

"I introduce at least one new trick a year," she said, not trying to hide her impatience. "I've been rehearsing this one several weeks now. What's the problem? This is just a variation of the bounce act I've done before."

"But you didn't do it with a mixture of lions and tigers. It's too dangerous—"

"Every act in the show is dangerous," she told him scornfully. "I'm a professional. I know what I'm doing. I've been working cats since I was fourteen, and adding tigers to the bounce will add flash to the act."

"It's fine just as it is. In fact, I thought you specialized in a picture act with a tableau finish. You don't need to take unnecessary risks just to jazz it up."

"You're out of line, Mr. Broderick. My judgment has never been questioned before. Pop trusts my professionalism. After all, it's my neck I'm risking. And how does it happen that a man whose only experience with a circus is a few weeks working as a roughneck is suddenly some kind of expert?"

The muscles in Wade's jawline tensed, his only sign of anger. "I don't pretend to be an expert. But a mixed rush act—four lions and two tigers coming at you at the same time—is too much of a risk for a—" He broke off, looking uncomfortable.

"For a woman? Is that what you're saying? Now it all comes out. You're a damned sexist, and I refuse to be dictated to by a sexist. I say the act stays just as it is—"

"And I say it goes out. And while you're at it, I think it's time you retired Leopold. He's a danger not only to himself but to you. That big male tiger, Bennie, is already challenging his leadership. One of these days they're going to clash, and you're going to be right in the middle."

The rage smoldering inside Tanya burst into flame. She stalked toward Wade and shook her finger at his face. "Don't you dare make snide remarks about Leopold! He's my most valuable lion. And anyway, what does a josser—" she scornfully emphasized the circus word for a rank amateur "—like you know about running a circus? You think your money gives you the right to tell us what to do, but you don't fool anyone. The way you strut around the lot, giving orders and poking your nose in where it doesn't belong makes me sick at my stomach. Sure, some people toady to you, but all the time they're really laughing at you behind your back—"

She broke off, staring at Wade's cold expression

and narrowed eyes, aware that she'd gone too far. For one thing, what she had said wasn't true. Rightfully or not, Wade had managed to acquire the trust of the whole circus, and no one was laughing at him behind his back. But she met his stare, refusing to retract her words. After all, it was his fault she'd lost her temper! He had driven her to it, insulting Leopold and criticizing her act.

Suddenly she'd had enough. With a swift movement she whirled and rushed away, leaving silence—and she was sure disapproval—behind her.

Marshall came to her trailer later. "Well, you had your say. You told the boss off good and proper. You feel any better?"

"I feel awful," Tanya confessed ruefully. "I made a bloody fool out of myself. I never should have said that about people making fun of Wade behind his back. But he gets me so mad, Marshall, and then I lose my temper and. . . and say stupid things."

"Mad, yes. Mad as in you're crazy about the guy."

"That isn't true—I hate him!"

"Uh-huh. Every time the two of you get within fifty yards of each other, the air almost ignites."

There was a brooding look in Marshall's deep-set eyes, a resignation, as if he had suddenly made a decision. "Look, my young friend, why don't you end the open warfare with Wade, for your own sake as well as everybody else's? The man says he originally came here because he needed a vacation and because he's always been fascinated by circuses. Why is that so hard for you to believe? There's always a circus buff or two hanging around, some of them from pretty high places—including that United States senator who joins the joeys whenever he gets the chance."

He paused to take a breath and to study her set face. "Is it so hard to believe that when Wade learned the circus was in financial trouble, he decided it would be a good investment? It sounds a little crazy, but it very well might be true. Certainly the changes he's made are for the best. He's put new spirit in this operation, and at the least, he's earned the chance to prove himself. A couple of the old-timers have been downgraded, true, but that had to happen eventually—"

"What are you talking about?"

"You know, Bruno and Cookie. Cookie is grumbling a bit, but he's really happy to be out of it. He finally admitted to me that his eyes have gone bad, which explains the rotten food lately. You know he never would allow any of his helpers to do much of the actual cooking. And Bruno will still be with the circus, even if he won't be catching for the Anderson twins any longer."

"Are you saying that Cookie and Bruno have been *fired*?"

Marshall gave Tanya a closer look. "I say, you didn't know, did you? And I've let the cat out the bag. I guess Cookie and Bruno haven't told you yet because they knew how you'd take it. You're pretty defensive about your friends, little one."

Tanya swallowed an impulse to scream. "When did all this happen?"

The evenness of her voice must have fooled Marshall, because he looked relieved.

"At the last business meeting. Bruno is going to stay on as a rigger and also as a trainer. Wade said that his know-how shouldn't go to waste. To tell the truth, I think Bruno is a little relieved. He told me privately he's been concerned lately that his timing was a tad off. And Cookie—well, you know how the food has gone downhill this year. Wade retired him, gave him a more-than-respectable pension. He's already hired some dude who used to work for Ringlings to take over the cookhouse.''

"Cookie gone.... What else is Wade planning? Who will he get rid of next," Tanya said bitterly.

"Wade has the best interests of the circus at heart, Tanya. I'm convinced of that now. Did you know that he arranged for Octavia to go to a health farm to help her kick her drinking habit? She'll be leaving in a couple of days, but she'll rejoin the circus later, in a few weeks. Who knows? If she licks the booze, maybe that will help her lick the depressions, too.''

"And nobody bothered to tell me any of this? This...this outsider is tearing up everything Pop has done through the years, changing everything around. He may have fooled the rest of you, but not me. I'd do anything, anything at all, to get control of the circus away from him. And if I ever did get the chance, no matter what it takes, that's just what I'll do, so help me!''

"Shh...lower your voice," Marshall said, glancing out the open window. "That snoop O'Brien just walked past. He's got a big mouth—you don't want that kind of remark to be repeated.''

"I don't care...I'm so miserable, Marshall. Everything is changing. Wade came here and turned everything upside down. And it's only a hobby, some kind of whim to him. When he gets tired of playing circus, off he'll go to something else, but by then, everything will be changed. It won't ever be the same again.''

"Nothing stays the same forever," Marshall said sadly. "Change is inevitable. The past few years have been special, but it had to happen sooner or later. People do grow older. We get ailments and have to quit, or simply get burned out. One of these days I expect I'll have enough of circus life and go back to England, find myself a place along the Cornish coast and settle in for the long haul.''

It was at that moment when Tanya burst into tears. Marshall took an immaculate handkerchief from his jacket pocket and silently tucked it into her hand. She stopped crying almost immediately and, a little shamefaced, blew her nose, and then told him she'd wash the handkerchief and return it later. Marshall nodded; there was a strange expression on his face as he studied her. She started a little when he put his hand out abruptly and brushed a strand of hair back from her face, a rare gesture from a man who hated to be touched.

''Poor Tanya! You hate change because you're afraid to face life,'' he told her. ''All that passion and fire just below the surface, and yet all you dare to show is anger. It will tear you apart if you don't learn to handle it. And I blame myself as well as the rest of us. We were too protective, never allowed you to be disappointed about anything for long. We protected you too much, and now you're a grown woman with a woman's emotions and you don't know how to handle frustration except to turn it into anger. Take some advice from a man who has spent his own life hiding his feelings behind clever words. Don't be afraid of your emotions. If you love, show it. Fight for it with all you have. It's long past time for you to grow up. With luck, you'll come out of all this a wiser person, and I have a hunch you're going to be one hell of a woman someday.''

After Marshall left, Tanya sat in the darkening

trailer, too emotionally wrung out to move. When she heard another knock, she sighed and called out an invitation to come in, expecting Pop or Alice or Octavia, come to chastise her for being rude to Wade. But it wasn't one of her friends. It was Wade who opened the door, came in, then stood looking down at her. "May I have a word with you?" he said when she only stared at him.

"Oh, say your piece. Don't bother to ask," she said.

He was silent for a moment, as if assessing the bitterness in her voice. "Why are you sitting here in the dark? Why don't you turn on the lights?"

"Why should I bother? You won't be staying." But the growing darkness suddenly seemed too intimate, and she switched on a lamp.

"Tanya, we have to get a few things straightened out. You know that I can't put up with your insolence and insubordination. It sets a bad example for the whole circus."

"So fire me," she said recklessly. "And when you do, be prepared for some of the others to walk out, too."

"You'd do that to your friends just because of your pride?"

"Pride! It has nothing to do with pride. You came here pretending to be one thing and all the time you were laughing at us for being so stupid and gullible!"

"So that's it. You think I deliberately lied to you. As for laughing at you—Tanya, I've never laughed at you. You're the last person in the world anyone would laugh at. With your loyal heart, you're a rarity in this crazy world. But your loyalties are all mixed up. I can't allow you to go around defying me in public and undermining my authority. So I suggest we set up some kind of ground rules. You don't have to be friendly—though God knows I'd prefer that—but you do have to be polite. And no more insults. Do you understand? Also, it isn't fair of you to speak for your friends. If they have any criticisms of me, they should come to me with them.''

Tanya felt a rush of guilt. She had spoken as though her friends had been complaining about Wade, which of course wasn't true. In fact, it was their acceptance of him that exacerbated her anger.

''I shouldn't have said that,'' she said stiffly. ''They aren't laughing at you behind your back.''

''There.'' He was smiling at her. ''Was that so hard to say?''

''Don't think this means that...that I intend to hide my opinions in the future. I think you're bad for the circus because you want to take over completely and push Pop out. Is it your ego? Can't you stand being in second place? Is that why you bought the circus, so you could be a little tin god again? When you came here as a josser, it must have really hurt your ego to have to take orders from other people. Is that why you bought the circus—to pay them back? When are you going to fire Flat Iron, your old boss, as you did Cookie and Bruno? He must be next on your hit list.''

Wade's face was pale. ''You little fool, when was the last time *you* took orders from anyone? You walk all over Pop and the other old-timers. Oh, sure, you help them out and cover up for them as long as they treat you like a little princess. That's why you don't want any changes, isn't it? You don't want to give up your devoted followers, your own little kindgom—''

The blood rushed to Tanya's head. She flew at Wade, wanting only to make him be quiet, to stop his hurtful words. As he stepped back to avoid her, he lost his balance and fell, pulling her down on top of him. For a moment she lay stunned, and then it was too late to escape, because his arms had tightened around her and he was holding her so close that her face was crushed against his chest. She heard his heart thundering under her ear and knew that he was very angry—or was it something else that made his heart beat so fast?

At some point she stopped struggling. Was it when he cupped a hand behind her head and kissed her, or when his supple tongue invaded the softness of her mouth and sent her senses reeling out of control? Or was it when his hands, their touch so sure, moved down her back, settling around the curve of her hips and holding her tightly against his own quickening body? All she knew was that suddenly she didn't want to escape. What she wanted was to be even closer, and she resented the layers of clothing that separated them and thwarted the need she could no longer fight.

She felt a coolness on her back as he pushed up her T-shirt, and the touch of his hands on her bare skin drove her wild. She writhed against him, unable to stop the convulsive movements of her hips. With a quick twist he rolled over, taking her with him, until she was staring up, not down, into his face. In the lamplight his eyes had a feverish look, and his mouth seemed fuller and softer and very erotic to her heightened senses. When he kissed her again, her own lips parted helplessly, permitting the invasion of his knowing, insidious tongue.

And then, unbelievably, he was rolling away from her, leaving her feeling bereft and frustrated and, above all, ashamed. What was wrong with her—was she losing her mind? She detested this man, and yet she wanted to hold him there, to beg him to make love to her.

Wade's voice was like a dousing of cold water. "What are you trying to do to me, Tanya? This hot-cold, on-again-off-again business is driving me crazy. Is that what you want? Is this your way of...of tormenting me? A prelude to another practical joke?"

Tanya didn't move for a moment. Then she rose quickly in one fluid movement and whirled away from him. She straightened her clothing quickly, restoring it to order. When she turned to face him again, she discovered he was standing, too, watching her.

"If you ever touch me again for any reason at all," she told him, "I'm going to yell 'rape' at the top of my lungs, and everybody in the circus will think you tried to attack me. So this is a warning—stay away from me in the future. If you have anything to say to me, do it in front of other people."

Wade's lips twisted into a smile that held no amusement. "You don't have to worry about that. I won't bother you again. But think about this. I instigated that first kiss, yes, but you cooperated fully with the rest of it. You're a tease, Tanya, a cheat—and I don't like cheats."

After Wade had gone, closing the door behind him quietly, Tanya turned off the lamp and undressed in the dark, not wanting anyone to see her lights on and drop by for a visit. But she didn't sleep. She lay in the dark, confused and bewildered by the betrayal of her own body. For the third time she had almost surrendered to a man she disliked, a man she didn't trust, someone to whom she was only another female body he happened to find desirable. And the worse shame of all was knowing that once again the only reason he hadn't taken her was that he had been the one who pulled away.

CHAPTER TEN

IT WAS TWO WEEKS since the circus had left Florida. Wade was in the kitchen section of the comfortable motor home he'd leased for the duration of the tour, spooning coffee into an electric coffee maker, when someone rapped smartly at the door. He added a final tablespoon of coffee and plugged in the machine before he went to open the door.

At first, since no one seemed to be there, he thought his ears had played a trick on him. Then his gaze dropped—to meet Marshall's sardonic stare. The little man, dressed in a Harris tweed jacket and turtleneck and sporting a deerstalker hat, looked as if he'd just stepped out of an English hunting print.

"We don't all come up to your eye level," Marshall quipped.

Wade grinned down at him. "Nor do we all come up to your intellectual level."

Marshall's eyelids quivered, which may or may not have meant he was pleased by the compliment. When Wade invited him inside, he climbed the metal steps with his usual aplomb and settled himself on a leather footrest. Leisurely he examined the luxurious furnishings of the van. "I see you came out of the closet with a bang," he said.

"I like comfort. I understand you do, too," Wade countered, and won a sour smile.

"I thought it was time the two of us had a talk,"

Marshall said, glancing toward the closed door of the bedroom. "Did I come at the wrong time?"

"I'm alone—and I'm not expecting anyone. I just plugged in the coffee maker. Care to join me? Or would you prefer a cup of tea?"

"Coffee's my thing. I abhor tea. It always tastes like medicine to me. That's one of the reasons I left England."

"And the other reason?"

"Well, you might say I was an embarrassment to my family. So I removed myself voluntarily."

"Their loss, our gain."

"Yes, indeed. I could have been the first don at Oxford who couldn't see over the lecturer's podium without climbing up on a ladder."

"Why don't you go back—and the hell with them?"

"Oh, I like my life here. I have all the advantages and none of the problems of a settled life."

"And maybe you've been too busy playing nurse-maid for the past few years to think about anything else?"

Marshall's chiseled features hardened. "Most people do what they want to do, and make excuses later. I never bother. I elected to stay on with Pop's circus for my own reasons. It had nothing to do with Tanya."

"I don't believe you. I think too many of you took on the job of being Tanya's surrogate parents. She isn't sure just what her role is—the lone chick or the mother hen to the lot of you. I think she needs to grow up—"

"And you think you're the one to ease her into womanhood!" Marshall shook his head. "No, my fine cockadoodle, you are *not* the right man for

Tanya. She doesn't need a fly-by-night Romeo who is only interested in taking her to bed. What she needs is a strong man who will cherish her and love her for what she is, who won't try to mold her into his own image of what a woman should be. She needs someone strong enough to give her plenty of space and let her be herself. And I don't think you're that man. You'll be getting bored with the circus one of these days, and then what happens to Tanya? She's a woman of strong emotions and great depth of feeling. When she gives her heart, it will be permanent. Which is why I thought we should have this little talk."

Wade knew his eyes were cold, but he did his best to keep his tone light. "You think that's what I want? To have an affair with Tanya and then simply... walk off into the sunset?"

"What else—unless you have marriage in mind. Is that it, Wade? Are you going to ask her to marry you? If so, that would be an even worse disaster."

Wade rose and went to stare out the window. The sinking sun had almost dropped behind the trailers and vans that lined the opposite side of the row. A glancing ray fell across his face, but he felt chilled, not warmed, by its heat. "No, I can't marry Tanya," he said finally. "She'd be miserable in my world. And anything else would be wrong, too. So you see, we don't really need this little talk. I've already decided there can't be anything between Tanya and me."

"I'm delighted to hear that, although I don't agree with one thing you said. Tanya could fit into your world or any other world if she chose to. The circus encompasses everything that the outside world does—in microcosm. We have our royalty, our com-

moners, our losers and our clowns, and Tanya holds
a special place here, just as she would anywhere, I
suspect. But I wouldn't want to see her married to
you. She needs tenderness, understanding, someone
to cherish her for her good points and yet help her to
control her impulsiveness and make sure that temper
of hers doesn't get out of hand. I don't think you're
man—or maybe I should say, human—enough to
handle her. It's possible you're more computer than
you are human."

Wade was silenced by a sudden realization, one
that made his heart twist with pity. Marshall was in
love with Tanya. He loved her as a man, not as a surrogate parent. How ironic that this man, who understood her so well and could probably give her the
kind of caring she needed, had been forced to become her confidant and mentor instead, simply because of an accident of birth.

"You're right," he said heavily. "I'm not the man
for Tanya. If I promise to stay away from her, will
that set your mind at rest?"

"Frankly, I wish you weren't even in the picture,"
Marshall said. "But yes, I'll settle for your promise.
You're a hard man, but you're fair and honest.
Which is enough for me. I only hope you can hold
out. Tanya has a very strong and special appeal."

Wade offered his hand. Marshall shook it, but he
let it drop almost immediately. "And I guess I'd better get into my patent leather shoes and top hat for
the evening crowd to ogle," he said.

"Do you mind being stared at?" Wade asked impulsively.

"Everybody asks me that, and the truth is, I regard
what I do as a job, neither bad nor good. Sometimes
a tip will get a bit rowdy, but most of the time they

only look and ask a few rather polite and not too objectionable questions. I seldom get heckled, and most people are genuinely interested in this miniature man in their midst. I like traveling, seeing new horizons all the time. I also like going to bed at night, knowing that I'm surrounded by friends, that the next day will bring new experiences. It's the best of all worlds for a misfit like me. I feel more at home here than I ever did with my own family, to whom I was only a bloody freak, someone to be kept out of sight when friends called. And of all the circuses, this one is the best. Not the most profitable or the best known, but for the people who are with it, it has no peer.''

He paused to give Wade a searching look. ''If anything should happen to close it down, it would be a disaster to a lot of people who don't fit into a world that scorns them. What would Jojo, the dog-faced man, do if he didn't have the security of the circus? He's a person of sensitivity. Have you ever noticed that he never eats in public, not even in the cookhouse? And Too Tall Tim—he's a gentle man, psychologically unable to defend himself against bullies. Here, he's safe and happy. And there are others. . . .''

Again he paused, this time for a thin smile. ''In case I haven't told you this yet, I'm grateful that you saved the circus from bankruptcy. All of us are.''

''Except Tanya.''

''Oh, she is, too. But you hurt that prickly pride of hers, not telling her who you were and letting her think you were a drifter. She accepted you anyway, and now she feels like a fool. But she'll come around. I don't know your motives for buying into Pop's circus, but I hope you keep what I say in mind if you should ever—well, just keep it in mind.''

"You're still not completely reassured about my intentions toward Tanya, are you?"

"I think you mean what you say—for now."

"You don't have to worry. I'm not exactly in favor with Tanya at the moment, and I doubt matters will improve. And even if they did, I meant my promise."

"Oh, I'll still worry—that's my favorite indoor sport." Marshall slid off the stool, put his hat back on and, with an airy wave of his diminutive hand, was gone.

Wade sat over his coffee for a long time. When he found himself wondering how much he'd meant his own assurances to Marshall that he wouldn't let his relationship with Tanya develop beyond simple friendship, he pushed away his cup. Feeling restive, he decided to join Pop at his station near the Big Tops back door, where he supervised the Big Show twice a day.

As always, the bustle behind the Big Top in the canvas-covered compound where the performers gathered to wait their turn to go on was endlessly fascinating to Wade. Although he was careful to stay out of the way of the hurrying clowns, prop men, animals and artistes, the right to be there was a "perk" of his position as co-owner that he wasn't about to forgo.

Rank hath its privileges, he thought, and one of the privileges he exercised daily was a thorough canvassing of the circus lot. Only to himself would he admit why he found so many excuses to go to Clown Alley, and why he never missed the opportunity to see the Big Show unfold before an audience.

It was the sights, the color, the movement of the whole circus that intrigued him, as well as the smells: horseflesh, mingled with the leather odor of the harnesses the rosinbacks wore; sun-warmed canvas and the hay along the bull-line near the menagerie tent; the subtle, civet scent of the big cats; and the mustiness of the clowns' tent, which was always redolent of grease paint and cheap talc and the starch in the stiffened cotton bows so many of the joeys wore.

Inside the Big Top was a different set of odors: the characteristic vinegar scent of the elephants, which always reminded Wade of brine; the pungency of tanbark, laid down to give purchase to the hoofs of the ring stock; the aroma of roasting popcorn from the stand outside the entrance. Even the tickets that the customers presented at the door had their own dry, acrid smell, like wet ashes. It was a world of illusion, of sleight of hand, on the border line between what was real and what was make-believe, a will-o'-the-wisp world, here today and gone tomorrow.

But it's not the world of a dyed-in-the-wool businessman, Wade thought, suddenly depressed. He, too, would be here today but gone tomorrow. And then what? What did he want to do with the rest of his life after he'd left here? And how long would it take him, once he was back in New York, to return to reality?

His eyes morose, he watched the second walkaround of the clowns as they filled in the time gap between acts while the propmen tore down the Big Cage in the center ring. The walk-around was a montage of bulbous noses and blubber lips, of outrageously grotesque costumes and tumbling bodies, broad pantomimes and exaggerated expressions of joy or woe or malice, all accompanied by the whoops, guffaws, chuckles and shrieks of the audience.

He had purposely missed Tanya's act, but he knew

exactly how she must have looked as she'd faced the big cats—the pride in her straight and slender back, the challenge in her amber-colored eyes, the radiant smile with which she acknowledged the applause of the audience at the end. Oh yes, he could see her every move in his mind's eye. Would it always be that way? When he left here for good, would he spend the rest of his life remembering how soft Tanya had felt in his arms, remembering how her eyes had burned when he'd kissed her breasts, how her lips had yielded beneath his?

"So what do you think of the new gag the clowns cooked up?" It was Pop's quick, sharp-edged Chicago voice. He pointed out the tiny float on which Bumbles, the panache clown who dressed in women's clothes, was riding, his white face beaming beatifically, unaware that the first half of the "skin" act—in this case two men wearing a horse's costume—was following him, devouring the flowers on his hat one by one.

"It's a winner," Wade said with certainty.

"Yeah. The audience loves it—the ones that bothered to come out in this lousy weather to see the show. I'm glad tomorrow is breakdown day. I don't like playing to Mr. Patch."

"Mr. Patch?"

"You know—a small, watcha call patchy, crowd. The chamber of commerce in this burg didn't do their job and see that we got the right kind of publicity."

"Why didn't you ask for a guarantee in the contract?"

Pop shrugged. "I thought I did. Guess I slipped up there."

Wade started to ask how that could happen, then

changed his mind. This was not the time to question Pop's forgetfulness. But he made a mental note to check over any new contracts in the future. A thread of thought came to him, making him frown. That business of the contract that never reached the fairgrounds in Texas—had that been Pop's fault, too? If so, no wonder Tanya had been so incensed when he'd told her that if he were boss, she would have been docked for that mistake. . . .

He realized that Pop had noticed his preoccupation and was frowning at him. "The tempo is faster than usual tonight," Wade said quickly.

"The crowd was so thin, I told John to speed it up. That way we can get out of here early and get a good night's sleep."

"John Cohen is a good man," Wade said, stating the obvious.

"Yeah. It takes more than a deep voice and a gift for gab to be a good equestrian director. The timing is a real pain in the keister. Especially when you get a prima-donna type like Maria Kahn."

Pop paused to stare up at the circus's solo female aerialist, who was working the web, doing a one-arm flange to the accompaniment of the audience's chanting as they kept count of her turns.

"She's good—and she knows it," he went on. "Always preening and running over her twelve minutes, milking the applause as long as she can. But John can handle her. Once, in Peoria, when she was really dragging it out, he called for the top lights to go off and then introduced the cannon act. That brought her down in a hurry. She was spitting fire, but he just stared her in the eye and told her, mild as honey, that he didn't care if she was the Queen of Sheba, she only had twelve minutes to do her act."

Wade laughed. At that moment the clowns came rushing through the back door, scattering in all directions like confetti before a high wind. "What would the circus be without its clowns," he said, almost to himself.

"Yeah. They're the peg you hang your circus on. If you don't have a good crew of joeys, you're dead. They fill in when there's an emergency and keep the crowd happy, no matter what. And part of their jobs is keeping a sharp eye out for anything that could hurt the other acts—y'know, like a broken bottle or a loose rope or a stray dog."

"Sometimes they act as if they could murder each other, but the next minute they're buddy-buddy again."

"I figure it takes a certain temperament to be a clown," Pop said, nodding. "Most of them never really grew up, and they love the applause, love being the center of attention. I guess you know that each one cooks up his own pantomimes, plans his own costumes and supplies his own props?"

"Like Emmett Kelly with his cabbage leaves?"

"Ole Emmett could do more with that damned cabbage leaf than a Shakespearean actor with a whole stageful of props."

"Is that envy I hear in your voice?"

Pop fixed him with a glum stare. "Everybody wants to be a clown. You wouldn't believe the prominent men—mayors and educators and even big business tycoons like you—who beg to be allowed to put on greasepaint and prance around in the ring."

"So how do you discourage them?"

"I don't. If they're persistent enough, we put them in the act. Makes for good public relations. That's why we call them 'friends of the circus.' The joeys go easy on them, not like they do apprentice clowns. Now those are the boys who really take the water.''

"Take the water?"

"You know—they get smacked with the paddle, bowled over in the chases and doused with water through a funnel stuck in their belts. They're always the back half of the skin acts, and they get handed the toughest, hardest role in all the spectaculars. You can tell a true clown by how he reacts to all this. The naturals love it. They're never happier than when they're being smacked with a board in the carpenter act or being run over by the fire engine in the burning-house drill. Of course, some clowns are ex-acrobats or tumblers. They turn to clowning after they've been hurt and can't do their skill act anymore. It's one way of staying on with the circus. They bring what talents they had to their new profession, which is why you see a lot of acrobats and pratfalls and the like.''

"It's all very complicated. Not the way I thought at first," Wade said.

"If you got your ideas from books or the movies, I'll guarantee you got it wrong. No one has ever shown circus life as it really is on the screen. Guess that would be impossible.''

Wade nodded. So many of his own ideas had changed since he'd joined the circus. For one thing, he had discovered that most of the old clichés about clowns were false. They weren't addicted to melancholy, nor did they live in thick makeup in order to hide from the world. Most of them had very healthy egos and were eager to be recognized by their audience, both in or out of costume. The height most aspired to was to be a "producing clown," one who would dream up new versions of the old gags, invent-

ing new props and twists to the classic clown reper-
toires.

"You wouldn't have a few ambitions along that
line yourself, would you?" Pop said, his smile thin.

"Maybe," Wade admitted. "But it's too late for
me. You need to have a lot of the boy in you to be a
good clown, and I don't think I ever really was a
boy—or so a friend once told me."

"Well, could be you're wrong. I still put on the
paint once in a while."

"You were a clown?"

"That's how I got started in this business. But I
had other ambitions, so I saved my money, found
myself some backers and went into the production
end. But I've still got a big soft spot for the joeys.
That's why sometimes I put on the paint and let them
knock me around."

"Were you an auguste?" Wade said, pronouncing
the word *ah'-goost* as the clowns did.

"No, I was a panache—tramp outfit, black eyebrows on white paint, a turned-up nose that looked
like I would drown if I got caught in the rain. Red
mouth painted into a big dumb smile."

There was a rare enthusiasm in his voice that silenced Wade. Although he had first-hand knowledge
of Pop's compassion for other people, the circus
owner was usually a man with little to say; this was
the first time since Wade had bought into the circus
that they'd had a conversation that could be described as personal.

Pop turned away to answer the question of one of
the performers, and Wade resumed his silent watch
from the wings. In the arena, the flow of the acts
went on. The vivid costumes became a multicolored
blur, a sharp contrast to the brown tanbark, the gray

elephants, the brown canvas sides of the tent. And the sounds—the screams of the crowd, the loud, open sound of the cornet and the shrill penetrating wail of the clarinet as the band did a "gallop," a high-speed number used for entrances and exits. It was written two beats to the bar, and this particular one was titled "Caesar's Triumphant March."

In the center ring, where the elephants were finishing their performance, the head bullman shouted, "Tails! Tails!" and the gray behemoths, as graceful as dancers, curled their trunks around the tail of the elephant in front of them and trotted briskly out of the arena. As they passed Wade, he wondered if one of them could be his old friend, Maisie. If so, she must have forgotten him. No friendly trunk reached out in his direction, and the pairs of bright eyes, so world-weary in their rolls of wrinkles, merely looked him over and moved on.

Overhead a flier soared from a pedestal and did a three-turn somersault. There was a slapping sound as his hands connected smartly with the catcher's. They swung outward, and when the flier's trapeze, sent hurling toward him by a fellow performer, was in position, he did a quick flip-flop and made a dazzling return as the band fanfare rose, holding the action suspended in time, the scene caught by sound and held in unforgettable beauty.

The three aerialists did backward flips into the net, one by one, then took their bows. They looked so otherworldly it was hard to believe that the male flier had a penchant for garlic, the female was in the midst of a torrid romance with one of the equestrians, and the catcher, who had replaced Bruno in the act, was already gaining a reputation for being quarrelsome.

But the circus, Wade reflected, would absorb his

personality flaws, tolerate his shortcomings as it did others'—as long as he did his job. Where else was this possible?

The band changed to a lively show tune as the aerial-ballet women, who were billed as the Montrose sisters, though they weren't related, ran out into the arena, their smiles almost as dazzling as their spectacular new costumes. Wade watched them idly as they hooked their feet into loops in the web ropes and started their ascent to the pedestal, fifty feet above the arena floor. His body stiffened when he recognized the smallest one, who was wearing a blond wig.

Tanya. What the devil was she doing out there? Since the influx of new personnel, she had not been called upon to fill in as she once had. So why was she substituting for one of the Montrose "sisters"?

Pop finished his low-voiced conversation with one of the performers and turned back to Wade.

"Why is Tanya working the traps?" Wade asked, not trying to hide his disapproval.

Pop shrugged. "It's Shirley—she caught a summer cold. Nose all stuffed up, can't breathe. I asked Tanya to fill in. She won't do any of Shirley's specialties, just the web work and a couple of simple swings and turns on the traps."

Although not totally reassured, Wade returned his attention to Tanya. He watched with hard eyes as she reached the pedestal, then poised gracefully—her smile radiant and her arms flung wide—between the other two women. As the one who would be doing the simplest tricks, she would have her turn first. The equestrian director introduced her from below as "beautiful Shirley Montrose," and she stepped forward to grasp the trapeze, looking like a butterfly in her yellow satin costume with its flirty fringe. Then she flung herself into space and made a graceful two-turn swing before grasping the reaching hands of the catcher.

He swung her back and then released her as one of the other fliers gave her trapeze a carefully timed push. Tanya whirled around with her body erect, stopping all vertical movement for one breathcatching second before she took the bar again. It was a simple move, but extremely effective when done right. Wade let out the breath he was holding, but his relief was short-lived. As Tanya leaned backward, still holding the bar, the catcher smacked his hands together and yelled, "Now!" and she swung outward again and, at the height of her swing, let go. For a moment her graceful body was suspended between the top of the tent and the earth, then the catcher caught her and swung her upward again, and a moment later she had caught her own trap on its upward swing and was returning to the pedestal to take a bow, her arms extended, her smile wide.

She stepped back, out of the way, letting the other women take their turn. Although their moves were much more complicated, Wade realized that it was Tanya who was the crowd pleaser, and he thought of words like *charisma* and *stage presence*. Later, when she joined the other two as they slid down individual ropes, stopping midway to do a series of one-armed flanges and turns, he watched her with puzzled eyes. Her smile looked fixed, as if it had been painted on her face, and her skin had a waxy look under the heavy makeup.

He turned to Pop with a question. "If Tanya was trained as an aerialist, why did she become a lion trainer?"

Pop shrugged. "It was her choice. She's always

been crazy about animals. She used to sneak off and sleep in the cage with old Leopold. Of course, he wasn't old then. And the elephants—they were like her nursemaids. When she didn't want to do her lessons or her chores, she'd go out to the bull-line, crawl under their bellies and those elephants wouldn't let anyone come near her. How she used to laugh at us! You couldn't stay mad at her even when the trick she played was on you. But she always was a good sport when the tables got turned on her and would laugh right along with the rest of us.''

"She hasn't changed much.''

"Yes, she has. She isn't playful like she used to be. I can't remember the last time she played one of her practical jokes on someone, unless it was when she sent you all over the lot, looking for old Maisie.'' There was real regret in Pop's voice. "Our little girl is growing up. Well, it hadta happen. She's almost twenty-two. You can't stop time.''

Wade discovered he was smiling. He was remembering a little girl who had played under the feet of the elephants, and who had tormented him unmercifully, trying to get his attention. So that girl *had* been Tanya. How strange that she was still tormenting him, but in a different way.

"So after Lars had his accident, he couldn't work the cage no more,'' Pop was saying, and Wade gave him his full attention. "By then Tanya knew almost as much about handling the big cats as Lars did. He finished training her, and she took over his act. I don't think she ever really wanted to be a flier, though she still works out with the catcher sometimes so she can fill in for any of the aerialists who's out sick. Just hasn't got the heart for it, I guess.''

Wade nodded, watching Tanya, who was finishing

her flanges and being lowered to the ground along with the other two women.

"Tanya's mom was the best flier I've ever seen," Pop said. "It was like she was born to fly through the air. Never a false move, never a slip or a mistake. Even the time when she got light burn—y' know, from the spotlights—and couldn't see for a few minutes, she went right on with her act, did it by instinct and timing."

"And yet wasn't she killed in a fall?"

"A rope ring broke. It never should have happened. The rigger had just inspected those rings, but they say it was metal fatigue, a one-in-a-million accident. And since she never used a net—" Pop shrugged his narrow shoulders; there was a bleakness in his eyes as he added, "So then we all got together and talked it over and... well, we decided to sort of adopt Tanya. She's a true child of the circus."

"Not a child—not any longer," Wade said.

Something in his voice made Pop stare at him. He turned brooding eyes upon Tanya as she finished her bows and ran lightly toward them. "You're right. And it's high time the rest of us got used to the idea that she's a woman now, I guess."

Tanya hurried past, pausing only to give Pop a wan smile and mutter something about getting out of her tight costume. Wade watched the next round of acts, and although the new equestrian troupe was spectacular, he found his attention wandering. Pop, looking harried, was called away to settle a problem with the lighting, and on impulse Wade decided to check up on Tanya. It was possible, if summer colds were going around, that she was sick. Something had been wrong with her when she'd hurried off.

Since it was a warm night, the outside door to Tan-

ya's trailer was open to catch the evening breeze. As
he came up to the trailer he could see Tanya through
the screen. She was sitting on the sofa, still in costume, her arms and legs hanging limply at her sides,
her head resting against the back of the sofa and her
eyes closed. Despite the pink blush on her cheeks, her
skin had a gray look, and she seemed completely
wrung out physically. This was such a contrast to the
energy she usually radiated that Wade stopped to
stare at her, his hand still extended to knock.

My God, she's scared, he thought in sudden realization. *She's scared stiff of heights....*

He didn't stop to consider that since she had been
so careful to keep her fear from her friends, she
would probably resent a stranger who had discovered
her secret. His only thought to comfort her, he
pushed the door open, went inside and, without a
word, took her in his arms. For a moment she stiffened, then she was slumped against him, burying her
face in his chest, accepting the mute comfort he offered.

After a while she straightened and pulled away,
not looking at him. "I guess I caught a chill somewhere."

"It isn't a chill," he said softly. "Why don't you
tell Pop that you're scared to death to go up on the
traps?"

"I—I can't. It would be like thumbing my nose at
all my mother stood for. She was great, the best there
was. She could have gone to Ringlings or any other
circus in the world and done the star turn, but she
loved this circus, and she wanted me to be just as
good someday. I—I always hated it, maybe because I
knew I could never measure up to her. Finally I told
her I wanted to train cats, as my father had. We

quarreled. She was afraid of animals and was sure they would claw me—or even kill me as they had my father. But I wanted my own way and I yelled at her, said some...some terrible things. She was hurt, so hurt. Her eyes were so sad and wounded looking. Then she left to do the matinee, and I never got the chance to tell her I was sorry because that was the day she fell..."

Her voice shuddered to a stop.

Wade put his arm around her shoulder. "Don't talk about it, Tanya. It's tearing you apart. Don't say any more—"

But Tanya shook her head. "I want to talk about it. This is the first time I've ever wanted to. That afternoon, after she left, I went to see Leopold. I had a good cry, and then I knew I had to tell her how sorry I was that I'd said those things, and I would be a flier if that's what she wanted. But when I went to the Big Top, it was just in time to see her fall. I heard the sound when her body—"

She stopped, swallowing hard. "So you see, I never told her that I was sorry. I went on with my training, even though it was worse after that. It was my way of...of making it up to her. But later, when Lars got hurt so badly, he offered to coach so I could take over his act. I couldn't resist his offer. It was what I really wanted to do. Everybody thought it was a wonderful idea. Female animal trainers are a great drawing card for a circus. I've never told anyone how I feel. I guess I was ashamed to admit I was a coward."

"Not a coward. Everybody is afraid of something. I wouldn't go into a cage with a lion if my life depended on it," Wade said ruefully.

Tanya giggled. "Not even Leopold?"

"Well, maybe—but not that male tiger. He scares the bejesus out of me."

"I guess you're right. Everybody is afraid of something." She gave him a searching look. "How did you know, Wade? No one else has ever guessed, not even Marshall."

"I didn't—not until I had a sudden flash of intuition just now when I came up to the door and saw you sitting there, looking as if you were ready to cave in." He smiled at her wince. "So you've never told anybody, and when you're called upon to substitute for one of the aerialists, you go ahead and do it, and then you go back to your trailer for a good cry."

"I don't cry. Usually I just throw up."

He couldn't help smiling. She gave him a reproachful look and started to say something. The sob that escaped her throat must have caught her by surprise, because she cupped her hands over her mouth, her eyes wide and startled. And then the tears were flooding her eyes and running down her cheeks. Instinctively he gathered her into his arms and rocked her back and forth, letting her cry it out.

But even as he buried his face in her sweet-scented hair, a warning sounded in his mind—*Danger! Danger!* His promise to Marshall came back to him, and he knew that if he stayed any longer, if he didn't leave immediately, he was going to do something very foolish—like kissing those tears off Tanya's face.

AFTER WADE WAS GONE, his departure as sudden as his arrival, Tanya washed her face and changed into jeans and a blouse, all the time trying to make sense out of his visit.

Wade had shown a side of himself that she hadn't

known existed—tender and compassionate and warm. And yet, there at the end, he had reverted to his old ironic self, telling her that little girls with big fears should stay off the swings. Had his tenderness been a spurious thing, a very small part of his total personality? Or was it the real Wade, the one locked inside that hard, impenetrable shell?

She shook off the questions, and because she wasn't ready to go to bed and didn't want to be alone, she went in search of Pop. She found him in the silver wagon, sitting at his desk. Since she had her own key, she didn't bother to knock. She unlocked the door and was inside before Pop realized she was there. He was slumped in his battered old swivel chair, staring down at a large ledger that was open in front of him, his forehead creased with worry lines. As she studied him with puzzled eyes, a painful thought came to her. How old he looked, as if a coating of fine dust had sifted over his hair and skin, washing out their color.

And thin. In the past weeks Pop had lost weight his lean body could ill afford. Was it the strain of having Wade underfoot all the time? True, Wade hadn't interfered nearly as much as she'd expected, but maybe just having him around was a constant reminder to Pop that he'd given up more than half the circus and was no longer in command.

Pop looked up and saw her standing there; there was something furtive about the way he quickly closed the black ledger lying in front of him. "How long have—I didn't hear you come in," he said.

"Which isn't strange, since I just this second got here." Pretending not to notice how quickly he had closed the ledger, she added, "I thought you might be hungry, so I brought you some of Alice's raised doughnuts. They're fresh—she just made them this morning.''

"Great. I'll get us some coffee." But before he left his desk, he slid the black book into the top drawer. Later as they chatted casually about circus affairs— the lameness of Sabu, one of the elephants; the elopement of a married candy butch with a cashier half his age; a scheduling problem that had just come up— Tanya knew that Pop's attention was straying. Once, when her spoon clattered against her mug, he jumped nervously.

He was reminiscing about his early days in the circus, something he seemed to do more and more of lately, Tanya thought, when the boss rigger came to the door with a problem. Although Pop hurried away, Tanya accepted his invitation to stay and finish her coffee. But after he was gone, her eyes were drawn toward the desk. Something was seriously wrong with Pop, and it was connected with that ledger.

Briefly she fought a war with her conscience, but in the end her concern for her old friend won out. Even so, it was a while before she overcame her scruples enough to open the desk drawer and take out the ledger. A small flat book fell out and clattered on the floor. Although she picked it up, recognizing it as a bank deposit book, she was too busy studying the name embossed on the front of the ledger to open it. Why had Pop been staring down at the ledger in which the accounts of the circus's reserve fund were recorded, looking almost ill with worry?

The reserve account was the circus's hedge against a rainy day—not an ordinary one, but a catastrophe such as a fire, or a natural disaster like a tornado, or even a long series of ordinary rainy days. It was also the account to which the performers and other permanent employees donated a small percentage of their earnings every payday so they'd have something to fall back on for their own emergencies, such as a long illness or family problems. Although it was an informal arrangement, it worked very well, so why had Pop put the book out of sight, almost as if he didn't want her to see it?

A few minutes later, after she'd examined the ledger and the bankbook that had been with it, she found the answer to her questions. As she stood there, staring down at a record of heavy withdrawals that had almost depleted the account, she felt a weakness in her knees, a quivering in the pit of her stomach.

She sank into Pop's desk chair and buried her head in her arms, trying to make sense out of what her eyes told her was true. Pop was an embezzler—no, that couldn't be true! However bad it looked, he would never cheat his friends—unless it was a choice between them and saving the circus.

And even if he had taken the money, maybe it wasn't really embezzlement. After all, he was in charge of the fund—or was he? Oh, God, if he'd drawn out the money *after* the sale, then he was accountable to Wade for any withdrawals.

Feverishly she slipped open the book again and studied the withdrawal record. Her heart sank when her worse fears were realized. All the money had been drawn out after the sale, which meant that Pop had broken the law and could be sent to jail.

"It would kill Pop to be shut up in a cell," she whispered aloud. A mental picture of Pop, his thin shoulders bent and defeated, sitting in a gray prison cell, made her cringe inwardly. A sob forced its way through her tight throat muscles. She couldn't let that happen. She had to find a way to keep Pop out of jail even if she had to take the blame herself. But no, that wouldn't do. He would never allow that. She had to think of something else.

Maybe if she went to Wade and appealed to his... to his what? To the tenderness he'd shown her tonight, just before he'd made that ironic quip and left her so abruptly? How could she know if that tenderness was real? Maybe it had been an act. No, she couldn't take that kind of chance, not with so much at stake. Whatever she did to save Pop, telling Wade the truth wasn't the way—which must have been Pop's decision, too, or else why hadn't he gone to Wade himself?

Wade could never understand what had driven Pop to do such a thing. Whatever the reason, it must have had something to do with saving the circus. Had those back taxes he'd owed the IRS driven him to raid the reserve fund? Whatever the case, she couldn't take a chance on Wade's mercy. He had described himself as a hardheaded businessman, and from all the evidence, it was true. After all, he had no loyalty ties with Pop. To Wade, Pop would simply be a man who had succumbed to temptation and embezzled funds that didn't belong to him.

However, Wade did have one weakness that she might be able to take advantage of—if she dared. When he'd held her so close tonight, his arousal had been unmistakable. It wasn't love. She knew that now. But it was a weapon she could use if only she had the guts. Could she, who had always prided herself on her honesty, deliberately use her femininity to win concessions from Wade? If so, how far was she willing to go? All the way? But that would be... It was an ugly word that made her wince. Did her loyalty to Pop demand she go that far?

Tanya gathered up the ledger and bankbook and returned them to the desk drawer. She finished her coffee, which was cold now, then rinsed the mugs under hot water and set them on Pop's sink to dry before she went back to her trailer to get ready for bed. In the future she'd have to be careful about acting normal so no one would suspect that anything was wrong. Because she had made up her mind. She would do whatever it took to save Pop—starting with an attempt to cultivate Wade's friendship. And that meant she mustn't make any mistakes in front of Wade, who had once told her how observant he was.

CHAPTER ELEVEN

TANYA STOOD IN FRONT OF THE MIRROR in her tiny
dressing room, staring at her own image and trying to
view herself as if she were a stranger. Since the white
spotlights of the arena washed out color, she used
makeup judiciously when she was performing. At
other times she seldom bothered with more than a little lip gloss; her mouth was a natural dark pink and
her eyelashes were thick and long and very dark.
Now, trying to see herself as Wade did, she wondered
if he thought her casual hairstyle was too plain and
her skin tone too dark—"tawny rose," a newspaper
feature writer who had done an article on the circus
had once called it.

Carefully, using the techniques that Octavia had
taught her, she applied a layer of cherry-bright lip
gloss, underlined her high cheekbones with blush,
tipped her eyelashes with mascara and twisted her
thick mane of hair into an elaborate knot at the base
of her skull. For a long time she studied herself in the
mirror before she shook her head. No, this wasn't the
real Tanya Rhodin. This was her professional face,
the way she looked under the bright lights of the Big
Top. If she suddenly blossomed in makeup, everybody would tease her, and besides, she didn't want
Wade to become suspicious of her sudden turn-
around and think she was stalking him, did she?

She creamed her face and wiped off the lip gloss,

blush and mascara, but she brushed out her hair until it fell, glossy and thick, to her shoulders instead of bundling it up under one of her beloved caps as she usually did during the morning when she was busy with her cats. Although she pulled on a pair of jeans, as always, she hunted through her closet and found a rust-colored jersey that enhanced her coloring and brought out the tawny shade of her skin. Still not satisfied, she tied a brown-and-gold designer's scarf, which had been a birthday gift from Marshall, around her neck before she left the trailer.

Finding Wade without making it apparent that she was looking for him was a bit more complicated. As she drifted around the backyard, the lot and the midway, making excuses to drop in at any place she thought he might be, she found it hard to hide her nervousness. *I'd make a terrible spy*, she thought ruefully, when she found herself stuttering as she told Alice and Too Tall Tim that she'd just dropped by their trailer to find out if they'd picked up any new magazines during their last stop.

She tried the silver wagon and discovered Pop with his feet up on his desk, engrossed in a racing form, which he put aside quickly when he saw her standing in the door. Although Wade wasn't there, she talked to Pop for a few minutes before she left to check out the cookhouse, then Clown Alley, where she was greeted with ribald remarks and a flood of teasing about training her to be a lady clown. She drifted on, this time for a tour of the concession stands, which were already bustling with preparations for the afternoon crowds.

But it was at the menagerie that she finally located Wade. He was standing a few feet away from the bull-line where the elephants were tethered, watching

Maisie, the grande dame of the troupe. There was such an odd mixture of amusement and sadness on his face that Tanya paused a moment, feeling like an intruder. But Wade must have caught a glimpse of her from the corner of his eye because he turned to stare at her, his expression wary.

"That's Maisie," she said, her tone casually friendly. "She's my favorite of all the elephants. I used to play under her when I was a kid, but she never once stepped on me. I'm sure she thought I was one of her offspring, because she'd run anyone off who tried to come near me."

"Which is how you got out of doing your lessons and your chores, right?"

"Now who told you that? Marshall, or Pop?"

"Or Octavia or Alice or Too Tall Tim or Gogo or half a dozen others, all of whom are full of stories about Tanya as a toddler, Tanya as a teenager, Tanya as the fearless star of the circus."

There was an ironic note in his voice that didn't bode well for her plans to butter him up. Rather than start anything that might lead to another disagreement, Tanya hastily changed the subject.

"Why were you watching Maisie?"

He hesitated, then said, "It's this thing I have for elephants."

"Good or bad?"

"Good. I admire them."

"Well, let me introduce you two," she said, unable to resist a relatively harmless joke. Maisie, for all her docility, had a disagreeable little trick with newcomers. If she decided that she didn't like one—and she wasn't partial to strange men—she turned out their jacket pockets with her trunk and then showed her backside to them.

As they drew close to Maisie, the giant animal's small, intelligent eyes examined Wade from top to bottom. When her trunk snaked out, Tanya stifled a giggle. But her amusement turned to disbelief when the facile gray trunk curled lovingly around Wade's arm, then touched his face as if she were kissing him.

"She likes you," she said wonderingly.

"Is that so hard to believe?" Wade's voice sounded a little husky; if it hadn't been crazy, she would have said he was deeply touched.

"Well, she doesn't usually like strange men." To her chagrin, there was a note of jealousy in her voice.

"I guess it's my fatal charm. It gets the ladies every time," he said, and she saw that he was laughing at her.

She bit back a rude remark. "You can't be all bad if animals like you," she said sweetly.

"So you believe that old saying, do you? What about hardened criminals who have faithful dogs?"

"What about them?" She dismissed the subject with a wave of her hand, then gave him her most demure smile. "Why don't you treat me to a cup of Cookie's coffee and a danish—" She broke off, remembering that Cookie no longer presided over the cookhouse. At his retirement party, he had been in very high spirits, but underneath she had sensed his reluctance to leave. Even so, he hadn't said a single critical word about Wade, and somehow that had made her even more resentful.

"I'm sorry about Cookie," Wade said. "It was something that had to happen. With Cookie's eyesight failing so fast, he couldn't handle his job anymore. The men do such hard physical labor that they deserve good, hearty meals three times a day, especially since they often can't get to a restaurant—and a steady diet of concession-stand hamburgers and French fries is ulcer fare. Cookie was pleased with the...the arrangements we made for his retirement.''

Tanya forced back the retort that trembled on her lips. Did part of her resentment stem from the fact that she hadn't been the one to realize why Cookie's skills had deserted him so quickly? There had been so many clues besides the deterioration in the quality of the food, such as the kitchen accidents that he'd blamed on his helpers' carelessness. But why hadn't he told his friends that he was losing his eyesight? Was it pride, of which Cookie had such an abundance?

"I do think you could have let him finish out the tour," she said stiffly. "Cookie used to run the best cookhouse in the business. Everybody said that. He deserved better treatment."

"It was his own choice, Tanya. Cookie wanted to get settled in his new home before the lights went out altogether."

She knew he was right. Cookie had told her the same thing. Even so, she was silent, not willing to admit that she had been unfair.

Wade shook his head. "Always so loyal to your old friends, aren't you? And how about new ones? Do you feel the same way about new ones?"

There was a deepening in his voice that made her stare at him, only to discover that it was impossible to look away. When he reached out and took her face between his hands, her body felt so nerveless that she didn't even attempt to escape. Instead, to her later shame, she closed her eyes, her mouth tingling in anticipation of his kiss. But he only touched his lips to her forehead before his hands dropped away.

Although she managed a cool smile, the intensity of her disappointment warned her that she was playing with fire. If she persisted in encouraging him, it could only mean further assaults on her own emotions, and she was finding out that she was very vulnerable to the appeal of this man. She felt it when he looked at her, when he spoke—and when he touched her, her reaction was almost overwhelming. By going on with this scheme was she opening herself to eventual heartbreak?

She realized that Wade was watching her, and she forced herself to answer his question as if nothing had happened. "I value all my friends, the new as well as the old."

"Which does call for a celebration. How about that coffee and danish you mentioned, or do you have some unfinished business here?"

Even though she was sure it was an idle question, she answered it carefully. "I came to see my old nursemaid, Maisie. I have a treat for her." She produced the banana she'd swiped from the cookhouse. They both laughed as Maisie's supple trunk snaked out to take it from Tanya's hand. Methodically, with a delicacy a master chef might have envied, the elephant peeled the skin, ate the pulp inside, then daintily devoured the skin, too.

"I remember that trick from—" Wade broke off.

When he didn't go on, Tanya prompted, "From what?"

"From something I once read in a book about elephants."

They walked toward the cookhouse, talking easily, and this casual friendliness set the pattern for the days that followed. At least once a day they would meet. Tanya made very sure of that, even if it didn't come about naturally. For the first time in her life she consciously set out to charm another person—and found she had a natural talent for it.

As the days went by she realized that Wade's wariness had vanished, and he was regarding her in his old friendly way. What surprised her was that she felt the same way toward him. For one thing, it was astonishing how many things they found in common. Earlier, before their conversation about elephants, she had assumed he was indifferent to animals. Now she discovered that he was an active member of a well-known conservation group and devoted not only money but a portion of his busy life to the organization, which was dedicated to the preservation of the world's endangered species and other natural life.

When she expressed her own views on animals in captivity, he listened intently, even though she knew he didn't agree.

"When people get the chance to see the beauty of live animals, not just view photographs or movies of them, they are more willing to invest their emotions and time in conserving the ones still in the wild," she told him earnestly. "My cat-training act is pure entertainment, but nobody watching it can be untouched a little by the grandeur of the big cats. I try never to let them lose their dignity, because I want the audience to realize that these superb animals have as much a right to share our world as we do. Which is why I don't degrade them by having them perform silly tricks or dress them up in crazy hats."

"Not even old Leopold? He does look rather like an overgrown kitten when he rubs up against you, you know."

Wade was lounging on Tanya's sofa, looking remarkably at home in the small trailer. She had invit-

ed several of her special friends—Pop and Marshall,
Too Tall Tim and Alice, Bruno and a few others—to
a barbecue since it was a still day between two long
engagements.

Her trailer was parked at the end of a row of vans
and trailers, which gave the party a degree of privacy,
and after they had eaten the charcoal-broiled ribs and
chicken, the salad and roasted ears of corn and the
strawberry shortcake she'd provided, they had sat
out in folding chairs under the darkening sky for a
long time, swapping yarns and talking.

When others, drawn by the voices and laughter,
drifted up, they had been invited to join in, too, and
it had been the kind of relaxed and casual evening
that Tanya enjoyed most.

Too Tall Tim and Alice had been the last to leave.
She had expected Wade to leave with them, but he
had insisted on helping her clean up, an offer she had
rejected from others but accepted eagerly from him,
because it gave them a chance to be completely alone
without much risk of interruption, a chance she'd
been hoping for.

After the last paper plate had been gathered up and
dropped in the trash cans, and the last coffee cup and
spoon dried and put away in her tiny cupboards,
Wade had stayed on as if he hated to leave, sipping
the glass of wine she'd offered him and talking casually about everything and anything.

The evening had been full of shoptalk, good-
natured wrangling and endless anecdotes, most of
which she had heard dozens of times before. It was
obvious from the first that Wade was having a good
time. Although he was not really one of them, the circus people had treated him with a friendly reserve
and, Tanya knew, with genuine respect....

She came out of her reverie with a start, realizing that Wade was looking at her with curious eyes, still waiting for an answer to his question about Leopold.

"Leopold is special. I always tell the audience that he's unusually tame and I was practically raised with him, so he regards me as a fellow lion."

"More like a bewitching tigress," Wade murmured, his eyes glinting.

She pretended not to hear the compliment and added, "I don't want them to lose their awe of the big cats. Just to understand them and be willing to give them space in this world we all share."

He nodded. "I'll go along with that." He hesitated. "I had a great time tonight. I saw the circus people in a new light."

"What do you mean by a 'new light'?"

"As ordinary people. Maybe it's because there's nothing more ordinary than a barbecue in someone's backyard."

"Well, they aren't ordinary people." Despite herself, her tone was short. "You have no idea what it's like for Jojo, for instance, to do something as normal as go to a supermarket for a loaf of bread or into a gas station to fill up the tank on his cab-over rig. That he does it anyway and doesn't hide himself away in his RV is so incredibly brave of him. He's a truly gentle person. He's aware that his facial distortion upsets some people. I know there's a strong belief that sideshows should be banished, that they exploit human misery, and maybe that's true, to a degree. But what else would these people that others call freaks do with their lives? Where would they go, and how would they earn a living? Most have been badly mistreated by the outside world. Here they have the dignity of knowing that they are wanted, that they can earn a decent living and that they have friends and a home.''

"Marshall said something like that to me once,'' Wade told her. "And of course he—and you—are right. But isn't it a shame that anyone has to be exhibited like an animal in order to be accepted?''

She shook her head. "I don't think any of them really minds. In fact, most of them love the attention. Maybe it's compensation for having been rejected or ignored so often before they came here.''

He stared at her so long she felt uncomfortable. "What is it? Did I say something wrong?''

"You said something right—so right that it surprised me. You're very articulate, you know. You don't speak like the others, and yet you've spent your life with the circus.''

"Marshall never allowed me to use too much jargon. He coached me in grammar and made me study hard.'' She sighed, remembering the arduous drills he'd put her through. "I used to rebel sometimes, but he has a will of iron. It was easier to just go ahead and do my lessons so I could go out and play.''

"Well, he did a good job on you. You could pass—''

He broke off. When she realized what he'd been about to say, a rush of anger went through her. It was all she could do to smile as if she hadn't caught the significance of his broken sentence.

But the smile must not have been convincing, because Wade added, "You're angry at me. I should have finished that sentence. I meant to say that you could pass at any level of society. And I meant that as a compliment.''

"Taken as one,'' she said, and quickly changed the subject. They chatted quietly, reliving the party. Tanya was laughing about one of Marshall's more virulent remarks, this one to the pompous bandmaster, Acey Brenner, when she realized that Wade wasn't listening. She looked up, and what she saw in his eyes brought a flush to her face.

He reached forward and ran the back of his hand along her cheek. "You're beautiful—not lovely or cute or pretty, but truly beautiful. And you don't realize it, do you?"

Since his tone was serious, not teasing, she thought a moment, then gave him an honest answer. "I guess I'm too busy to worry about how I look."

"Which is just about the answer I expected," he said, smiling.

"Well, I do stay pretty busy. Do you think I should do more to . . . you know, fix myself up?"

"Don't change a hair on that lovely head." Wade leaned toward her and kissed her lips. Although it was an undemanding kiss, the blood rushed to her head, and before she had time to think, she was returning the pressure, her lips opening beneath his. He made an inarticulate sound deep in his throat, and then she was pressed tightly against his hard body, and his lips, his tongue, were plundering her mouth. She inhaled deeply, liking the male scent of his body, but when she snuggled closer, signaling her willingness for him to continue, he released her with a groan. "I'd better leave before I forget a promise I made."

"A promise? I don't understand—"

"I don't want you to. Let's just say that it's getting increasingly hard to remember that you're only twenty-one."

"Twenty-two—or at least I will be in another week."

"That's a very special birthday. Will your friends give you a party?"

"Of course. Every year they have a surprise party for me, and every year I'm surprised as hell."

"You're lucky. I can't remember anyone ever giving me a birthday party, surprise or otherwise."

"Not even your mother?"

Wade took his time answering. "My mother was very busy with her own life," he said finally. "For one thing, she usually held down a job—between pregnancies."

"And your father? Was he busy, too?"

"My father died when I was six. I was the oldest of five boys—by seven years. And if you're adding up dates, they're my half-brothers. Since my mother lost interest in her offspring once they grew beyond the baby stage, you could say that I was their surrogate mother and father as well as older brother."

"Then you don't come from a wealthy family?"

"Just the opposite. My mother worked as a secretary, and I was holding down part-time jobs by the time I was sixteen. I worked full-time while I went to college, but I struck it lucky in one aspect. It seems I have a knack for electronics. I invented a gadget that electronic companies wanted. So I got the right backing, started my own company, and after a long hard pull, things worked out well for me."

"Are your brothers in electronics, too?"

"The one next to me is studying to be a doctor, a surgeon, and the twins are both electrical engineers. They're partners in their own business now. My youngest brother is going into law. With his natural charisma and his penchant for hard work, he'll probably be the senator from California one of these days.

There was a quiet pride in his voice, and a sudden realization came to Tanya. If Wade hadn't come from well-to-do people as she'd assumed, then someone had helped his brothers through school, and the likeliest candidate was Wade. Was *this* the chink in his armor—a strong sense of responsibility? The fact that he'd been so quick to jump to Leopold's aid the day someone had tossed a broken bottle into his cage bore it out. Was this how she could reach him and get Pop off the hook? Maybe now was the time to appeal to his sympathy, while he was full of good spirits and in a mellow, relaxed mood. . . .

"You look so pensive," Wade said. "Are you thinking of the siblings you never had?"

"Something like that," she lied. "I would've liked having brothers and sisters, but of course I've been so lucky that it seems wrong to want more. You had four brothers and a mother, but I had a dozen mothers and fathers. That's why I'm so grateful—to Pop in particular. He's been a wonderful friend. I guess I'd forgive him anything because of that."

She gave Wade a sidelong look. "I'm sure you feel the same way about your family—that you'd forgive them anything?"

"No, not anything." There was a grimness in his voice, a chill in his eyes, that made her wince. "Some things, like the betrayal of trust, I find it impossible to forgive. When I was eighteen, my mother ran off with a man who had taken her fancy, leaving my brothers to the mercy of social agencies. It was three years before I finally got custody of them. It was a bad time for all of us. It left me distrustful of. . .of other people."

"You never forgave her for deserting her family?"

"Forgive? What does that mean? I've never let

down my guard with her. I only give people one chance. After that, if they betray my trust, I cut them out of my life."

Tanya quickly changed the subject to hide her dismay. A few minutes later Wade rose and stood looking down at her. He was smiling now; it was hard to remember the hardness that had been in his eyes when he'd talked about his mother's desertion.

"I want to ask you a favor, Tanya, and no nonsense about refusing me. These past few days we've become good friends, and I want to do something special to celebrate your birthday. We'll be in New Jersey in a few days, and since we have another still day, I'd like to take you out to dinner. You told me once that you've never been to New York except to look at the lights from the New Jersey shore. It would give me a great deal of pleasure to show you my adopted town at its best. You will accept, won't you?"

A thrill of excitement ran through Tanya—until something else occurred to her. "But I haven't anything fancy to wear, and the schedule for the next eight days is so tight I won't have time to do any shopping."

"Leave that part to me," Wade said, his eyes crinkling with amusement. "Just say yes, and trust me. Let me play fairy godmother, although I never saw a less likely Cinderella in my life. I guarantee you'll have something appropriate to wear for a night on the town. Let's call it the second part of your birthday gift. Is the answer yes?"

"Yes," she said, feeling ridiculously happy at the thought of spending an evening alone with him.

It was only after Wade had gone, first kissing her lightly on the forehead, that her thoughts took a dif-

ferent, more calculating turn. She had been looking
for the right moment to approach Wade about Pop,
to appeal to his compassion as well as his sense of
responsibility by pointing out that if Pop went to
prison, it would adversely affect the whole circus.
What better time than during a long evening alone
with him?

With luck, she could persuade Wade to allow
Pop—and all their friends, who were sure to rally to
Pop's help—to make restitution, and she would get
his promise that he wouldn't file charges for embezzlement.

CHAPTER TWELVE

EARLY THE NEXT MORNING Wade made a phone call to his psychiatrist friend, Larry Glover.

"Hello, stranger," Larry said when he heard Wade's voice. "How's the big circus tycoon?"

"So you know about that. News does get around."

"I can read. There was a delightful, tongue-in-cheek article in the *Times* about the businessman who ran away and joined the circus. Really heart wrenching. For about a month there, you were the main topic of conversation of your crowd. You mean you haven't been bombarded with curious phone calls—"

"No, but then I have been out of touch," Wade said, not liking the direction of the conversation.

"Even from the stunning Monica? I hear she's tearing out her hair because a live one got away."

"Yeah, well, that relationship cooled off quickly. We...let's say we have different interests in life."

"But you gave her quite a rush when you came back from your circus jaunt last fall, didn't you? So what happened? Or does that come under the heading of 'none of your busines, Larry old pal'?"

"It didn't work out. Let's leave it at that."

"Closed subject—provided you tell me what happened during your original sojourn with the Peeples Circus. You were moody as hell the few times I saw you this winter, and when you refused to talk about it, I assumed the adventure had been a disaster.

Then, out of the blue, you closed your apartment, left a message on your answering machine saying something about going on another cruise and dropped out of sight. Until I read that article in the *Times* and heard the gossip, I didn't even know that you'd bought into the Peeples Circus. Is that any way to treat a friend?''

"It's a lousy way to treat a friend, especially one with a curiosity bump as large as a walrus, but I've been busy, and besides, I had some things to work out."

"Like paying off a debt to a man you credit with setting you on the track to fame and fortune? If that's what was bugging you, why didn't you just put up the money to bail his circus out of its financial troubles? You didn't have to get involved personally in the running of the circus. What *really* gives?"

"I believe in keeping an eye on my investments— and that isn't why I called. I want to ask a favor."

"Just name it. It's done. I owe you a couple."

"Not so fast. I'm asking the favor of Irene, not you."

"Oh, the plot thickens. What's this all about?"

"Just put her on the phone, okay?"

"She's not here. She went on a shopping binge in Paris with her sister, and that's going to cost me a bundle. She'll be calling me tomorrow morning. Until then, she's out of touch."

"Dammit, I was depending on her fashion know-how."

"Why don't you tell me about it and then I can brief her when she calls. No problem about her doing the favor. She dotes on you."

"Okay—no, maybe I'd better forget it—"

"What is this? You're acting very skittish. Are you hiding something?"

"Nothing like that. I want to...to buy a gift for a friend. It's her twenty-second birthday, and I'm taking her out for a gala evening in New York next weekend. She doesn't have the right clothes for a night on the town or the time to do any shopping, so I thought Irene might do it for her."

"Consider it done, even though this is going to cost me! She'll come back with one outfit for your friend and three more for herself. Well, so be it. Give me the details, and I'll get her cracking on it. She can express the stuff from Paris—at your expense. And you're in good hands. She's a whiz about such things. But first I want to hear all about this mysterious lady."

"Okay, my elephant-child friend, I'll satisfy your curiosity. But no cracks, no advice and no inferences just because I have this impulse to buy a gift for a very special person, understood?"

"Understood. I'll keep my opinions to myself even if it chokes me. So give me details—size, coloring, that sort of thing. When Irene calls me, I'll pass it along."

"According to the circus wardrobe woman, Tanya's dress size is seven, shoe size five. As for her coloring... You remember that poster in my den, the one of the woman animal trainer? The colors were right on target, except that Tanya's eyes are a deeper amber."

"So the lady does exist. Are you sure she's just a friend? She isn't the real reason you went into the circus business, is she?"

"Nothing like that," Wade said, his tone short.

"Uh-huh. Well, I hope it's 'nothing like that' if a

really heavy relationship such as marriage is involved. It wouldn't have a prayer of working out. For one thing, if it's Tanya's twenty-second birthday, you're ten years older, my friend. And the background differences is enough to make this old psychiatrist get the bends. Don't you agree?''

Wade was a long time answering. "Look, I don't need any of your advice—professional or otherwise. And it's a moot question because Tanya is just a friend. Okay, I have a soft spot for her. I knew her as a kid. It *is* possible for a man to be good friends with a woman, you know.''

"Maybe, but I don't think in this case you're telling me everything. But okay, I did promise not to give advice. Just be careful. You're a vulnerable dude, for all your worldly outlook and business acumen. And you're dealing with something here that's new to you. Just don't do anything you'll regret all your life—and that's absolutely the last bit of advice I intend to give you.''

"And not a minute too soon. If you want to take another look at that poster, I'll call the building super and tell him to give you access to the penthouse.''

"I just might do that. Irene'll be in seventh heaven, being able to draw upon your bank account for a shopping spree, even if it is for another woman. Can I tell her she has carte blanche?''

Wade hesitated, fighting doubt. Irene was a shrewd, perceptive woman, but would she understand that Tanya was not a sophisticate, that she would look out of place in an *haute couture* gown?

"Yes," he said finally. "Tell her to spend what's needed for a gown, shoes, jewelry, the works—including a wrap. Something suitable for dinner at...

oh, the Changing Seasons. But no fur. Irene knows my views on that. And my friend holds the same views. Be sure to mention that Tanya is only twenty-two. She isn't the ingenue type, but she isn't a sophisticate, either. In fact, she's rather...earthy. Tell Irene to keep that in mind while she's shopping."

"You can trust Irene. She cut her teeth in the fashion business, you know. Your little friend will look like a princess."

"She *is* a princess, and that's part of the trouble," Wade said. He hung up before Larry could ask the next obvious question.

It was done, Wade thought as he turned away from the phone. Although he was having second thoughts, he couldn't disappoint Tanya now. Larry was right about one thing. He intended to be very careful that the evening remained a one-time outing, the gesture of a friend treating another to dinner and a floor show. And after it was over, then maybe it was time for him to gradually withdraw from the circus and return to real life.

TANYA WAS GETTING READY for the evening performance when she heard a rap at the screen door. Because it was so warm outside, she had opened all her windows to let in a cool breeze. Unlike some of the other trailers, hers didn't have air conditioning, a luxury she wasn't able to afford because she was saving her money to buy a new truck. She threw on her robe and went to unlatch the door and let Alice in. The expression on her friend's face told her that something was up even before she saw the packages in Alice's plump arms.

"This stuff was delivered to the silver wagon just a few minutes ago." Alice's eyes were bright with curiosity. "Maude asked me to bring them over. They're addressed to you, and the return address is a Dr. Laurence Glover, New York City."

"There must be some mistake. I don't know anyone by that name," Tanya said, disappointment flattening her voice. For the past week she had waited for Wade to say something more about his dinner invitation, but although he had been as friendly as ever, there seemed to be a wall between them again, making her wonder if he had changed his mind. Her first thought on seeing the packages was that this must be the birthday present he'd promised her. But obviously there had been a mistake, because she didn't know any doctor, much less one with a New York address.

"Well, the packages were sent to you care of Pop, so let's see what's inside," Alice urged.

After a moment's indecision, Tanya opened the largest box. Her breath caught sharply when she lifted off a layer of tissue paper and saw the gown inside. It was mist green, a concoction of fine lace and a soft, delicate material that she knew must be real silk. When she took it out of the box and held it up against her body, she realized that when the gown was worn, one shoulder would be bared. A clasp of tiny green jewels set in gold was pinned to the shoulder, the garment's only ornament.

"Are those emeralds real?" Alice said in an awed voice.

"Surely not," Tanya said. "But they're lovely— and the dress is just my size. I've never seen anything so beautiful!"

"Look—there's an envelope! It's pinned to the tissue paper."

Tanya's hands shook slightly as she took an ivory-colored card from its matching envelope. "It's from a friend of Wade's, a Mrs. Glover," she said finally. "She hopes I like the gown she chose for me, and that I'll have a wonderful time in New York."

"Wade bought you the gown?" There was speculation in Alice's voice. "And he's taking you out to dinner in New York? When?"

"Tomorrow night. He. . .he asked me last week. I told him I didn't have anything to wear and he said I wasn't to worry about it, that part of his birthday present was something appropriate for dinner in New York. I didn't expect. . .oh, Alice, I can't accept an expensive gift like this! It must have cost a small fortune."

"A fortune to us, pocket money to him" Alice said, shrugging. "Why don't you see what's in the other boxes?"

Tanya opened another box and gasped out loud. An exquisite silk velvet evening wrap, so soft she wanted to bury her face in it, lay wrapped in tissue paper. It was the same mist green as the gown, and they obviously were intended to go together. When she slipped it over her shoulders, it seemed to snuggle against her skin, promising enchanted evenings ahead.

The smaller boxes yielded gold evening slippers, which consisted mainly of tiny straps, an exquisite set of creamy silk lingerie and a gold evening bag. It was when she was exploring the bag that she found two jewelers' boxes inside. She opened the largest one first, and her heart seemed to turn over as she stared down at a necklace of exquisitely wrought gold links, each set with a tiny emerald. A few seconds later, a pair of emerald earrings winked up at her from the second box.

Only half-aware of Alice's steady stream of comments, she touched the necklace with her fingertip, knowing that if she didn't accept the gifts and have her evening in New York with Wade, she would regret it all her life. But she would be careful not to lose an earring, she told herself, because later she intended to return the expensive jewelry to Wade. But for just one night, she would play at being Cinderella. She even had an excuse to salve her conscience. If she hoped to influence Wade in Pop's favor, it was important to please him, and he obviously drew some pleasure from giving her these lovely presents.

"You've decided to accept them, haven't you?" Alice said, sighing. "Well, who can blame you? No, I'm not going to lecture you, hon, but I do want you to be careful. It's so easy to have your heart broken when you're young, to believe that someone has more serious intentions than. . .than he really does. I've seen the electricity between you two when you're together. Everybody has. We're all worried about you, even though we've kept our mouths shut. You're a woman now, and you have to make your own mistakes, only. . .only don't get your hopes up too high."

She got to her feet and began gathering up the tissue paper. "There, I've said my last word on the subject. You're a big girl now. I guess I'll always worry about you. You were my little girl for so long—what would this old circus be without you?"

She bustled off, but before she left she gave Tanya a fierce hug.

Feeling strangely lost, Tanya stood in the doorway, staring after her friend, before she finally went to hang up the gown and change into her costume for the evening performance.

IT WAS MUGGY in the bay bottoms where the fairground was located, but tonight, Tanya hardly noticed the closeness in the air, even though all the windows were open to cool the trailer off as she finished dressing for her dinner date. Octavia was helping her—and giving her a steady stream of advice, which Tanya listened to absently, most of her thoughts on Wade, who was already waiting outside.

Not entirely to her surprise, Wade had had quite an audience when he'd come to pick her up a few minutes earlier. If he was annoyed at the sight of Marshall and Pop and several others who just happened to be standing outside the trailer talking when he arrived, at least he didn't let on. His voice as he'd greeted them had sounded normal to Tanya's anxious ears. In fact, at the moment he was laughing and joking with Pop, who was teasing him about his recent encounter with an officious local authority.

"I think I'll have to turn over the patch man's job to you, Wade," she heard Pop say. "You handled that fellow like he deserved, and still didn't make no enemies. How you'd learn to be so slick?"

"Running a business that employed several hundred electronic nuts was quite an education in how to deal with people. All computer types are...let's say they're rugged individualists. I had to be nursemaid, boss, father confessor and sometimes a diplomat to keep them happy—and working hard."

"You sure know how to deal with officials. That fellow didn't know what to say when you mentioned you was friends with his boss, the mayor of this burg. Were you telling the truth about that?"

"I've met the man a time or two," Wade admitted. "But the friend part was stretching it."

"Well, it worked. I don't think we'll have any

trouble with permits and zoning violations during this run like we did last year. Lord, the chiselers were so thick around here we couldn't hardly wade through them. I guess they saw all that loose change in the silver wagon and figured we were rolling in dough. If I had a dime for every Annie Oakley we passed out last year to the local police and fire inspectors and city councilmen, I could retire.''

"We shouldn't be bothered too much this time. And speaking of money, the auditor told me to remind you about the reserve-account books. Could you round up all the pertinent material sometime soon?''

To Tanya's straining ears, Pop seemed to take a long time answering. "I'm a little rushed right now, what with this tight schedule and the tax business coming up, but I'll get that letter off in a day or two and have the clerk at the home office get the ledger out of my safe-deposit box. Don't know how I come to leave it behind this spring—''

Marshall's clipped voice cut in, and the conversation shifted to other things. As she slipped into her dress, then turned so Octavia could zip up the back, Tanya felt a strange reluctance to go outside and face her friends. Would they sense something else—the way her heart jumped so alarmingly every time she heard Wade's deep voice?

"Stop daydreaming, girl, and turn around so I can put this necklace on you," Octavia said crossly. She had volunteered to help Tanya dress, and to "do something with that mop of hair."

Tanya had had her reservations, but since she didn't want to hurt Octavia's feelings, she had accepted her offer of help. Now, as she studied herself in the mirror, she found it hard to believe that this was the same Tanya who had worked beside Moon that morning, cleaning out the cats' cages and helping the bullmen wash down the elephants after two of the handlers had quit.

That Tanya had looked like a boy in her cap and jeans; this one was a mature woman, glowing and radiant. Her eyes seemed more green than amber, as if they had stolen color from the emeralds she wore around her neck, and her skin glowed with health. Octavia had arranged her thick hair in a soft style that flowed from a central part to her shoulders, hiding her small ears so that only an occasional flash of green fire revealed that she was wearing emeralds.

Octavia had also insisted that Tanya wear make-up—a touch of mascara to emphasize the brilliance of her eyes, a careful application of coral lip gloss to make her mouth seem lush and mature, a shading of blush along her cheekbones and a touch of powder to complement the natural matt finish of her skin. And the dress fell in a soft line from one shoulder down to the tip of the glittering gold slippers. Deceptively demure when she was standing still, it revealed more than it concealed when she moved, giving enticing hints of her lithe young body.

Despite Wade's compliments, Tanya had never thought of herself as beautiful. Her idea of beauty was the fragile pink-and-white perfection of her mother. But now she had an acute sense of the power she could exert over men—if she were so inclined.

"What a sensation you would've made in the Old Country," Octavia sighed, her hooded eyes reminiscent. "When I think of the emeralds and rubies and diamonds the men showered upon us—men were much more generous about their romantic attachments to theatrical women back then. Why, a smart girl could retire young and live off the jewels given to her by admirers. But times have changed. Today men want so much for so little. But Wade is a generous man. I'm sure he'll see that you're taken care of, love.''

As the meaning of Octavia's words sank in, Tanya whirled on her angrily. "If you mean what I think you do, you're wrong, Octavia! Just because Wade gave me a few presents, that doesn't mean I intend to...to be his mistress! We're friends and nothing more.''

The wrinkles around Octavia's eyes and mouth deepened as she gave a knowing smile. "A man like Wade won't be satisfied with friendship for long. No, he wants you, and that's how it should be. But what worries me is how *you* feel about him. A woman in love sometimes forgets to look after her own best interests. So don't be foolish or too hasty. Make sure that he understands what it is you expect from him before you allow him any...any liberties.''

Ignoring Tanya's silence, she added fretfully, "I should have talked to you about this earlier. There are ways to please the men, to tie them to you and win concessions—yes, I'm afraid I've neglected your education shamefully. You grew up so fast. It seems just yesterday that you were plaguing me to tell you stories about my rich industrialist, the one who gave me my diamonds.'' She sighed deeply, and Tanya knew that she was thinking of the treasures she'd been forced to leave behind when she'd escaped from Hungary after some scandal, which she never talked about.

Tanya bit her lip to hold back another sharp remark. Octavia meant well, she just saw things differently than most people did. As for learning how to please a man, surely just being yourself was the way to do that.

She folded the velvet wrap over her arm since it wasn't needed yet, kissed Octavia's heavily rouged cheek and murmured a soft "Thank you" before she went outside. From the expressions on her friends' faces when they saw her, she knew they were as surprised at her transformation as she had been. She had been expecting an audience, of course. There were few secrets around a circus, but she wondered how Wade was taking it behind his calm smile.

"Well, well, our little girl is all grown up," Marshall said. There was a cutting quality in his voice, which always seemed surprisingly deep for his size. "All you need is a white horse, Wade—and maybe a couple of bodyguards for Tanya."

The two men exchanged glances. "Take good care of her, Wade. She's very special."

"I know how special she is," Wade said.

As if his words were a signal, the others chimed in with their compliments. As she smiled at them, Tanya caught an expression in Wade's eyes that startled her. He looked wistful, not at all like the confident, unflappable man she knew him to be, and she wondered if he had been taken aback by such an uproar over what was really an ordinary dinner date.

Did he understand what lay behind all the casual teasing, the laughs and jokes? Her friends were telling him they were concerned about her evening out with a man who was not really one of them. Did Wade realize that? If so, was he insulted? Or did that sadness she saw in his eyes stem from something else? Briefly Wade's own words came back to her. He had been a surrogate father very early, he'd said. Had there been times when he'd resented it, when he'd grown tired of always having to be the strong one his family leaned on?

The car waiting for them at the edge of the housing area was long and shining, a rented limo with New York license plates. The chauffeur driving it was dressed in matching gray; he jumped out with alacrity to open the door and help Tanya inside. Wade must have caught her look of awe, because he told her dryly, "I'm giving you the full treatment. Tonight you're Cinderella, and this is the modern-day version of the coach and footmen. There's even a bar. Would you like some wine?"

She hesitated, then shook her head. This was a once-in-a-lifetime evening. She wasn't about to dull her senses with alcohol.

"I hope you don't mind if I have a Scotch. I need a drink after that inquisition."

"They mean well," she said quickly. "I guess they're afraid—" She broke off, appalled at what she'd almost said.

"I know what's bothering them. The subtle message they were giving me with all that friendly chatter came through loud and clear. But it wasn't necessary. I'll be a perfect gentleman, even though I'm very susceptible to beautiful women with chestnut brown hair and dark amber eyes. You truly are a work of art tonight—almost as enchanting as a certain tomboy I know who wears crazy caps when she works out with her lions. You're sure to knock 'em dead at the Changing Seasons."

"The Changing Seasons?"

"Where I've made reservations for dinner. The food is superb—they have one of the finest French chefs in the country. Later I thought we'd go dancing and take in a floor show at one of the nightclubs. Do you like to dance, Tanya?"

"Oh, yes. Octavia taught me, but not the latest

steps, I'm afraid. She was a ballet dancer when she was young—"

"Among other things," he said.

"You heard—" She broke off, her cheeks flooding with heat.

"Octavia's motherly advice? Part of it, enough to know that like your other friends, she has your best interests at heart." To her relief, he dropped the subject and added, "Don't worry about the latest steps. The club we'll be going to after dinner is into the Big Bands revival. Fox-trots, waltzes, rumbas, perhaps a tango or two."

"I'm surprised that you—" Again she stopped, wishing she could control this habit she had of blurting out her thoughts.

"You're surprised that I know how to dance? Because of my great age?"

"Of course not," she said with dignity. "I did wonder if maybe you'd been too busy to do much dancing in your life."

"As it happens, I love to dance. I even took a few lessons—for business reasons. When I was getting started and looking for backers for my company, I learned that one way to make a good impression on potential investors was to guide their wives around the dance floor. At first I had to grit my teeth, but to my surprise I learned to like it."

Tanya smiled at his wry tone, but she couldn't help wondering what else he had learned during his drive toward success. Was buying clothes and jewels for women part of it?

"I can't keep the emeralds, you know," she said abruptly. "They are much too expensive. I only wore them tonight because they look so perfect with the gown."

She expected an argument, but he only shrugged. "As you wish. But I hope you change your mind. No strings attached, Tanya. They're the gift of one friend to another."

She didn't answer. Part of her realized that Wade had just made it almost impossible for her to return the jewelry. She also felt... Was it disappointment? Could it be possible that she had wanted Octavia's assumption that Wade planned to seduce her tonight to be true?

She shook off the disturbing thought, and as they drove toward the glittering lights of the city, she felt a rush of excitement. As if he sensed her change of mood, Wade took her hand and held it tightly. "Relax and enjoy this evening—as I intend to," he said softly.

Before she could answer, he bent his head and kissed her, but not on the forehead this time. His lips were surprisingly soft for a mouth that looked so firm, and for a moment she felt his tongue against hers and the melting sweetness that always surprised her so much. Then he pulled away, and his smile was ironic, as if directed at himself rather than at her.

"Sorry. I couldn't resist. I've been wanting to do that ever since you appeared in the doorway of your trailer, looking like a star-touched mermaid in that dress."

Her laugh was a little shaky. "Thank you, but mermaids don't live in trailers, and the ones who try living on land come to very sad ends."

"Not this mermaid. She's going to have a happy, fruitful, fulfilling life. Surely Octavia must have read your tarot cards and told you this a dozen times?"

"Not exactly. She sees happiness ahead for me, but only if I'm careful and don't make any mistakes.

And she always sees trouble in my cards, too,'' Tanya said, sighing.

"Just what you saw in my cards—if you really did. What was it you told me? That I was a man at the crossroads of life—the Hanging Man, I think you called it. You were right about that—and about a woman who was out to play practical jokes on me."

"That was awful of me, wasn't it? I did it because of the way you looked at me the morning I started training Bennie. As if I were some kind of specimen that amused you."

"Did I do that? I'll tell you a secret. I thought you were the most exciting woman I'd ever seen in my life in that baggy sweater and those washed-out jeans."

"That wasn't how I read it. When you came into Octavia's tent, so polite and respectful, I realized you thought I was an old woman. I couldn't resist teasing you. I would've let it drop then, except for the way you stared at me when I was wearing Shirley's blond wig and her flier costume. I decided to teach you a good lesson."

"I was looking at you because your face was so pale. I thought you were sick. It didn't occur to me you were scared. It puzzled me that a minute later you were flirting with me like mad, inviting me to your trailer for a home-cooked meal. Since I've never been able to resist a mystery, I accepted your invitation."

"Then you weren't...you know, coming on to me?"

"You looked awfully fetching in that brief costume and that blond wig, but no, I wasn't coming on to you."

"We both made a mistake, didn't we?"

"Agreed. Tell me about Bennie. Are you still having trouble integrating him into the act?"

For the next few minutes they talked about her problems with Bennie, then about other circus business, until the streets of New York caught her attention. Wade fell silent, as if he realized her fascination with her surroundings as the view outside the limo windows changed from the warehouses and produce houses in the river bottoms to grimy streets seething with humanity and then to an area of tall apartment houses interspersed with brownstones. She was so fascinated by the ambience that she felt a stab of disappointment when the limo pulled up to a curb and stopped.

As she looked out at an expanse of white marble and wide brass doors, and the metallic canopy that sheltered the sidewalk, she couldn't help feeling glad that she hadn't worn her one and only long dress, which was two years old and hadn't been stylish even when Alice had made it for a Showman's League banquet.

As he waved off the doorman and the chauffeur and helped her out of the limo himself, Wade asked her, "What do think of the Changing Seasons?"

"It's. . . elegant."

"It's that, all right. It also looks like a mausoleum with all that marble and brass. But the food is special. You're in for a treat, Tanya."

Once inside the brass-trimmed doors, Tanya had only a moment to look around at walls covered with burgundy velvet cloth, handsome oil paintings depicting what she guessed were French provincial scenes, small tables that held what seemed to be an extraordinary amount of silver and crystal and snowy white linen, before they were greeted by the maître d', a slim man with a trim black mustache and a French accent. Although the restaurant was crowded and they were almost an hour late for their reservation, their table was still waiting for them. Tanya noticed that Wade was addressed by name by the maître d', who bowed them into their chairs, then raised a white-gloved hand to summon a wine steward.

Wade was looking over the wine list when a noisy group of six came into the dining room. Tanya couldn't help staring at the striking silver-blond woman in the midst of the group. Wade looked up and followed her glance; his face darkened and he swore under his breath. "Dammit. I might have known Larry couldn't resist satisfying that curiosity of his," he said, his tone savage.

"Are those people friends of yours?" she asked.

"You might say that. Right now I'm not so sure—"

"Wade! Is that really you?" The blond woman's voice was light and very clear. She came toward them, both hands outstretched to Wade. If she noticed Tanya sitting across the table from him, she gave no sign of it. "Where on earth have you been keeping yourself? And why haven't you called me, you naughty man? I've been devastated, not knowing what happened to you!"

Wade rose and kissed the cheek she offered him. "I've been very busy with—"

"With your circus. Oh, you are a quixotic one, aren't you? What *do* you find interesting about such a grubby business as a circus?"

Tanya stiffened; despite herself she knew that her eyes flashed fire. The woman smiled and gave her an appraising look. "Is this one of your little friends from the circus? Fascinating—oh, we must join tables! We're all dying to hear about your adventure, and to ask you about circus life."

She beckoned to the others, and there was a flurry of activity as someone summoned help in putting together tables for eight instead of two. By now Tanya knew that the blond woman's name was Monica Clarkson. Her escort, who had a decidedly English accent, was either Denny or Benny Earle, and one of the other couples was introduced as "the Martins—surely you know Elissa and Bob, Wade?" But it was the second married couple that made Tanya's face relax into a genuine smile.

"Oh, so you're Mrs. Glover!" she said warmly. "I want to thank you for—"

"Heavens, call me Irene," the woman cut in quickly. There was a warning in her eyes that puzzled Tanya. Although not pretty, she was elegantly thin and her smile was warm, her voice quick and light. "And happy birthday, my dear. Wade told Larry—that's my husband over there, the one who's staring at you—that he was taking you out for dinner tonight."

"Oh, a birthday? Is *that* what this celebration is all about?" Monica's perfectly arched eyebrows rose slightly. "Is it your eighteenth, Tanya?" she added, her voice honeyed.

"I'm twenty-two," Tanya corrected. "Wade was kind enough to ask me out to dinner when he found I'd never been to New York."

"I see. And where did all this take place? Did you have to come far?"

"Only from New Jersey. The circus starts a three-day engagement there tomorrow."

Monica made a small moue. "New Jersey—the end of nowhere. Well, you have my condolences. Why on earth didn't you hire the Garden, Wade?"

"Another circus has a monopoly on the Garden."

Wade's voice was dry. "You may have heard of it—The Ringling Brothers?"

"We're just a small circus," Tanya said. "We couldn't draw a big enough crowd to fill Madison Square Garden."

"And what do you do at the circus, Miss...uh, Tanya? No, let me guess!" The malice in Monica's eyes warned Tanya. She braced herself for another barbed remark. "Oh, I know! You're a...don't they call them kooch dancers? Or do you wear a funny costume and greasepaint? Are you a lady clown?"

"I'm an animal trainer," Tanya said, unruffled by the woman's rudeness. She wondered why Wade was so quiet. Was he embarrassed because his friends had caught him out with a circus woman so much younger than he was?

The man who had been introduced as Larry Glover spoke up. "Tanya trains lions—and tigers. I understand she's one of the few women trainers in the business."

"A lion tamer—how droll," Monica said.

"Not a lion *tamer*," Tanya corrected. "Circus people never call them that. No one really tames a wild animal, but they can be trained, with patience and understanding."

"And with a whip?"

Tanya held fast to her temper, knowing she was being baited. "A cat who has been trained through fear and bad treatment is a very dangerous and treacherous animal. It's like working with a time bomb, because eventually a mistreated lion or tiger will turn on its trainer. The only safe way is to convince them that you are the boss—the leader of the pride. That way, they may test you over and over, but it's out in the open, something you can control."

"My. All I've ever wanted to know about lion training—and more," Monica said mockingly. Her dark blue eyes flickered to Wade's expressionless face then back to Tanya. "What a lovely gown. Did you make it yourself?"

"Not unless her name is Jacques La Rue," Irene said quickly. "That *is* a La Rue original, isn't it, Tanya?"

Tanya nodded, wishing she were anywhere but there. Before the entrance of Wade's friends she had been so happy and excited. What had happened to the evening alone with Wade that she'd looked forward to so much?

"I think we'd better order," Wade said. "Tanya and I have another engagement later."

"Oh, I hoped you'd go with us to see the midnight show at the Marionette Room," Monica said quickly.

"Sorry—and I'm afraid I can't invite you along with us because it's a private party," he said.

It was all Tanya could do to hide her relief and joy. Wade didn't want Monica along tonight, or was there another reason for his quick excuse? Did he think she needed protection from the other woman's hostility? The suspicion didn't sit well with her pride. Unconsciously she tossed her head, making her hair swing around her shoulders. She'd like to tell him that this Monica person was an amateur next to some of the catty women she'd dealt with. What did he think circus life was—a Sunday-school picnic?

Still angry, she studied the menu, at first to have something to do and then with real interest. She was looking at the entrées when Monica's voice, much too sweet, intruded. "I think I'll have the *jambon de Parme*." She leaned toward Tanya and said in a penetrating whisper, "That's ham, dear."

A trickle of anger ran through Tanya, and she forgot her resolution to hold on to her temper. "Yes, I know. But I think I'll take the *saumon en croûte au beurre blanc*," she said, just as sweetly, but in perfect French. "So often it's difficult to get fresh seafood while we're touring."

Monica's mouth tightened ominously as Larry gave a hoot of laughter. Tanya couldn't help glancing at Wade to see how he'd taken this exchange. He looked so grim that her heart sank. Did he resent her rudeness to his friend? Didn't he realize that Monica's whisper had been intended to put her down, not help her?

The group chatted quietly while they waited for their food. To Tanya's relief, both Larry and Irene Glover made sure that she wasn't stranded in a pool of silence by asking her questions about her work and listening with obvious interest to her answers. As far as Monica was concerned, Tanya could have left the table, and her escort and the other couple followed her lead, as if they were afraid of offending her.

When she heard the Englishman—Denny or Benny—ask Monica how her father's senatorial campaign was coming along, she put two and two together and realized that the "daddy" Monica kept dragging into the conversation must be the senator from New York, Senator Clarkson. Was that why Wade sat there so silently, speaking only when addressed directly? Was he sorry he'd brought her to a place where his friends were?

The food, as Wade had promised, was superb. Despite her troubled thoughts, Tanya enjoyed every bite. The *pâté feuilleté*, the fish-shaped pastry that surrounded the fillet of salmon she'd ordered, was flaky and tender, and the accompanying sauce had an unusual flavor she couldn't quite identify, although *beurre blanc* was familiar to her. She tasted it on the tip of her tongue, trying to place the subtle difference from the one she had prepared often under Marshall's supervision. Monica must have been watching her, because she asked, "Is something wrong with your salmon? Is it too rich for you?"

"The food is wonderful. It's just that I can't identify the herb in this *beurre blanc* sauce."

"Oh, come now! You don't have to play the gourmet with us—we're all friends here," Monica drawled. "I'm sure that sauce has all the standard ingredients."

Tanya felt a warning heat in her face, but she refused to look away from Monica's scornful smile. "Yes, I know that you are all Wade's friends. And I don't pretend to be a gourmet. But the sauce does have an unusual flavor. I thought it might be a touch of tarragon, but that seems such a strange herb for a *beurre blanc* sauce."

The waiter came up to refill their water goblets, and Monica beckoned him to her side. "Would you please ask the chef if he has seasoned the *beurre blanc* sauce with tarragon?"

The waiter gave Tanya's stiff face a worried look. "Is *madame* allergic to tarragon?"

"No, just a little argument we'd like to settle," Monica said impatiently.

"Ah, yes, Monsieur Duval does add just a rubbing of fresh tarragon to that sauce. He's quite an innovative chef, you know."

There was complete silence at the table as he finished filling the water goblets. When he was gone, Monica smiled thinly and said, "I seem to owe you an apology, Tanya. I must admit I didn't expect

a. . . a circus girl to be an expert on French cooking.''

"I'm not an expert," Tanya said, deciding on honesty. "But my friend Marshall Dillingham is a fine amateur chef. He taught me a lot about French cooking.''

Monica's eyes narrowed; she gave Wade an arch look. "Do you have a rival for Tanya's affections, Wade?''

"Tanya has many friends, both male and female," he said shortly. "Marshall Dillingham is one of them.''

"Really? Does he work for the circus, too?''

"He does.''

"And what does he do? Tame—oh, sorry! *Train* lions, too?''

"No, he's a. . . He performs in the ten-in-one show. He was also my tutor.''

"You mean he has a teaching certificate? Why would a teacher join a circus?''

"Probably for the same reason a computer whiz did," Larry interjected smoothly.

The Englishman leaned forward, his eyes bright. "I say! You wouldn't be talking about the Earl of Dillingham's oldest son, would you? I did hear rumors that he'd joined an American circus.'' He paused as if considering what else he knew about Marshall, and Tanya braced herself for his next remark. To her surprise, when he went on, he only said, "The circus must get in the blood. Marshall took top honors at university, and I know he was offered a teaching position at Oxford. Well, well. Will you tell him Denny Earle said best and all that? He'll remember me, I expect. I used to chum around with his nephew, Arthur.''

In her relief, Tanya gave him her most radiant

smile. Although she regarded Marshall's size a matter of small importance, she also knew she didn't want to hear Monica's questions about what it was like to have a midget for a teacher.

There was an ugly look in Monica's eyes as she glanced at her escort, and he wilted back into his chair. "I see I have a lot to learn about circus life. And here I thought it was so sordid. You know, grubby people with grubby backgrounds. I'm so glad we ran into you tonight, Wade. I'll have a lot to tell your old friends tomorrow about your fascinating new...interest."

"I'm sure you will. I'm delighted that you have something new to talk about. And I'm afraid we have to be leaving. It's getting late, and we do have another engagement."

He beckoned for the check, and during the flurry of goodbyes, Larry Glover, his clever face amused, touched Tanya's arm and whispered, "Go get 'em, tiger!" a remark that didn't make much sense to her, though she sensed it was well intended.

But she nodded and murmured a soft, "Do tell your wife that I'm very pleased with the gifts."

Wade and she were standing in the lobby, waiting for the doorman to summon their limo, when she asked, "Are we really going to a party now?"

"That was just an excuse to get you away from them."

"Why would you want to do that? Are you ashamed of me?"

The surprise on his face gave her a warm glow. "No! I was ashamed of them—or at least of Monica. She was a real bitch tonight."

Tanya suspected that Monica was always a bitch, a suspicion she didn't voice aloud.

"And I did say it was a private party—I just didn't add that it was for two people only. As it happens, there's something I want to show you. I intended to do it later, but why don't we postpone the dancing until another night?"

Tanya was so bemused by the implication in his words that there would be other nights for dancing that she didn't ask him what he was so eager to show her. As Wade helped her into the limo, all she was conscious of was the touch of his hand on her elbow—and the heady knowledge that the evening hadn't yet ended.

CHAPTER THIRTEEN

WADE WAS SILENT, obviously lost in his own thoughts, as they drove through the streets of New York, and Tanya was too busy watching the people, the cars and the lighted shop windows to want to talk, or to ask any questions. It seemed only a few minutes before the limo had pulled up in front of a white brick apartment building and the chauffer was helping her out. Wade spoke quietly to the uniformed man, who nodded and tipped his cap before he got back in the limo and drove away.

Tanya was beguiled by the firmness of Wade's hand as he took her arm and guided her into the lobby of the building. A uniformed man sitting behind a small desk was watching a row of video monitors, all of which seemed to show empty corridors. When he saw Wade and Tanya, he nodded and said a polite "Good evening, Mr. Broderick. Glad to see you back," before he returned to the monitors.

At Tanya's questioning look, Wade told her, "Security—and one reason the maintenance fees here are astronomical, even though the building is a co-op. And in case you haven't guessed, this is where I live when I'm in New York. I also own a condo in Cupertino, California—near my old plant—which I'm in the process of selling, and a lodge in Aspen, which I intend to keep."

Intrigued by the idea of anyone owning three

homes, Tanya was silent as he led her toward an elevator. "The apartment may be a bit stuffy—it's been shut up for a couple of months now," he went on. "But I left orders that it be aired out every week when the plants are watered. Let's hope my houseman's been doing his job."

As they waited for the elevator, Tanya stared up at the bronze floor indicator, feeling tense and confused. Why was Wade taking her to his apartment instead of to the nightclub he'd mentioned? Did he want to be alone with her, or had he decided it was too risky taking her to a place where they might run into more of his friends?

She started when Wade broke the silence between them to say abruptly, "You didn't feel at all at a disadvantage with my friends. Even her poison didn't really bother you, did it?"

"Are you talking about your friend Monica?"

"No, she isn't my friend. She once was...let's say that we once had a relationship. I don't think we were ever friends."

Tanya swallowed hard under a sudden rush of pain. Was he saying that he and Monica had been lovers? What had happened? Had they had a lovers' quarrel and broken up?

"I'm not sure what you mean," she said. "Why should I feel at a—what did you call it? A disadvantage?"

"No reason at all. But Monica took such pains to let you know she is Senator Clarkson's daughter. That didn't intimidate you?" There was a probing look in his eyes now.

"Well, I've never met a senator's daughter before, but I have met several politicians, including one senator who is a Friend of the Circus. He's very nice and not at all intimidating. So why would meeting Senator Clarkson's daughter bother me? As for her poison, as you called it, I knew she was being catty because she was mad at you, not me. I felt sorry for her because it must be very painful, being so jealous. I wouldn't have flared up like that if she hadn't run down circus poeple. That really got me mad. I guess you think I was pretty rude to her?''

"I thought you were marvelous," he said, and again there was something in his eyes that made the heat rise to her face.

The elevator doors opened, and an elegantly dressed middle-aged couple got out. They exchanged nods with Wade, and the woman gave Tanya a curious look before they hurried away across the gleaming floor of the lobby. A minute later, Wade and she were rising in the elevator. Tanya studied the muraled wallpaper that covered the upper half of the elevator's interior. She had to smile. An English hunting scene seemed so incongruous for a city elevator.

Wade caught her smile and guessed its reason. "New York overkill," he commented. "You should see the mural they had before—sailing vessels during a storm. It was enough to make you upchuck."

She laughed at his dry tone, then asked, "Which floor do you live on?"

"I have the penthouse."

"Like in the movies?"

"Like in the movies. And if you're worried about conventions, we won't be staying long."

Unaccountably, Tanya felt a pang of disappointment. To cover it she asked, "What is it you want to show me?"

"Something that will please you."

Since it was obvious he didn't intend to say more, Tanya was silent, too, as she stared at the bronze needle inching across the indicator. A minute later they had reached the penthouse floor, and Wade was inserting a key in a wide paneled door and ushering her into a spacious room. Tanya's breath caught with pleasure as she stared at the deep rugs, the paintings, mostly pastoral, on the walls, the comfortable-looking chairs and sofas covered in a rich, nubby material, a subtle contrast to the exquisite Oriental silk screen that covered half of one wall. Wide doors led out onto a terrace, and several plants in huge ivory-coloured containers added warmth and hominess to a room that should have been aggressively masculine but instead looked inviting, as if it welcomed guests.

"It's lovely," she said finally.

He shrugged. "I turned the job of decorating it over to a professional, but I vetoed most of her original ideas and told her I wanted comfort, simplicity and no frills. She won out on a couple of items, but the rest is exactly what I asked for."

"It's very nice. Of course I don't have anything else to judge it by since I've never been in a penthouse apartment before."

"And yet you look right at home here, just as you look as if you've always worn emeralds—and Jacques La Rue gowns."

A laugh escaped Tanya. "I'm sure Monica suspected you'd bought these clothes for me even though your friend Irene wouldn't let me thank her for picking them out. I didn't mind if Monica knew—unless it was embarrassing to you."

Wade stared into her eyes as if trying to read her thoughts. "I made a mistake about you, Tanya. You can hold your own anywhere, just like Marshall said.'' He touched her cheek lightly. She waited, her heart beating very fast, for him to kiss her, but instead he took her hand and pulled her toward another door. ''Come along. I want to show you something.''

The room he ushered her into was obviously a den...no, more like a library, she thought, staring at a wall of books. Then she saw the framed circus posters and the display case filled with clown masks. For a long time she studied her own image on one of the posters before she turned to Wade.

''Did you bring that poster back with you last fall?''

''No. Look at the date. It's three years old.''

''You've had that poster for three years?''

''When I bought it I assumed that you were someone the artist had dreamed up. And yet deep down, maybe I always knew you were real.''

Tanya's laugh sounded too husky to her own ears. ''Barney Comstock did the poster. He's an old friend of Pop's. They started out in the business at the same time. He was an advance man who did posters on the side. He's retired now but he still takes a few commissions from old friends. I always thought this one made me look sort of fierce.''

''As if you're challenging the world to a duel—one you probably would win,'' he said. ''And why are you frowning? Aren't you pleased that I liked that poster so much I put it up there with all those antiques?''

''I was thinking it seems so strange that you knew what I looked like even before we met.'' She hesitated. ''The first time I saw you, I had the feeling I'd known you somewhere before, which is really crazy—''

"Not so crazy. We're old friends, Tanya, dating back to when you were a tousle-haired little hellion who used to torment a bullhand who took his duties very seriously by playing under his elephant—"

"Are you...? But you can't be! His name was Rick!"

"Short for Broderick. That's what my family used to call me when I was a kid."

"So that's why Maisie took to you so quickly! Why didn't you tell me?"

"Maybe I enjoyed turning the tables on you. You made my life hell, you know, putting worms in my bunk and tying my shoelaces together and a few other assorted things."

She gave him a stricken look. "I wanted you to notice me—and when you left so suddenly I was sure I'd driven you away. I cried for weeks—" To her horror, her eyes filled with tears. She turned away, not wanting him to see them, especially since she wasn't sure why she was crying. Then Wade's hands were gripping her shoulders, turning her around, and she buried her face in his chest to hide her wet eyes.

"That isn't why I left," he said softly. "I had to go back to my brothers, who needed me. And I never was really mad at you. In fact, if I could have chosen a kid sister, she would've been just like you—spunky and lively and sparkling with energy."

But that wasn't what Tanya wanted to hear. She didn't want to be Wade's kid sister. What she wanted was to have him to put his arms around her and kiss her, to admit her into his heart....

She pulled away so she could see his face. "Now I know why you stared at me so hard that first day. Did you recognize me as the little girl who used to play under your elephant?"

"Not at first. But of course you *were* the woman in the poster on my library wall. Until then I wasn't sure if you really existed."

"Well, I'm real enough."

"Yes, you are. And if I'm not careful, I'm going to start breaking a lot of promises, implied and otherwise," he said. He left her and went to open the doors of a cabinet, revealing a small, obviously well-stocked bar. "Sherry okay? Or I can get some ice cubes from the kitchen and fix you a mixed drink."

"Sherry is fine. Just a few drops." She sipped the amber-colored liquid as she wandered around the room, examining the posters, then the masks in the exhibit case. Recognizing one, she laughed and pointed it out. "That's Wee Willie's mask. He was with Ringlings before he came to us. The mask maker must have known him then."

When they had finished their drinks, Wade took her glass and asked, "Would you like to see the view? It's pretty spectacular from the terrace."

Although his voice was casual, she thought she read a reserve in it, and she wondered if he was sorry he'd brought her here. For a long time they stood at the waist-high terrace wall, staring down at the lights of the city, while Wade pointed out landmarks and the dark strip that was the East River.

"Up here, the city seems like fairyland," she said finally. "But down there, it's so different. Do you feel untouched by all the things going on in the streets—poverty and crime and hunger—up here in your ivory tower?"

"Not untouched. I've never let myself forget where I came from. I do what I can. You know my interest in wild-life preservation—I feel just as strongly about preserving the quality of human life."

Somehow she wasn't surprised. She had watched his easy conversations with Jojo, the dog-faced man, and knew that Wade was a compassionate person. And no one who loved animals as much as he did could ever turn his back on people.

"Why is it that some people are so lucky, and others never get one break in all their lives?"

"I don't know. I wish I did. I was one of the lucky ones. It wasn't just hard work that made my business a success. Some of it was pure luck."

"Marshall says you're a multi-millionaire. He showed me an article about you in a news magazine. How does it feel, being so rich?"

"Do you really want to know? Or are you needling me again?"

"I guess what I'm really asking is why you stay with the circus. The posters in your library tell some of the story—at least, why you joined in the first place. But why did you come back? You'd already had your little adventure. Why buy into a shaky business and then concern yourself with it personally?"

"I think you must know the answer to that, Tanya." Wade took her by the arms and pulled her close. For a long time he stared into her eyes, and what she saw there, the torment and wanting, sent a wave of heat through her own body. Without thinking of consequences, she slipped her arms around his neck and lifted her face for his kiss. At first, when he stiffened, she thought he would pull away, but instead he lowered his mouth to hers.

It was a hard, fierce kiss; the pressure parted her lips, admitting his tongue into the warmth of her mouth. A core of fire, a hunger, grew deep inside her, so urgent and strong and overpowering that she pressed herself against his hard body, wanting a closer intimacy, not content with just a kiss this time.

There was no hiding Wade's response. When she felt the tautness of his arousal against her thigh, it sparked a corresponding quiver. Instinctively she yielded, her giving way to his maleness a mute invitation for him to possess her. His kiss deepened and became a total ravishment of her mouth. A sweetness, as if the blood in her veins had turned to warm honey, invaded her as she pressed against him, frantic to feel his hands on her body.

"I didn't mean for this to happen, Tanya." Wade's voice had a tortured sound. "I only meant to kiss you, but I can't stop now. I want you, Tanya. More than anything else in the world, I want you—"

"Then take me, Wade," she whispered against the strong column of his throat.

At her words he lifted her in his arms. She felt his breath against her throat, and she buried her face in his shoulder, regretting the clothes that separated them. He kissed her again, a long, lingering kiss that promised more delights to come, and she relaxed against him, feeling incredibly desirable.

His bedroom was shrouded in shadows with only the lights of the city outside the windows to illuminate it, but he didn't bother to snap on a lamp. As he threw back the spread on an immense brass bed, using only one hand as if he couldn't bear to be separated from her for even one moment, she felt her first shyness. But it vanished when he set her on her feet, then touched her gently, running his hand over her hair and along her cheek.

"So soft—you look so competent and cool, but the feel of you gives away your secret. My Tanya, the one in my arms, is warm and passionate and sexy...."

"And *my* Wade seems so fierce sometimes, but his eyes give him away," she said dreamily, fascinated by the way his voice deepened when he said her name.

He kissed her lips, then the softness of her throat. His hands trembled slightly as he unpinned the clasp at her shoulder. The dress fell away into a rippling heap at her feet, and he touched her bare shoulder with his fingertips, tracing a line to the bit of lace that covered her breasts.

He undressed her slowly, taking his time, and as his hands lingered on her body, she felt an upwelling of eroticism that was new to her. Whatever happened tomorrow, whatever this night of love might cost her, she knew that it would be worth the price.

When she stood before him nude, she felt proud—proud that her breasts were full and firm, that her waist was narrow, her hips softly rounded. Staring into her eyes, Wade undressed quickly, and when she saw his taut, strong body, when she saw the proof of her effect on him, she felt confident and unafraid.

He lifted her and held her against his chest, and the wonder of her naked flesh against his, of their two hearts beating as one, was so strong that she felt faint for a moment. Then he was lowering her to the bed. As the down comforter yielded beneath her, its silkiness felt incredibly sensuous to her sensitized skin. Wade knelt beside the bed and pressed his mouth to her breast. She wound her fingers into his thick hair, wondering if it was possible that the storm of passion that shook her was strong enough to stop her heart.

His kiss this time was gentle at first, but she felt the shudders that went through his body and knew he was holding back his passion at great cost to himself. But she didn't want his gentleness, not when her own body was aching, burning for consummation. With a cry she pulled him over so that he lay on top of her, and when she felt his hardness invading the soft valley between her thighs, she writhed frantically, driven by a primitive force, wanting to feel him inside her, unwilling to wait a moment longer.

But Wade rolled away. The strain lines beside his mouth and the blaze in his eyes revealed what it was costing him. "Not yet," he said hoarsely. "I want this to be good for you, too. And it isn't time—not yet."

He lowered his head and kissed her, his mouth and tongue tasting her softness, just as, a few minutes later, they tasted her breasts, lingering on the tiny peaks that were so sensitive to his touch. She moaned with frustration when he prolonged the sensation by gently sucking each one in turn. His hands drifted lower, caressing the taut muscles of her stomach, exploring the small indentation of her navel, then the soft triangle below as she yielded to his touch, opening herself to him. He drew in a deep breath, and she expected him to take her then, but again he pulled away.

With hungry eyes she stared at the strong line of his shoulders and the tangle of brown hair on his chest, which was so surprisingly soft. She gazed longingly at his legs, his strong thighs, the proud maleness of his aroused body.

"I want to touch you, too," she whispered. "I want to do the things that please you—"

"I'm not sure I can handle that." His voice had a strangled sound. "If you touch me, I'm not sure I can hold off."

"I don't care. I want to know you as you know me." She ran her fingertip around the contours of his taut upper lip, so straight and uncompromising, then over his lower lip, which was fuller, more sensuous. She explored his eyebrows, touched her tongue to the deep crevice of his ear, then traced a line along his throat to his chest.

As he had done to her, she caressed his taut nipples with her tongue and discovered they were sensitive, like her own, and hardened at her touch. Like a child exploring a new toy for the first time, she ran her hands over his muscled rib cage, then down to his lean thighs. When she bent and pressed her lips to the shaft of his maleness, he muttered a husky, "Oh, God! You're killing me!" and then he had pulled her down beside him and was kissing her, fondling her, caressing her with frantic haste.

She was aware of his body heat and his scent, a mingling of his cologne and pure maleness, and when the sweet agony of desire became unbearable, she wrapped her arms around his neck, urging him closer. He lifted himself above her, and in the shadows of the room, the pupils of his eyes seemed to have no bottom as he parted her willing thighs with his knee. She surged up to meet him, offering herself to his thrusting urgency, admitting him into the citadel of her heart as well as her body.

A shivering ecstasy filled her as he joined his body with hers. There was a momentary sting, more ache than real pain, then the world around her became tinted with color, as if she were seeing it through a rainbow.

Somewhere in the room someone was moaning, and she wasn't sure if it was Wade or herself, nor did she care. As she moved in perfect unison with Wade, their bodies attuned to the same rhythm, she was sure they must be floating in the air, because she could no longer feel the comforter beneath her. At the same time her body seemed infused with an incredible sensitivity, and she felt Wade's ecstasy as well as her own, as if they shared minds as well as bodies.

Deep within her, in the very core of her being, there was an explosion, a pulsating, spiraling intensity of sensation that penetrated every nerve of her body. Her last thought as she yielded herself up to pure rapture was a deep thankfulness that it was Wade who had initiated her to this wonderment, this most glorious of intimacies.

CHAPTER FOURTEEN

TANYA WAS AWARE of an urgent voice calling her name, of hands touching her face, and warm breath on her cheek. She smiled drowsily, filled with a languor that was both sensuous and debilitating. She whispered "Wade?" even before she opened her eyes to stare up into his worried face.

"Tanya—oh, God, did I hurt you? I tried to be gentle—"

"Hurt me?"

"I knew it was the first time for you and I tried to hold back, but I lost control. When you fainted—"

"Fainted? But I've never fainted in my life!"

He let out a long breath, and a teasing expression replaced the strain on his face. "What you just did was a good imitation," he said dryly.

He gathered her up in his arms and pressed her head against his chest. Although diverted by the tingling sensation that ran along her spine as his fingers caressed the sensitive nape of her neck, Tanya asked, "What happened? The last thing I remember was—"

She stopped, then burrowed into his chest to hide her hot face as she remembered her wildness and abandon in Wade's arms. Had she really cried out for him to take her, to end her torment? Could that have been the same touch-me-not who wouldn't even allow a boy to give her a French kiss, who had clawed at Wade so frantically, trying to consummate the raging passion in her body? And what must he be thinking now? That she was so cheap and easy that she would actually beg him—she winced painfully—to fill her emptiness?

"I think your first experience with making love was so overwhelming that you simply passed out," Wade said, answering her question. He cupped his hand under her chin, lifting her face so she was forced to meet his searching eyes.

Automatically her hands slid around his neck. Her fingers brushed an abrasion on his naked shoulder, then another; when she realized that her own nails had put those scratches into his flesh, she could have died with shame.

"I'm sorry about. . .about the scratches," she faltered, closing her eyes to shut out the sight of his face.

When Wade didn't answer her, she opened her eyes and saw that he was smiling, a strange smile that seemed to hold more pain than amusement.

"Sorry? Oh, Tanya, you have a lot to know about men! At the moment I feel very. . .humble. And unworthy."

A smile got away from her and tilted the corners of her mouth. "But it won't last," she said slyly. "Any minute now you'll be your old arrogant self again."

Wade laughed down at her. "Look who's talking! My friend Larry once told me, when he saw that poster of you, that you looked like a young tigress. I'm forced to agree. Were you ever afraid of anything, Tanya?"

Only of heights—and of losing you, she thought. She pretended to be giving it some thought before she finally shook her head. "Not of any person or animal," she answered truthfully.

"I thought as much. Anyone who can face down a cageful of lions twice a day wouldn't be fazed by anything, not even a barracuda like Monica."

"Something about her must have attracted you or why would you have a...a relationship with her?"

Wade settled down on the side of the bed, his eyes steady as they met hers. "When I first met Monica I thought she was charming, gay, a lot of fun. But when our relationship looked as if it would develop past casual friendship, I pulled away and stopped calling her. Then she instigated a meeting, and that's when she announced she wanted to have an affair with me, but that there were a few ground rules—nothing heavy or serious, no permanent ties. Of course it was just a ploy, but like a fool I fell for it. Then she began a campaign to get me to marry her. Oh, she was subtle, but it didn't take a brick falling on me to realize the true story. When I reminded her of the ground rules she herself had set up and told her I would never marry her, she let her claws show. I'm not blaming it all on her. I was at fault, too, but I never played games with her and pretended it was anything more than sexual attraction."

Tanya felt a deep heaviness of spirit. Was Wade trying to say that he felt the same way about her—sexual attraction and nothing more? She fought against a distressing quiver in her lower lip; to hide it, she put her hand up to cover her mouth. "If she was in love with you, she must have been very hurt that you didn't feel the same way about her," she said finally.

A look of distaste came into Wade's eyes. "Monica doesn't love me, never did. I'm not sure if she's ever been in love. Possession is more her game. She wanted to smother me, and she also wanted a rich husband. When I found out she was telling people we were secretly engaged, that ended it for me.''

Tanya must have shivered, because Wade tucked the edges of the comforter around her shoulders. ''I'd like to keep you here in my bed all night, but your guardians are undoubtedly sitting up waiting for you. I don't think I can take on the whole circus. Pop and Too Tall Tim, and Bruno—maybe I could handle those three. But not Marshall—not with my energy so low right now. Very shortly we'll have to get dressed and start back to New Jersey. I suspect our chauffeur is having fits, wondering what's keeping us.''

''He's waiting for us downstairs?''

''I hope so. I told him to come back in half an hour, which was about an hour ago. This was a total surprise to me, Tanya. It wasn't planned. I had no intention of making love to you tonight.''

The coldness inside Tanya deepened. She shifted the position of her legs under the comforter, not looking at him. ''Not to worry,'' she said stiffly. ''You aren't under any obligation just because we made. . .had sex. Nothing has really changed.''

''Oh, but it has. I've been fighting it for weeks, trying to be sensible and make myself believe that what I feel for you is just chemistry, that I'm too old for you, that it wouldn't work. But now I know it has to work, because I can't live without you. I'm crazy about you. And after tonight I know that you feel the same way about me. I want to marry you, live with you, start a family with you. We'll work out our differences. Just say that you love me, that you'll marry me, Tanya. Tell me you can't live without me.''

A wave of thankfulness took away her breath for a moment. Her hands shook as she mutely touched his face. With her fingertip, she outlined his proud, strong nose, the high, smooth planes of his cheekbones, his sensitive lower lip.

"I love you. I'll marry you because I can't live without you, Wade," she said finally, her voice vibrant with relief.

He kissed her, and the touch of his lips, so familiar now, sent a fresh wave of hunger through her. She gave a tiny moan, and her lips opened under his, telling him without words that she was ready for love again. She felt frustrated when he pulled away, his face strained.

"No. Not until we're married. What happened tonight was spontaneous, something so overpowering that I don't think either of us could have stopped it. But you deserve an old-fashioned courtship, Tanya. I didn't realize it until now but I guess I have a streak of the puritan in me. God knows I want you, but I think we should wait—and the wedding had better be pretty damned soon or I may forget my resolutions!"

Although she pouted at him, she was secretly touched by this evidence that he treasured her and didn't regard her as an easy conquest. Blissfully she sank back into the thick downy pillows, deliberately seductive, and had the satisfaction of seeing his eyes darken and his lips tighten with desire. She smiled up at him, feeling treasured—and very, very sexy.

Being Tanya, she also felt a need to puncture his male assumption that she would go along with everything he decreed.

"You're probably right," she said, sighing. "But I do hope there'll be time for Octavia to give me some lessons on how to please a man. Or maybe I should do a little experimenting on my own with other—"

She broke off with a little scream when he gave the

end of her hair a hard tug. "That's enough of that, you little tease. I should have added that the wedding will be soon, *if* you agree."

She gave a low laugh and nodded. He kissed her again, a lingering kiss that sent the blood surging up to heat her skin, and suddenly she was sorry she had agreed that they shouldn't make love again until after the wedding.

"You're right. The wedding had better be very, very soon," she murmured against his ear.

He threw his head back in a laugh. She studied him with such intensity that he asked, "Why are you staring at me like that?"

"You so seldom laugh out loud. You should do it more often."

"And you laugh all the time. I think I fell in love with your laugh first of all. Or maybe it was your wacky sense of humor. We'll make an odd couple— an old sobersides businessman and a pixie of a girl who trains lions and likes to play practical jokes."

"I also have a terrible temper," she confessed.

"You do, you do. And so do I. Yours is like a summer storm. It clears the air and is soon over and forgotten. But I can't seem to shake mine off that easily. I'm afraid I have a streak of ruthlessness in me that gets in the way of my judgment sometimes. I'll try to change, but I'll take a lot of getting used to, Tanya. I'm not going to be easy to live with."

"Then we'll just have to be careful with each other, won't we?"

"It's a bargain. And speaking of bargains, I think our engagement calls for something spectacular in the way of a wedding present. I'd get you the moon if I could, but since that's not available, how about a honeymoon trip around the world? Or a diamond so

big it will weigh down your hand, or a Rolls, long
and sleek, with brass fittings?''

Tanya started to tell him that the only wedding gift
she wanted was a simple gold ring—and his love. A
sudden understanding stopped her. Despite the
humor in his eyes, she sensed Wade meant what he
said. He was a generous man who enjoyed lavishing
gifts on those he loved, and he would feel cheated if
she didn't ask him for something special. Another
thought came to her; her heartbeat quickened and
she suddenly found it hard to breathe. It was a long
moment before she felt she could safely speak without her voice giving away her inner tension.

"Anything, Wade? Anything at all?"

"Anything within my power to give—and you'd
better take me up on my offer quick. I'm in a particularly generous mood tonight. After all, my woman
just said yes."

She forced a smile at his jocular tone. "There *is*
something that only you could give me. But it's very
valuable, much more expensive than a Rolls-Royce
with brass fittings."

Wade studied her with thoughtful eyes. "Name it
and it's yours," he said finally.

"I want you to turn over your circus shares to
me," she said in such a rush that it sounded like one
word.

She saw Wade's face change, and watched the old
wariness return to his eyes. She was sure she'd made
a mistake, one that would not only ruin any chance
she'd had to save Pop, but would end her own happiness, too.

"You're serious about this?" he said quietly.
"This isn't just some whim?"

"I—I didn't plan to ask for the circus, no, but it

isn't a whim. I owe Pop and Marshall and Bruno and Too Tall Tim and—oh, so many people—a debt that I can never repay, but this would be a start. If I owned those shares, then they'd know they'd have security for the rest of their lives. Pop would continue to have the support and advice of his old friends—he already has their complete loyalty—and they would make sure he didn't get into financial trouble again.''

Wade's expression was unreadable; she wasn't surprised when he withdrew his hands.

"This would make you happy, Tanya?"

"Very happy. And in return, as my gift to you, since I can't afford an expensive present, I'll agree to live anywhere you like, even if it means—" she swallowed hard "—giving up the circus. I'll make you happy, Wade. I promise you'll never regret asking me to marry you."

"You'd do that for me—give up the circus?"

"I'd do just about anything for you, Wade," she said, and because she meant it, her voice rang with sincerity.

"Then I can do no less for you. Okay, on our wedding day I'll put my shares of the circus in your name. You can do anything you like with them."

"And I meant what I said, too. Anywhere you want to live is fine with me."

"Even New York?"

"Of course. It's very... very nice here," she said bravely.

Wade shook his head, his smile teasing. "Oh, we'll come here often to shop and go to the shows and take advantage of the things that only New York can provide, but for the time being I think we should spend the first year of our marriage with the circus, don't you?" He laughed when Tanya nodded so vigorously that her hair tumbled over her forehead. "After all, you did sign that contract when I insisted that all the performers have one, and it still has another eighteen months to run, if I remember correctly. Besides, you wouldn't want to leave Pop in the lurch in midtour, would you?"

In answer she threw her arms around his neck. The comforter fell away, revealing her naked breasts, and Wade's eyes took on a feverish glow as he cupped his hands around them, then bent his head to kiss each dark tip. For the next hour there was no more talk about returning to the circus, but they said many other things—some foolish and lighthearted, others profound.

When they finally did return to the fairgrounds, it was so late that the eastern sky was showing the first light of dawn. But it didn't matter. As soon as Pop and Marshall, who had been napping at opposite ends of Tanya's couch like a pair of worried fathers, confronted them, Tanya blurted out the news about Wade's proposal, and what had looked to be a tempest quickly turned into a celebration.

DURING THE NEXT FEW DAYS Tanya was surrounded with a haze of happiness, shot through by moments of dazzling pleasure. True to his word, Wade made sure that they were seldom alone. As he courted her decorously, under the indulgent eyes of the circus, she lived for the moments when he kissed her goodnight, when his hard arms held her and she felt his body against her own feverish flesh. Dreamily she went through the motions of normal life, while every part of her yearned hungrily for her wedding day, which was approaching much too slowly to suit her.

The only real flaw in her happiness was an occasional bout of conscience. She assuaged it by telling herself that her original plan to make up to Wade in order to influence him on Pop's behalf didn't really matter, nor did the fact that she'd tricked him into promising to turn over his share of the circus to her. After all, she was marrying him because she loved him, and she intended to devote her life to making him happy. What did it matter that she'd taken advantage of his generous streak to help out an old friend?

It may have been her preoccupation or simply a fluke that caused the accident. When she went into the Big Cage two days before the wedding, she put everything else out of her mind as she always did, but perhaps this time she didn't completely succeed. For one thing, all the big cats had been particularly nervous and difficult to handle the past few days, and from Bathsheba's kittenish behavior and long, sultry glances in Leopold's direction, she knew that the fact the tigress was in season again was the cause of their restlessness.

Bennie, always unpredictable, was slow to obey commands that he usually took in stride, and even Leopold, the most reliable of her animals, seemed spooky when she sent him up on his perch. He twitched his tail and gave an uncharacteristic "ooh-aw," which shook the arena and started the other male lions roaring. At her sharp "No, Leopold!" his golden eyes seemed sulky as they shifted away from her stern gaze.

With the instinct that was part of her trade, she gave Acey Brenner, the bandmaster, the hand signal that meant she intended to cut her act a few minutes short, knowing he would soon cue in "The Stars and Stripes Forever," the circus's "chicken" song, which

told the other performers there would be a change in
the routine and signaled the clowns to gear up and
come out earlier than usual on the walkaround that
ended the matinee performance.

Since Bennie was giving her the most trouble, Tanya snapped a command at him in German to go down
the chute first. He twitched his tail and jerked his
head sideways as he gave a silent snarl. Then, to her
dismay, instead of bounding toward the chute, he
leaped across the cage toward Leopold, catching the
old lion unaware. In a moment the cage was filled
with their snarls and a tangle of claws and fangs.

There was no time to separate them, not with the
other cats still in the cage. She had to trust the cagemen, Moon and Charlie, to hose them down with
water to stop the fight. Quickly she sent the other
lions, starting with Moana, the youngest of the
lionesses but something of a leader among the females, down the chute. Since Bathsheba was quiet,
watching the affray between Bennie and Leopold
with aloof eyes from her perch, Tanya let the young
tigress stay while she cleared out the lions.

She was aware that the fight had ended when Bennie, his fur matted with the water Moon and Charlie
had applied with the full force of the pressure hose,
stalked toward her. With a snap of her whip, she kept
him at bay, and although he eyed her malevolently,
he finally responded to her command and the frantic
rattling of the chute gate and followed the others
down the chute.

With the part of her mind that was always attuned
to the audience, Tanya noticed that the quality of the
crowd noises had changed even before she caught a
streak of tawny fur where it shouldn't have been and
realized the tigress had left her perch. She whirled,

the chair in her hand poised, prepared for a charge, but it didn't come. As she stared at the two remaining cats, she finally understood the crowd's hoots and shouts of laughter.

It wasn't fighting that the tigress was interested in—it was love. And Leopold, who always favored love over war, was cooperating fully with Bathsheba. Although she knew her face was pink with embarrassment, Tanya motioned to Moon, who was grinning widely, to break the two lovers apart with a judicious stream of water from the hose. A few minutes later the cage was empty except for Tanya.

Pop and Wade were waiting for her at the back door after she'd taken her bows to an audience that was still laughing and applauding loudly.

"I don't know whether to laugh or give you a good shake," Pop grumbled. "You almost bought it, kitten."

Tanya gave him a reassuring hug. "I know—but it's over now. Bennie challenged Leopold for the leadership of the pride, and won. Which is what he's been itching to do all along. There won't be any more trouble."

Gogo, the head of the clown troupe, came up with a complaint, and after a pat on Tanya's shoulder, Pop went off to settle one of the interminable disputes among the sometimes irascible clowns.

Wade spoke for the first time. "How badly is Leopold hurt, Tanya?" Although his voice was quiet, she sensed the worry the fight must have caused him.

She gave him a reassuring smile. "The fight looked a lot worse than it was. A tiger does a lot of scratching and biting, but the lion is usually the most dangerous fighter because he heads for the jugular vein. A couple of years ago, when Leopold was still in his prime, Bennie probably would have been badly mauled or even killed. Leopold will be okay, but we'll have to watch both of them to make sure their bite marks don't get infected.''

Wade's eyes took on a twinkle. ''I didn't know tigers and lions were so compatible.''

Tanya hid a smile. ''Oh, they do mate, but it isn't usual. They can even have cubs—half lion and half tiger.''

He gave her a deadpan stare. ''Remind you of anyone you know?''

She felt a blush starting at her throat. ''I don't know what you mean.''

''Oh, I think you do. Right now you're blushing so hard you look like you have a sunburn. And the resemblance isn't really valid, because I mean to remain king of *my* pride for a long time. I'm even thinking about going back into the marketplace with one of my old partners. He's starting up an electronics business to market software. It wouldn't be a full-time thing—I could divide my time between California and wherever the circus is. Of course, when we start our family, it might be a different story.''

A family...yes, she'd like to have children, sons and daughters who looked like Wade. Impulsively she gave Wade a kiss before she went off to check on the cats.

She found Leopold licking what were obviously only a few scratches, but she felt guilty all the same. It could have turned out so differently. Well, she had been warned. Wade had told her that Leopold could be hurt in a fight for leadership of the pride, but she hadn't been willing to let an old friend go out to pasture. Now she had no choice. When they returned to Florida, she would arrange for a retirement spot for him, perhaps at the wild-animal retreat that Lars Larsen managed. If there was room for him, he could live out his remaining years in peace.

She sighed and turned away, leaving Leopold in Morris Vaughn's expert hands, thankful that the menagerie boss knew more about the medical treatment of the big cats than most veterinarians. On her way back to her trailer, she decided to stop by the silver wagon to see Pop. There was something she had to discuss with him; she had already postponed it much too long. So far she hadn't told Pop that Wade was giving her his circus shares for a wedding gift. She had put it off because she knew it would be tricky, reassuring Pop that he no longer had any worries about the shortage in the reserve-fund account yet at the same time not letting him suspect that she knew about it. But time was running out. Arrangements had to be made to transfer the stock back to Pop, and the sooner she told him the better, if only because it would relieve his mind.

She was approaching the silver wagon when she heard angry male voices. Not wanting to intrude, she paused outside the door and waited impatiently, only half listening to the raised voices. One was Pop's, but it was a few seconds before she realized the second voice was O'Brien's. What was *he* doing in there, arguing with Pop? She thought of the burly roughie's hot temper and her muscles tightened, even though she didn't move. Pop had handled dozens of such men in his life. He wouldn't appreciate her interference.

"I ought to knock your block off," O'Brien was saying. "If you weren't such an old geezer, that's just what I'd do. Where do you get off calling me a grifter? Okay, so I stiffed that drunk out of a few bucks—so what? Hell, he was so tanked up he would've been ripped off by someone else before he got home. And you ain't firing me because I've already quit. I wouldn't work in this fleabag circus if you paid me double.''

Tanya heard a sound behind her and turned to look into Wade's grim face. When he started past, she grabbed his arm. "Pop can handle it," she said in a low tone. "It's that hothead O'Brien. I've heard rumors that he's been shortchanging the customers since he started working as a candy butch in the Big Top. I guess Pop finally caught him at it. He'll make a lot of noise, but he wouldn't dare touch Pop or he'd be blackballed by every circus and carnival in the country—''

She broke off as the screen door slammed open and O'Brien, his fleshy face red and angry, came barreling out. He must have heard her final words because he stopped, scowling at her.

"Well, well—if it isn't the queen of the circus! Too good for the likes of an ordinary working man, ain't you? You're just another female on the make, and you finally caught yourself a rich one, didn't you? As for you, Mr. Fancy Dan Broderick—" he transferred his glower to Wade's angry face "—you think you're getting something special when you tie the knot with this one, don't you? Well, she's planning to take you to the cleaners. The whole circus is in on it—they all know what she's doing. She's been planning this for a long time. I heard her talking to her dwarf friend, Marshall. She said she hated your guts but that she'd do anything she had to to get control of the circus.''

He paused to give Tanya, who was stunned, a triumphant look. "See for yourself if you don't believe me. The truth's written all over her.''

"That's enough," Wade said coldly. "You'd better clear out before I make you eat your words."

The man gave a derisive laugh, but he sidled past, and by the time he rounded the corner of the trailer he was half running. For a long time Wade was silent, staring at Tanya with bleak eyes. Her face felt frozen, as if it were encased in ice, and she knew guilt was etched on her face. Even so, she tried to explain.

"It wasn't like that at all. I did say something along those lines, but that was just after we'd had a fight. I was furious at you that day—and anyway, that was before I realized I was in love with you. You have to believe me, Wade. I never planned to trick you. When you said I could have anything I wanted for a wedding present, I took you at your word. But I do love you and want to marry you—"

"There's an easy way to resolve this." Wade's lips hardly moved as he spoke. "Just ask me for another wedding gift. That will put the lie to what O'Brien said."

Tanya bit her lip. Turn down the shares to the circus? But how could she do that when it was Pop's one chance to escape retribution for embezzlement? No, she didn't dare back down, but maybe she could convince Wade that she really did love him, that she would be the wife he wanted....

"You promised me those shares for a wedding present," she said painfully. "If you really love me, you won't renege on your promise, and you'll trust me without my having to prove anything to you. You must know that I love you. Don't you have all the proof you need? How can you doubt me after... after what happened that night in New York?"

"All that little interlude proves is that you're a very passionate woman—and I already knew that."

The contempt in his eyes told her she had failed to convince him. "And I should have known. God, what a stupid fool I've been, but maybe I can be excused for falling for the act you put on. You're quite an actress. All that trembling innocence. Where did you learn your technique? Or was it just another practical joke, like sending the new boy to look for a left-handed wrench, something else the circus can snicker about?"

"That isn't true. I never—"

"What did you plan to do next?" Wade interrupted, as though she hadn't spoken. "To go through with the wedding and then, after I'd turned the stock over to you, run out on me and get a divorce? Or maybe you intended to carry out the charade a little further and try for more. What did you expect me to do when I realized, as I would have eventually, that you're a cheat and a liar? Did you hope I'd pay you off to get out of a bad marriage?"

She tried to answer, but he stopped her with a sudden gesture of his hand. "Were the rest of them in on it, like O'Brien said? Or was it a private scheme you cooked up to get yourself a circus—and a rich husband? You're worse than a prostitute. At least it's all up front with them—so much sex for so much money. They don't pretend to be something they aren't. Well, you don't have to worry now about putting up a front. There's no way I'd ever marry you."

"And the circus shares?" The words were wrenched out of her.

"You'll never get your hands on those shares. I don't intend to let the circus fall back into its old sloppy ways. I'm going to make my deal with Pop pay off. You can stay until your contract runs out, but then I want you to clear out. Since the cats belong to the circus, you have no claim on them, so you'll leave without them. Not that you'll have a hard time getting work somewhere else. Your kind always lands on their feet—like a damned alley cat.''

She opened her mouth to tell him that, though technically the cats were in Pop's name, she had taken a smaller salary the past four years to pay for them. But again it was pride, her old bugaboo, that stopped her. Wade waited a minute, but when she only stared at him, he stuffed his hands in his pockets as if he was afraid he might hit her if he didn't, turned on his heel and stalked away.

Tanya wanted to run after him and beg him to listen to her, but she became aware that Pop had come up to the door of the silver wagon and was standing there, watching her. Had he heard Wade's final words? No, Wade hadn't raised his voice, not even during the most virulent part of his verbal attack, and there was nothing in Pop's eyes except concern—and maybe a little disappointment.

"He'll be back," he said. "Whatever made him mad, it won't last."

"No, it's all over." She felt so exhausted suddenly that it was hard to move her lips. Her head buzzed, as if a dozen bees had taken refuge inside her skull, and she wanted to be alone, to huddle on the sofa in her trailer and pull a pillow over her head. "He warned me once that he only gives people one chance. I'm sorry, Pop—so sorry. I tried—I really did try to set things right. Maybe he'll remember that you treated him like a man while he was working here as a roughie, that you've become good friends these past few months. That may help. I wish—"

She didn't finish the sentence. She turned abruptly and stumbled off, ignoring Pop's anxious questions.

She returned to the haven of her trailer, and as she fell, facedown, on the sofa, a stray thought pierced her.

I'll have to learn to live without Wade, but what if the pain I feel right now never goes away?

CHAPTER FIFTEEN

THAT WINTER, for the first time in her life, Tanya felt at loose ends. Previously her life had been so busy and packed with things to do that she seldom had time for introspection. But since they'd returned to Florida, she found she had too much time for brooding—and regrets. Usually during the winter season she would be training a new cat or two, devising new routines and refining old ones. She would spend a lot of time visiting old friends like Lars Larsen and other circus people who had retired and settled in the Tampa Bay area. She would also be helping Alice plan and work on the next season's costumes, giving Gogo and the other clowns her well-considered opinion of their new routines, passing judgment on any new performer Pop was auditioning—and a dozen other things.

But with her own future with the circus so uncertain, there seemed little point in trying to improve her act or getting involved with preparations for the coming tour. So she worked her cats a couple of hours every morning, saw to their well-being with the help of Moon and Charlie, who were on winter-pay status during the four-month hiatus, and did little visiting or giving of advice.

It came to her as a shock to realize that for the first time in her life she was lonely. It was only now that she truly understood what Wade must have felt as a boy when he'd been constantly forced to be the strong one of his family, the one who was leaned upon, who never got a chance to be weak or scared. She felt a deep regret that she, who loved him, had added to his distrust of women, and she wished desperately that things had been different. If only they could have met as two people unburdened by the past, she with her overload of gratitude and he with his wariness of women—and his too-harsh judgment.

It didn't help that she felt estranged from her old friends. Although everybody had been kind and had asked no questions when she'd announced that the wedding was off, she'd sensed their puzzlement. Even Alice, who had always taken Tanya's side even when she was in the wrong, had finally suggested tactfully that maybe she should pocket her pride and "make it up with Wade." It was then Tanya realized that her friends believed she'd been the one to break the engagement—and that it was her pride keeping Wade and her apart.

Although this realization hurt, she gave Alice a noncommittal answer. If she had blurted out the truth and told her friend that Wade not only wasn't going to renew her contract but also intended to keep her cats, she was certain the circus people would have rallied around her regardless of their respect for Wade and his status as their employer.

But of course she couldn't allow that to happen. No matter how it hurt to know they thought she was in the wrong, how could she be the cause of trouble between her friends and the man who controlled the circus— and their futures? Even without her cats she could probably find work with another circus without too much trouble, but who would hire a group of aging artistes, most of whom were long past their prime?

So she kept up her charade, and when the time came to leave the circus for good, she would invent some excuse, such as telling Pop that she was restless and felt it was time to move on.

But the need to watch every word she said put a restraint on the most casual conversations, and she soon found herself avoiding her friends, staying by herself. Her only solace these days was Leopold. With him she didn't have to make excuses about why she hadn't been around to see him, or put on a big smile and pretend that everything was great, or dredge up safe subjects to talk about that wouldn't reveal her heartache.

The knowledge that the old lion would be left behind when they started out on the spring circuit added a special poignancy to the time she spent with him. She had already made arrangements with Lars to give Leopold shelter at the animal reserve near Sarasota. But she postponed their parting until the last moment and was using the extra time to be with Leopold as much as possible, brushing his already gleaming fur, feeding him so many tidbits that he was as plump as a cub.

She also mourned her inevitable separation from the other cats, all of whom were as individual to her as her human friends. There was Belle, so placid and complacent, who groomed herself several times a day, just as if she really were a reigning Southern belle, and who had already produced several litters of cubs. Two of her cubs, Remus and Romulus, were also part of the act, a lively pair who were natural clowns.

And then there was Chub, the most indolent of the male lions, who was afraid of fire but who was a whiz at strolling across a tightrope suspended above the stage, and Cleo, his half sister, who had a weak stomach and whose food had to be specially prepared.

Would a new trainer understand these things about her cats and take good care of them? Or would he bring his own animals, sell off her cats and break up the act that she had put together so carefully? If only she had enough money to buy them from the circus! Unfortunately, the cats cost many thousands of dollars each, not to mention the horrendous food bills and other expenses of taking care of them. Tanya was almost broke, living totally on her winter pay, because she had quietly used the power of attorney Pop had once given her to transfer her own small savings into the reserve-fund account, hoping to stave off disaster for Pop a little longer.

And it wouldn't do any good to try to make a deal with Wade to pay for the animals in installments. He'd made that very plain the one and only time he'd spoken to her after their quarrel.

"Make arrangements for Leopold to stay at your friend's reserve in Florida," he'd told her, his eyes reflecting the deep chill in his voice. "And don't bother to break in any new cats this winter unless you're willing to pay for them out of your own pocket—in cash. You won't be handling them after next year. If you want me to tear up your contract at the end of this season, that's agreeable to me. But you'll have to decide now so we can get a replacement before spring."

Only the knowledge that she couldn't afford to let him get under her skin kept Tanya from quitting on the spot. She swallowed the sharp words she wanted to throw in his face and looked him squarely in the eye.

"I have no intention of tearing up the contract,

and I wouldn't advise you to try, either. And in the future, if you have any orders, please relay them through Pop.''

Wade had met her stare with one of his own; if her words had pricked him, it hadn't shown. With a stiff nod he'd walked away, and soon after that he had left for a trip to New York and hadn't made another appearance before the circus returned to winter quarters.

It was in January when she saw his name in a *Billboard* column devoted to circus gossip and news.

''Wade Broderick, Pop Peeples' new partner, has been squiring Monica Clarkson, daughter of New York's senior senator, around New York hot spots these days. Rumor has it that wedding bells are in the offing. Way to go, Wade!''

The words ''wedding bells'' seemed to jump off the page at Tanya, cutting through her defenses like tiny daggers. She crumpled the paper into a ball, and then, because the pain was too much to handle, she clutched her chest with her arms and rocked back and forth as if she'd just taken a hard blow.

When she realized what she was doing, she dropped her arms and went into her tiny bathroom. She splashed cold water on her face to restore the color that had drained away when she'd read about Wade and Monica. Facing her image in the mirror above the sink, she put her fingertips at the corner of her mouth and forced her lips into the travesty of a smile.

''Smile, damn you, smile,'' she muttered, and even though it was a poor attempt and her lips wobbled around the edges, she did feel better.

Stoutly she told herself that Wade and Monica deserved each other. She didn't intend to waste another thought on the man.... But why was it that he could be so unforgiving of what she'd done and then turn right around and overlook another woman's short-comings so readily? He had called Monica a barra-cuda, and yet he had taken up with her again. Had he really been in love with her all along? Maybe his fling with a circus woman had been an impulse, a physical passion that had flared up briefly and then quickly burned out once she'd given herself to him.

As for their engagement—had he been sorry as soon as she'd accepted his proposal? Maybe he'd been looking for an excuse to dump her. No wonder he'd been so quick to believe the worst of her. He'd barely given her a chance to explain, as if his mind had already been made up. If he hadn't wanted to marry her, why hadn't he simply told her he'd made a mistake and asked to be let out of their engagement?

Finding her thoughts too unpalatable, Tanya felt a need for company. After she'd pulled a comb through her hair, she put on a sweater against the cold wind that so often blew in from the gulf in early March. Because there was no one else she dared to confide in, she went to see Leopold, needing the total acceptance she couldn't find anywhere else, not even from Alice or Marshall.

As she let herself into the old lion's cage a few minutes later, she made herself a promise. She would live each day as it came, and as soon as possible, she would make inquiries about finding a job with an-other circus for the following year.

WADE WASN'T SURE why he had given in to a sudden impulse to fly down to Florida from New York. He couldn't even blame the weather, which was uncommonly fine for March in New York. He wasn't need-

ed in Florida, that was clear. In fact, the circus had
run so smoothly at the end of the previous season
after he'd gone back to New York that it was obvious
it could get along quite well without his personal attention from now on. The new computerized system
with its customized software that he'd had installed
to keep track of ticket sales, tour scheduling and
purchasing, payrolls and tax records, was up and
running, and such money- and time-wasters as dupli-
cated orders and fouled-up scheduling were things of
the past.

As for personnel—Pop was a genius at bringing
out the best in people, in keeping them loyal and content. It was obvious to Wade that his help wasn't
needed along those lines, either.

So why the hell was he there, Wade asked himself
as the plane he'd leased touched down on the runway
of a small private airport near the circus's winter
quarters.

There *was* the matter of the reserve fund. So far
Pop had given the auditors a dozen excuses why he
hadn't turned over that ledger to them. Maybe there
was a plausible reason for dropping in to see Pop. It
was high time that he leaned on him and found out
what the devil was cooking with that account. Ten to
one the old guy had lost the ledger and was covering
it up. Not that Wade couldn't have taken care of it by
phone simply by having his auditor send for dupli-
cate information from the bank that handled the account, but it did give him an excuse to get away from
New York. After all, he should check up on his investment properties in person every so often,
shouldn't he?

In another week the circus would open the season
with a week's engagement in Atlanta, a full six weeks

before their usual starting date. With more indoor engagements scheduled this year, the need to be concerned about early-spring or late-fall weather had decreased. It had taken a lot of persuasion to talk Pop into agreeing to do fewer dates under canvas. It might be hard to smell popcorn from the stage of an auditorium, as Pop was fond of saying, but it did alleviate some of the worries and extend the season.

Prosperity in the form of higher pay was sure to ease some of the nostalgia pangs for everybody, even the old-timers. With the full force of a New York public-relations company behind the circus and better bookings all round, it looked to be a banner year—so why the hell did he feel so damned depressed?

And why was he still tormented by the memory of that night of love with Tanya. Why couldn't he forget her? How did it happen that Tanya, with her fiery temper, her devious—and oh, so convincing—nature, had managed to get under his skin and ruin other women for him?

He had gone back to New York with the idea of putting the whole fiasco out of his mind. In an attempt to forget Tanya, he had even tried to start up his old relationship with Monica, but it hadn't taken him long to realize that it wouldn't work. After escorting Monica around New York for a while, he had discovered that the old flame couldn't be rekindled, at least not for him.

When he'd finally told Monica, as diplomatically as possible, that he didn't intend to resume their affair, she had screamed at him like a virago, an experience he wouldn't want repeated. He might have felt sorry for her if she hadn't been furious enough to tell him that she'd only wanted to marry him for his

money. Since then he'd had no inclination to see
other women, and he saw little chance that he'd
change his attitude in the foreseeable future.

Wade had arranged for a rental car to be waiting at
the airport, and as he set out, his mood began to
change from depression to anticipation. As he'd
already discovered on previous visits, Florida could
be quite blustery in March, and the day looked to be
very windy. Even so, the sun had a golden quality
and he found himself whistling, something he hadn't
done for a long time. Since there was only light traffic, he made good time, and it was a little past noon
when he saw the small sign that announced he was
approaching the winter quarters of the Peeples Circus.

After he'd parked the rental car in a gravel-covered
lot next to one of the stock barns, he sat for a while,
staring at the collection of barns and storage build-
ings, the animal corrals and the fenced-in lot where
some of the circus people kept their trailers during
the winter months. Although the acreage, purchased
by Pop some twenty-five years earlier, had once been
a citrus farm, the explosion of growth in Sarasota
was fast encroaching upon its isolation. Only a few
orange and grapefruit trees were still scattered
around, and a housing project had sprung up a few
hundred yards to the south. There had already been
complaints about noise, odors and flies—all untrue,
Pop had assured him.

Eventually, though, the circus would have to move
farther out from town. It would be expensive, finding a place in land-hungry Florida that was large
enough to house so many animals. He would have to
set his lawyers to work solving that problem, but at
least there was still plenty of time. For now the circus

was comfortably settled in for the rest of the winter, and Wade felt a pang, knowing that he no longer was a real part of it. Oh, he meant to retain his fifty-one percent, of course, and he would be involved in the business end of it, but as for traveling with the circus again—no, that part of his life was over.

He got out of the car, but he didn't head for Pop's trailer immediately, as he'd planned. Instead he turned toward the barn where the elephants were housed during the winter.

For a while, he stopped to chat with Freddy, the head bullman, who was trimming the feet of one of the elephants, a job that needed to be done every three months. Maisie, who was tethered to a stake nearby, recognized Wade and trumpeted a welcome.

When he approached her, she curled her trunk around his arm in greeting before she slyly slipped a supple tip into his jacket pocket for sugar cubes he had put there earlier in anticipation of this visit. When she had finished exploring the rest of his pockets, he produced a loaf of raisin bread he'd carried all the way from New York in a zippered bag. He watched, smiling, as she stuffed the whole loaf into her capacious mouth, demolishing it in a few swallows.

"You're sure soft on that old female," Freddy commented. The head bullman rubbed his hand over Maisie's side, assessing the roughness of her skin. "She needs a good oiling—the skin dries out faster when they get this old."

"She's some kind of lady," Wade said.

"Yeah. I hate to see her slowing down. You can get real attached to these critters, like Tanya and her old lion. She's sure gonna miss him next season, but I guess he'll be happy with his new lady friends. I wouldn't be surprised if he didn't break some kind of record for fathering cubs. Can you believe it? That tigress, the one Tanya calls Bathsheba, has come up pregnant. Looks like we're gonna have ourselves a half-tiger half-lion cub or two around here.''

It was hard for Wade to hide his pain behind a smile at the rush of memories the man's words evoked. Had he really teased Tanya about the misalliance of Leopold and Bathsheba, and asked her if it reminded her of someone else?

He nodded at the elephant handler, gave Maisie's wall-like side a final pat and left the barn. An uncomfortable thought came to him as he walked across the weedy field toward the silver wagon. As a boy, after he'd returned home from his stint with the circus, he had missed the elephant he'd called Gray Lady. How much more would Tanya mourn for her cats if she were forced to leave them behind? After all, no matter what else she might be, she took better care of her cats than anyone else would. Surely he could afford to be a little magnanimous now that he was no longer personally involved with her.

He didn't realize where his feet were taking him until the musky odor of the cat barn invaded his nostrils. He stopped just inside the door to look around, noting with approval the cleanliness and roominess of the big cages, each with its own wire-covered run that extended into the pasture behind the barn.

He didn't see Leopold, although the female tigress, looking sleek and plump, eyed him with sleepy eyes from a nearby cage. Had Tanya already found a home for the old lion, or was he still here and in one of the other cages?

Quietly he moved along the row, looking into each cage. In one, the male tiger, pacing restlessly up and down, made a plaintive sound, as if asking a question. Wade gave him a mock salute and then smiled at the malevolence that immediately flared in the tiger's eyes.

He had almost reached the end of the line when he heard the sound of crying, soft and muffled. Even before he came to the last cage, he knew that it was Tanya—Tanya who never cried.

She was curled up in a knot beside Leopold, her face buried in his soft side, and Wade felt a strange reluctance to back away, even though he knew he mustn't humiliate her by letting her know he'd been a witness to her misery. When she gave a snuffling sigh, he knew the tears were over, and he edged backward, fighting a compulsion to open the cage door, go inside and put his arms around her and tell her he'd do anything in the world to make her happy.

But his distrust—and maybe his male pride, coupled with the fear of making a fool of himself again—was stronger than his desire to comfort Tanya. He turned away, left the barn and went in search of Pop Peeples, determined to get his business finished so he could return to New York.

He found the older man in the silver wagon, sitting with his feet up on his desk, drinking a beer. When Pop saw him, his face paled and his expression changed so drastically that a belated suspicion came to Wade. He had dealt with too many men in his time not to recognize guilt, and the likeliest thing Pop could feel guilty about at present was the reserve-fund account.

"Okay, Pop, what the hell's going on with that reserve fund?" he said briskly. "I want to hear your side of the story. How did you get things so screwed up?"

Pop's face seemed to age ten years under Wade's

hard stare. He set the beer can down and gave his head a hard shake, as if trying to clear his thoughts.

"I knew you had to find out eventually, but I was hoping...well, that I could hold you off until after the season starts. If things go as good as they did the end of last year, I figured I could put back the money without you ever knowing about the shortage. How'd you find out about it, anyway?"

"Never mind that. Tell me what happened."

"It was all them debts. I had borrowed up to the hilt to keep things going early last year, and when you bought in, I figured I could cover them okay without anyone knowing. But this guy I took out the loan with, he really got on my back, upped the interest rate when I had to ask him for an extension on the loan. And with the interest piling up and piling up until I couldn't see anything ahead but ruin, I... well, I borrowed from the reserve fund. I knew it was wrong. I didn't have no right to take that money without your permission since you were half owner of the circus, but I thought I'd be able to cover the shortage for sure by the middle of this season. I put all my profit-share money from last season back into the fund, but it wasn't near enough, of course. Look, I done wrong, dipping into that fund, but—"

"I want to see that ledger and any records connected with the fund," Wade said tightly.

Pop started to say something, but he took a closer look at Wade and stopped. His thin shoulders slumping, he fumbled in a hip pocket for a tiny key and unlocked the top drawer of his desk. Without a word he put a large ledger, a bankbook and a stack of withdrawal slips in front of Wade, then went into the kitchen to get himself another beer.

It took Wade a while to sort through everything.

When he was finished, he stared into space for a long time, trying to absorb the significance of what he'd found. "These deposit slips—you've already replaced forty thousand dollars?" he asked finally.

"Forty thousand? No, not that much. I had other bills I had to clear up, too. It was more like thirty thousand," Pop said from the doorway.

"But the deposit slips say differently. According to my figures, it's forty thousand."

"Well, maybe the bank made a mistake. I didn't pay any attention to those deposit receipts. I bank by mail most of the time, so I just stuck them in with the ledger when they came back in the mail. I didn't even open the envelopes, you'll notice."

In answer Wade reached for the phone to call the Tampa bank that handled the account. A few minutes later he turned away from the desk to face Pop. "So you borrowed money from Tanya," he said, not bothering to hide his disgust.

"Tanya? Hell, no! I wouldn't do that. She doesn't know anything about this—" He stopped and a look of consternation crossed his deeply lined face. "So that's what she was talking about the day you two split up. I never asked her any questions about it later because I figured she was so upset she didn't know what she was saying—"

"What are you talking about, man?"

"The day you two split up. After you walked away, Tanya was white as skim milk and shaking all over. She said she was sorry, that she'd done her best and she hoped... If I remember right, the way she put it was she hoped you'd remember that the two of us were friends. It didn't make sense, but I figured she was hysterical. I never brought it up later. She made it pretty plain she didn't want to talk about that day, see?"

"I still don't understand—"

"She must've found out about the shortage and put her own savings into the account. She has my power of attorney—it wouldn't be hard for her to do. God, I didn't want this to happen—that's her savings, all she's got in the world except her trailer. She's been saving to buy a new rig to pull her trailer 'cause her old truck's about shot. She only draws about half of what she could earn at any other circus, you know."

"So you've been taking advantage of Tanya all these years?"

"Hell, I wouldn't do that! It's this deal we have. She was only seventeen when she first started her act, too young to get the kind of credit she needed to buy her own cats, see? So the deal was that I'd buy the cats but she'd pay me back by taking half pay. I've been meaning to turn over to her the titles to those cats ever since her twenty-first birthday, but... well, they did add to the value of the stock inventory when I put the circus up for sale, so I put it off."

Wade stared at Pop's sheepish face, but he was seeing something else—the expression on Tanya's face when he'd told her, so arrogantly, that he meant to keep the cats. Why hadn't she argued with him and told him about her deal with Pop? Was it because she knew that even if she had clear title to the cats, she still didn't have enough money in savings to feed them and rent space for them until she got another job, much less transport them to another circus later?

He had misjudged her—God, how he had misjudged her! She hadn't wanted the circus for herself but to save Pop from prison. She couldn't have known that the last thing he would ever do was file charges against Pop for embezzlement. And that was his fault. She had every reason to believe he was a hardheaded businessman who put profit above everything else. She had even felt him out, asked him if he wouldn't forgive a good friend almost anything. And he'd answered no, he only gave people one chance. . . .

As for their engagement, she must have gone along with it because she couldn't see any other way to keep Pop from going to prison—or at least from losing the circus that was his whole life. Was that why she had let him make love to her? No, by God, she had wanted him as badly as he'd wanted her that night! She had responded to him with a fire and passion that couldn't have been faked. But as for love—it seemed so clear now that she hadn't really loved him, had only wanted him.

He couldn't even blame her for asking for his shares of the circus for a wedding present. How arrogant and materialistic he must have sounded, offering her a Rolls or a trip around the world or the biggest diamond he could find! No wonder she'd had no qualms about jumping at a chance to solve Pop's problem so easily. He, with his own strong feeling of responsibility, understood that. He would do the same to save one of his brothers from prison.

So it all boiled down to this. He had blundered into Tanya's life, thoroughly messing things up for her, and it was high time he set things straight again.

It didn't take him long to convince Pop that he didn't intend to prosecute him for embezzlement. He even stretched the truth a little and said that since the circus looked to be such a money-maker, he'd make up the shortage from his own pocket and include it as part of the original purchase price. It took a little longer for the two of them to work out an agreement for Pop to buy back the circus via a long-term, low-interest loan with a six-month delay before the first payment was due.

Two hours later he was heading back to the airport, after assuring Pop for yet another time that no, he wouldn't change his mind, that yes, he'd set his lawyers to work as soon as he returned to New York so they could handle the legal details.

"One of the first things I want you to arrange," he'd added, "is to transfer the ownership of the cats to Tanya. She's to be given clear title to them, but I want your word that you won't tell her I had a hand in it. I also don't want her to know I'm replacing the money she put in the reserve account. With the hard feelings between us and that outsize pride of hers, she's liable to refuse both deals. Just tell her you're taking care of it out of last year's profits."

As he headed back to the airport, Wade was aware that he could never come back to the circus, not even for a visit. It would be too painful. Life might seem pretty grim to him in the future, but at least he'd done what he could to repair the damage that his impulse to relive a boyhood fantasy had done to Tanya's life. He had no doubt that once the cats were in her name and she knew she could stay on with Pop, she would recover fast.

And who knows, he thought soberly. *In time I might even do the same.*

CHAPTER SIXTEEN

TANYA STOOD BESIDE POP at his customary place near the back door. They were watching one of the new acts, Tillie Bauer and her dogs, who were billed as Fifi and Her Friends, go through their paces in the center ring. Even as she smiled at the antics of the clever little French poodles, each fitted out in a tiny ballet tutu and a saucy hair bow, Tanya was impatient for the show to end so she could return to her trailer. The smashing success of the past two months had rejuvenated the circus, brightening even the dourest dispositions, but Tanya found that although she was happy for her friends, she felt like a stranger, as if she no longer had a right to be there among them.

I've finally grown up, she thought sadly. *It will never be quite the same again.*

She shifted restlessly, irritated by her own thoughts. It must be this engagement, at the same fairgrounds in New Jersey where they'd appeared the year before, that had stirred up so many painful memories. She bitterly resented their resurgences. She'd been so sure that she'd finally put the past behind her and had achieved inner peace at last.

Well, at least there was no longer any question of her leaving the circus next year. Pop had made that very clear before they'd left Florida. In fact, she had been the first to know that he was again sole owner of Peeples Circus.

"Wade and I came to an agreement," he'd told her after he'd called her into the silver wagon. "I'm buying back his shares in the circus. He gave me a really prime deal. Low interest and easy payments. I should be clear of debt in five years—and by the way, Tanya, I had the lawyers make over the titles to the cats to you. Not that it really matters, but I thought it should be spelled out nice and legal."

He paused to pull the end of his long nose, a sure sign he was embarrassed. "About the money I, uh, borrowed from the reserve fund—I've already replaced that money from my share of last year's profits. I've also got a check for you that covers the money you put in as well as the interest you lost by withdrawing your savings. I appreciate what you done, girl. I'm real ashamed that. . .that I got myself into such a jam."

She kissed his hard cheek and told him it was her pleasure, and if he suspected what it had cost her not to ask any questions, he didn't let on. Since then, they'd both pretended the whole thing had never happened, but there was a new closeness between them, an unspoken understanding—the only good thing that had come out of the whole business.

As for Wade, no one had seen him since his quick trip to winter quarters in March. When she'd found out later that he'd been there and hadn't even bothered to seek her out to say hello, it had hurt, but maybe not as much as it once would have. She still felt resentment that he'd had so little faith in her, but by now common sense and reason told her that in Wade's eyes, she really was the cheat he'd accused her of being.

As for Wade's allowing Pop to buy back the circus with such favorable terms, she wasn't really surprised. In fact, she should have expected it. How long could something as insignificant as a circus interest a man who had created a multimillion-dollar electronics empire from a "gadget" he had invented?

So Wade had gone out of their lives the same way he'd come in—without fanfare. She would never see him again, something she was learning to deal with day by day. Her life would go on much the same as it had before Wade had come into it. He wouldn't be part of it, but she still had her work, her friends, her cats.

Why, in time she probably wouldn't even remember what the man looked like! She would forget the slight unevenness of his teeth, those white, white teeth that gave his smile such brilliance, and the way his hair curled slightly at the ends when he needed a trim. She would forget how the tiny lines beside his eyes deepened, giving him away when he was trying not to laugh, and how she'd felt, the soaring feeling inside, when he'd touched her. . . .

And if she still cried occasionally when she was alone in her trailer, who was to know? She put on a good face in front of her friends. She was gradually coming to terms with the knowledge that no matter what new love might someday come into her life, she would never feel the total abandon that she'd felt in Wade's arms.

But she was young, with most of her life still ahead of her. She would survive. What was it they said? That time healed all wounds? Someday she would be her old self again, be happy and carefree, just as she'd been before Wade had disrupted her life.

But oh, for now, how she yearned to see Wade again, to talk to him, to know the sure touch of his hands as he stirred the fire inside her until it raged.

Most of all, she longed for the sweet comfort of his arms....

Pop spoke her name, and she realized he must have asked her a question. "I'm sorry—I guess I was daydreaming," she confessed.

"Yeah, daydreaming. You still miss him, don't you, kid?"

"Miss who?"

"Come off it. This is Pop. Never try to con a con man, remember? You miss that guy, and you ain't getting over it. Which makes me wish—" He broke off, frowning.

"Makes you wish what?"

"That I hadn't made that promise."

"You made someone a promise about me?"

"Never you mind. It ain't important."

"But I do mind. And you may as well tell me what it's all about. I'll just keep after you until you do."

"I know, I know. You always was a pesky kid. Okay—not that I know what good it'll do." Having said that much, he fidgeted with his clipboard, looking unhappy.

"Tell me, Pop. What was this promise you made— and who did you make it to?"

He sighed and gave his beaklike nose a pull, but he finally said, "To Wade. He found out you'd put your own money into the reserve fund because of... that fool thing I did. So he insisted on replacing it out of his own pocket. Hell, I didn't have that kind of bread, kid, or I would've done it myself! And then he made me promise not to tell you."

He looked so sheepish that she told him it didn't matter, she wasn't angry. But inwardly she felt confused and bewildered. Wade had replaced her savings—but why? As payment for the misery he'd put her through? No, he didn't care about that. He'd made it clear he didn't give a damn about her. In fact, he probably thought she deserved everything she'd got.

It was a mystery, but Pop was right. It didn't make any difference except that now she owed Wade a large amount of money. No way would she accept such a gift from him, not with so much bitterness between them. As soon as she could arrange it, she meant to send the money back to him with a cool "thank you but no thank you" note.

Wee Willie, one of the older clowns, came up with a new joke for Pop. Tanya studied Pop's too-lean face with detached eyes as he laughed heartily at Wee Willie's quip. He had changed lately, as if a great weight had been lifted from his back. For that, she was grateful to Wade.

Outside the band slid into "Born Free," her cue that the Big Cage was ready for her act. She straightened the collar on her tight-fitting tunic, planted a wide smile on her face and marched smartly out into the arena as the equestrian director's rolling basso introduced her as "the daring, the darling Tanya Rhodin! Watch as the little lady battles flashing fangs and sweeping claws, enforcing her will on a ring of snarling, roaring hate and fury! I give you Miss Tanya Rhodin!"

The capacity crowd roared their approval as Chub, the first of the big cats, came loping down the chute and into the cage. As she put him through his specialty, the tight-wire walk, followed by a leap through a series of flaming hoops so small it seemed impossible his body could clear them, she couldn't help thinking of Leopold. The last time she'd seen the old lion he had already acquired quite a harem, although, as

Lars had told her, he was too lazy to fight the other males. When the pride leader or one of the younger males challenged him, he retreated discreetly after a few token growls. Even so, several of the females were already vying for his attention and ignoring the other males.

"Not typical lion behavior at all," Lars said disapprovingly, shaking his head.

"Well, Leopold is not your typical cat. Maybe he'll start a whole new race of mild-mannered lions."

"If that ever happened in the wild, the lion species would disappear off the face of the earth in a few generations," Lars said gloomily. "I suspect the old boy's some kind of sport—what they call a mutant. Where do you suppose he gets all that sexual drive, an old-timer like that?"

"Good clean living, and a diet of strawberries and sour cream," she'd said promptly, and had earned one of Lars's rare laughs.

As she put the twins, Remus and Romulus, through their specialty, an exhibition of spinning that made the crowd gasp with wonder, she kept a close eye on the other cats. It wasn't true, she knew so well, that the longer a cat was in an act, the less dangerous he became. Actually, some of them became *more* dangerous, because they lost their respect for the trainer and developed contempt for human frailty. Tanya made certain her attention never strayed even one moment as she introduced the tigers and put them through the tricks they'd learned.

As usual, Bennie was sulky and difficult to handle, but his great leaping ability, the beauty of his sleek, lithe body and his massive head, tawny and well marked with wavy black stripes, added "flash" to the act. After the finale, the living pyramid of lions and tigers that always evoked gasps of awe from the audience, the cats responded to the rattling of the tunnel gate and the strident blast of trumpets from the bandstand that was their cue to disappear down the chute. Tanya bowed to the audience, pleased by their enthusiastic applause.

Her eyes drifted to the blue seats, the cheap ones to the far left of the auditorium. Her temples throbbed and her wide smile faded as she stared at a familiar face.

Wade's face.

The music changed to "Ponderosa," the clowns' cue to start the walk-around that completed the performance. Moving like a marionette, Tanya took her final bow and ran off. When she reached the back door ramp, she looked behind her, but the seat where she'd seen Wade—if it had really been Wade and not some aberration of her own mind—was now empty.

Since she was not in the mood to talk to anyone, she hurried away to her trailer. Questions seethed through her mind, questions she couldn't answer. If the man she'd seen had truly been Wade, why had he been sitting out there in the audience? And how should she interpret the look she'd seen on his face? If she didn't know it was impossible, she would have called it torment or grief or maybe both. . . .

But that was ridiculous! Wade hadn't even bothered to say goodbye when he'd left the circus last year, nor had he written or called her in the past few months, even though it would have been a simple matter for him to learn the show's tour route. He must have come tonight out of simple curiosity to see how the circus was getting along without him.

For the rest of the day Tanya was locked in a fog as she tried to straighten out her confused emotions. It was after the evening performance when Marshall came to her trailer.

"What the devil were you up to tonight?" he scolded. He had changed out of his tails and top hat and was wearing one of his impeccably tailored suits and a bowler hat, looking very much the English gentleman. "That was one sloppy performance—I was sure you were going to lose control."

"But I didn't," she pointed out sulkily.

"It only takes a few seconds. If you're getting arena fever and can't handle the cats any longer, you'd better toss in the towel and switch to something else. I don't want to be bringing flowers to you in hospital. They're too expensive these days."

Despite his attempt at humor, she knew he was genuinely worried. She smiled at him and said softly, "I'm sorry I gave you a scare, Marshall. It won't happen again. It's just that—well, I had a shock this afternoon. I guess I had that on my mind."

Marshall was silent a moment. "So you saw him in the audience," he said heavily. "I was afraid you would."

She shrugged. "It isn't important. I've put it all behind me. What Wade does no longer matters to me."

"And you're lying through your teeth. I don't know what happened between you two—although I have my suspicions—but it isn't over yet. And that's the problem. I think you should have it out with Wade, either make a clean break this time or patch it up. You won't get any peace until you do."

"If you're saying I should go to him, there's no way I would ever do that! There are too many things that— It wasn't a simple quarrel, something we can patch up. Wade doesn't want anything more to do with me, and I feel the same way about him."

"So why was he sitting out there in the audience tonight, looking as if the world had caved in on him? And why did it get you in such a state that you almost lost control of your cats?"

She started to deny that Wade had had anything to do with her preoccupation, but she realized that Marshall would never believe her. Instead she asked if he wanted something to drink, and when he told her he was taking Tillie Bauer, the dog trainer, out for a midnight snack, and was already running a bit late, she hid her relief and told him to have a good time.

But after he was gone, she didn't get ready for bed. Instead, she sat in her easy chair, staring into nothingness, her mind turning over their conversation.

Was it true that she would get no peace until she'd had it out with Wade once and for all? By coming here, he had stirred up the old pain that she'd thought she'd resolved. And there was the matter of the money, too. She had planned to mail him a check tomorrow; why not take it to him in person tonight?

She changed into jeans and a matching denim jacket and tied a scarf around her head. Although she was already having second thoughts, she slung her purse over her shoulder and left the trailer, locking it behind her. No matter what Wade's reaction might be when she appeared uninvited on his doorstep, she thought grimly, it would be better than this feeling of unfinished business hanging over her head for the rest of her life. Maybe by turning up without calling ahead and giving him warning, he would let down his guard and tell her the truth. He had taken time out of his busy life to make the trip from New York to attend the matinee performance—and she had to know why.

And if it ended in another quarrel? Well, maybe

that would put things back into perspective for her. Wade's appearance that afternoon had thrown her off balance, especially since it had come right on top of finding out that he had replaced the money she'd transferred to the reserve account. The first thing she intended to do was to put the check in his hands and tell him that now they were even, that she no longer owed him a cent. Maybe then she could get on with her own life and stop thinking of him every hour of the day.

She borrowed the menagerie's pickup truck, and as she drove along the uncrowded freeway toward Manhattan, she had the strange feeling that she had just left her own familiar world for an alien one in which she had no right to intrude. There were so many possibilities ahead for humiliation and more hurt. What would she do, for instance, if she found Wade entertaining a woman—say, Monica? Just hand him the check at the door, turn around and walk away?

Or did she have the courage to tell him she was sorry to interrupt his social life, but after all, it would only take a few minutes to have their talk, and she'd come a long way? Then she would ask why he had been sitting out there in the audience, watching the show. What if he denied it, or if he told her it was none of her business and then slammed the door in her face? Of course she might not even get that far. When the lobby guard checked with Wade and told him he had a late-night visitor named Tanya Rhodin, it was very likely he would tell her to get lost.

It took a while to reach Wade's apartment. She had to stop twice to get directions, and there was a long hunt for a parking space, but finally she was standing in front of Wade's apartment building. She was already prepared to talk her way past the guard, but when she went into the lobby she discovered that no one was on duty at the guard's desk. She stared at an open thermos bottle, a cup of coffee, still steaming a little in the air-conditioned coolness of the lobby, and a half-eaten ham sandwich. Something had interrupted the guard's midnight snack—maybe it was the monitors. One of them was gray. Had it gone out and required his attention?

Impatiently Tanya waited for a few minutes, and when no one came, she shrugged and went over to the elevator and punched the Up button. The elevator doors opened, and she stepped inside, pushing the penthouse button. As the elevator began its smooth, silent rise, she stared at the mural wallpaper and remembered Wade's ironic remark about New York overkill. Had they ever really communicated so easily, laughing and joking together as if they were the best of friends? It seemed impossible now, and yet how natural and uncomplicated being in love with Wade had once seemed.

The elevator came to a stop and the doors opened with a soft swooshing sigh. Feeling more nervous than she was willing to admit, Tanya stood in the small oak-paneled foyer outside Wade's apartment, trying to get up the courage to press his doorbell. When she finally did, she listened to chimes, like far-off bells, through the thick, paneled door. But no one came, not even when she pushed the button several times. And yet—she put her ear close to the door—music was playing inside. Someone must be there. Was it possible Wade was simply not answering his doorbell?

Anger and a reluctance to return to New Jersey without talking to Wade stiffened her resolve. She rapped smartly on the door, at the same time giving the doorknob a twist; to her surprise, it turned easily in her hand. When she pushed the door open, she saw that the living room was ablaze with lights, as if somebody had gone around the room switching on all the lamps.

She hesitated a moment, then squared her shoulders and called Wade's name in a firm steady voice. But there was no answer, and a trickle of fear went through her. If Wade was already in bed, then why had he left the living-room lights on? Was it possible that he was entertaining a woman...in his bedroom?

The thought of another woman in the bed she'd shared with Wade was so painful that she winced. No, she couldn't go barging into his bedroom, but there was no good reason why she couldn't wait until he came out.

Moving quietly, she crossed the living room, heading for one of the deep sofas that sat at right angles to the terrace doors. She had almost reached it when a sound stopped her. When it came again and she realized it was something as ordinary and normal as a snore, she put her hands over her mouth, stifling the hysterical giggle that rose to her lips.

It didn't take her long to find Wade. His lean body was sprawled on the floor between one of the sofas and the huge glass-topped coffee table. From his relaxed position, she knew he was sound asleep. Near his head a bottle was lying on its side, and as she bent over him, the odor of whiskey assaulted her nostrils, so strong that she wrinkled her nose in disgust. The front of Wade's shirt was wet, as if he'd spilled the whiskey all over himself, and from the flush on his face, he appeared to be very drunk.

Tanya sank down on the sofa and regarded Wade's supine body with a mixture of pity and disappointment. There was no question of talking to him while he was in this state. And yet how could she go away and leave him there on the floor to sleep it off?

She fought a battle with herself, one of many she'd fought in the past few months. In the end she knew she couldn't leave him in that condition without at least trying to get him to bed. For one thing, his clothes, even his hair, were soaked with whiskey. For another, if he didn't move soon, he would awaken in the morning with one devil of a stiff neck.

As she bent over him and laid the back of her hand against his flushed forehead, she felt an unexpected tenderness. There was something so...so vulnerable about him now, so at odds with the self-confident, always-in-control man she knew. Gently, forgetting her anger with him, she brushed the matted hair back from his wide forehead. His skin felt cold in the air-conditioned room, and she noticed he looked much thinner than the last time she'd seen him. Had he been working too hard? There were lines in his face that she didn't remember. Was it possible he'd been ill? Surely he wouldn't be drinking if he were recuperating from some illness.

Another possibility came to her, one that made her breath catch. Was it possible that Wade had been suffering, just as she had suffered, from their break-up? Maybe he had come to the circus because he wanted to have it out with her. Well, if so, he must have changed his mind once he'd seen her, because he'd gone away without talking to her or anyone else.

Wade muttered something under his breath and he looked so uncomfortable and cramped that Tanya made up her mind what to do. She would get him to bed and then she'd leave, give up her plan to talk to him. It had been a rotten idea, anyway. She slipped her arms under his shoulders, grasped him around the chest and forced him to a sitting position by propping him up against the sofa. He looked at her with glazed eyes as she urged him to his feet, but he struggled upward, with her help, and his docility touched her in some part of her heart that was always vulnerable to anything or anyone who was helpless and in need.

As she slipped her shoulder beneath his arm to support him, she staggered under his weight, but she braced herself and guided his wavering steps in the direction of the master bedroom.

Once he was moving it was easier, and she finally got him to the bathroom, where he stood swaying dangerously, his eyes bleary. Afraid that he might fall, she slid a rattan stool under his knees and eased him down. He slumped on the stool, his head and shoulders braced against the wall, eyes closed.

Quickly she ran warm water into the bathroom's huge sunken tub, then bent over him and began unbuttoning his shirt. It took her longer than she had expected to strip off his wet clothing, since he gave her no help, and she had time to wonder at her own lack of embarrassment as she got him back on his feet again and led him to the tub. When she helped him into the warm water, he gave a deep sigh and opened his eyes briefly to give her a long, unfocused stare. He closed them again, as if the soft bathroom lights were painful to his eyes, and submitted quietly as she soaped him thoroughly, then rinsed him off as if he were a small boy. Since there was nothing remotely boyish about his muscular virile body, Tanya had to bite her tongue to keep from laughing when he reached forward once and patted the water with his hands, making waves in the suds.

By the time she'd washed his hair, then poured water over his head to rinse off the suds, she was thoroughly soaked herself. She pulled Wade to his feet, dried him with a thick, cream-colored towel, then wrapped him in another towel before leading him into the bedroom.

With a long sigh he dropped upon the bed, his eyes closed. She lifted his legs and got him turned lengthwise on the bed, tucked a pillow under his head and then covered him, towel and all, with a comforter she found in a closet.

For a while after she'd tucked the comforter around him securely, she stood there, staring down at him. He didn't open his eyes, not even when she bent impulsively and gently kissed him on the lips. Since she was exhausted by now, and also very wet, she went back to the bathroom, took a quick shower to refresh herself, then wrapped herself in a thick velour robe she found hanging behind the door.

She curled up on the big easy chair in one corner of his bedroom, too tired for the moment to move. In a little while, she thought drowsily, she'd get up, put her clothes back on, even though they were damp, and return to the fairgrounds. But she'd leave something behind for Wade—a check that covered the money he'd returned to her savings account. He'd get the message, all right, the message that she didn't intend to take his charity or be obligated to him in any way.

A moment later she was asleep.

WADE WAS AWARE of an ache deep inside his skull even before he opened his eyes. Light struck his eyes, and although it wasn't bright, he groaned and buried his head in his pillow. God, what a hangover—he must really have tied one on last night. Funny, though, he couldn't remember coming to bed. The last thing he did remember, in fact, was sitting in the living room and reaching forward to pour himself another drink. He had...yes, the bottle had slipped from his hand and he'd made a grab for it just as it struck the edge of the coffee table, spraying him with whiskey. For some reason that was obscure to him now, this had struck him as funny, and he'd collapsed on the floor, laughing like a fool.

Past that point, he remembered nothing clearly. But he must have fallen asleep there on the floor, because he had a vivid memory that could only have been a dream. He'd dreamed that Tanya had come to him, had talked to him in that husky voice that haunted him so in his dreams—and when he was awake, too, if he was honest with himself.

He had felt so comforted as she'd undressed him, then bathed him in warm sudsy water. She had dried him off, wrapped him in a towel and led him to bed, and after she'd covered him and tucked him in, she had bent and kissed him....

God, would he never be free of her? Going to see her the day before had been a mistake. It had stirred up so many painful memories, and he'd tried to obliterate them with alcohol, a stupid move that proved how mixed up he was lately.

He'd probably suffer royally for it today, though the truth was, he'd never suffered from a hangover the very few times in his life when he'd had too much to drink. But never again. These trips into the past must stop. He had to put Tanya behind him once and for all. To continue to think about her, to devise fantasies in which he met her again and courted her properly this time, were insane. There were too many obstacles against picking up their relationship where they'd left off. Anything Tanya might once have felt for him was gone now. He had forfeited his chance when he'd been so quick to turn on her, to accuse her of being a cheat—and worse.

His thoughts were so painful that, in defense, he opened his eyes. The vertical blinds at the window were closed, but the trickle of gray light that crept in around the edges told him it was still early in the morning. What the devil had awakened him at this hour, anyway? It was much too early for his house-man to be rattling around in the kitchen—and besides, come to think of it, this was his day off.

In any case, he was awake now and badly in need of a cup of strong black coffee and maybe a couple of aspirin to stop the pounding in his head. At least he wasn't nauseated. That would be the last straw.

He started to get up, only to find that he was nude under the comforter that covered him, and that his legs were tangled up in a large bath towel. It was also obvious from the talcum powder that still clung to his body that he had taken a shower or a bath before retiring. He shook his head, then winced as a dart of pain ran along the back of his head. It must have been one helluva night if he didn't even remember that much.

He twisted the towel around his loins and started for the bathroom. He had just come around the corner of the big brass bed when he saw Tanya, curled up in a chair. Her cheek was resting against the padded arm of the chair, and her hair had escaped its clip and was tangled around her face, half hiding it. For a long time he was so stunned he just stood there, fighting the surge of joy that flooded him. So it hadn't been a dream, after all. Tanya had come here for...for whatever reason, had found her way past the guard without being announced. And how the hell had she managed that? Had the guard let her into the apartment, too? Whatever the explanation, she must have found him sleeping on the floor. If he could trust the vague flashes of his own memory, she had given him a bath and put him to bed before she'd put on his robe—because she'd been wet?—and gone to sleep in his chair.

So what did it all mean? Why had she come here? Had she seen him sitting in the audience the day before and followed him home to tell him to stay away from her in the future? But that didn't make sense. If she was that angry with him, she wouldn't have bothered to clean him up and put him to bed, which must have been a hellish job since she was only half his size.

Why hadn't she simply gone away and left him to sleep it off? Did this mean she was still concerned about him, enough to take care of him when she thought he needed her help? Or maybe he was reading more into this episode than it deserved. After all, Tanya was a caring and compassionate woman. She would have cleaned up a mongrel if she'd found it wet and cold.

And knowing this, why did he feel so damned touched that there were actually tears in his eyes? Tanya was fond of saying she never cried, but the evidence proved just the opposite. *He* was the one who never cried, not since he was a kid and he'd found out that big boys didn't cry—not if they wanted their mother to pay any attention to them. In order to earn an occasional word of praise—he already knew by then that it wasn't possible to earn his mother's love—he had stopped showing weakness of any kind.

But now he wanted desperately to get down on his knees, put his head in Tanya's warm, safe lap and cry like a baby. For as long as he could remember, *he* had always been the strong one who cleaned up other people's messes. Last night the shoe had been on the other foot. Tanya had cared enough about him to see to his comfort, and if he let her go out of his life, this woman with so much fire and passion and capacity for loving, he would be making the worst mistake of his life....

Wade didn't stop to apply logic or reason to the tide of emotion running so strongly through him. For one of the few times in his life he did a completely impulsive thing. He bent over Tanya, gathered her up in his arms and carried her to his bed. She murmured something that sounded like his name, but she didn't awaken, not even when he slipped the robe off her body and tucked her under the covers. When she turned to her side with a sigh, tucking her hand under her chin, he gave a low laugh, remembering the same gesture from the night he'd asked her to marry him and she'd dozed off after they'd made love.

He went to get a cup of coffee and to take a couple of aspirin, although his headache had vanished and he felt surprisingly good for a man who'd had too much to drink the night before. When he refilled the cup and carried it back into the bedroom, Tanya was still deep in sleep. For a long time he sat on the edge of the bed, sipping the coffee and watching the way her lashes curled over her cheeks, the slight pout of her upper lip, the way her breast rose and fell under the comforter, setting him on fire....

Unable to resist temptation, he took off the towel he'd tucked around himself and slid into bed beside her. He pulled her up close so that her head was resting on his chest, and as he felt her sweet warmth, he knew that this time he didn't intend to let her go.

Because of their closeness, he was aware of the exact second Tanya awoke. He saw the question in her eyes as she realized their nude bodies were pressed tightly against each other, so close there could be no hiding his arousal. For a long time they stared into each other's eyes, and then, wordlessly, she slid her arms around his neck, a mute invitation that stoked the fires inside him. He kissed her, taking his time, tasting the honey sweetness of her mouth, etching a path of kisses down her throat to her breasts, to the secret places that he knew no other man had ever touched, tasted, possessed.

With a little cry she came alive in his arms, returning his kisses and caresses wildly, without restraint, and he lost control, too, forgetting all the things they needed to say to each other in the rush of passion that raged through his body, searing him with an inward flame.

He had never felt so strong, so invincible as he did now, as if he could take on the world and fight it to a standstill. The yielding softness of Tanya's body, a willing vessel he was only too eager to fill, and the sweet scent of her hair, which reminded him of wheat ripening in the sun, bewitched him, and he lost all sense of time and place. Only the incredible surge and ebb, surge and ebb as they moved together in their own primal rhythm, mattered now. As he possessed her, he was possessed in turn, and as they reached that moment of intense pleasure together, he knew that if he died right then, it would all be worthwhile, because he had known Tanya in the most intimate sense of the word.

Afterward they talked, and as if neither of them

could stand the thought of being separated even a little, Tanya stayed in his arms. There was so much to say, so many explanations, and yet none of it seemed important next to the reality of being together again. When they finally ran out of words, he kissed her again, this time on her forehead, then each cheek, before he claimed her lips in a long kiss, a promise that he would never again desert her.

"If you want me to live in your world, I will," she said. "I want to give our love every chance."

"Your world, my world—they're both the same. I want to make the circus a permanent part of my life, too. It wasn't just you that I've missed these past months. I guess Moon was right when he told me that the circus can get in your blood. Even while I was organizing a new software company, I couldn't stop worrying about the circus."

He paused, an old memory surfacing. "I never told you this, Tanya, but it was Pop who talked to me like an uncle and persuaded me to return to my family when I ran away that time. He told me that if it was meant for me to be with a circus, I would return to it someday, but first I should get a good education, because that's what it took these days to run any kind of business right. Well, I got my education and I made my mark in the world, but I never forgot my first dream. That's why I collected circus memorabilia and why I was so quick to take Larry's advice. With you by my side, the circus is going to be my world now. I think Pop could use a helping hand, don't you?"

"He'd love that. He misses you, you know."

"There aren't many men who get the chance to fulfill their boyhood dreams—and who knows? I might fulfill another one, too."

She snuggled closer, her warm thighs entwined with his. "What other dream? To marry a lady lion trainer?"

He laughed and hugged her tight. "That, too. And if you won't laugh, I'll tell you a secret."

"A secret? I love secrets. I promise I won't laugh."

"You will, but I'll tell you anyway. I've always had the fancy that I'd make one hell of a good clown."

Tanya didn't laugh. Instead she kissed him and said, her tone indulgent, "I'm sure you will, Wade."

HARLEQUIN
PREMIERE AUTHOR EDITIONS

6 EXCITING HARLEQUIN AUTHORS
— 6 OF THEIR BEST BOOKS!

Daphne Clair
A STREAK OF GOLD

Marjorie Lewty
TO CATCH A BUTTERFLY

Anne Mather
SCORPIONS' DANCE

Jessica Steele
SPRING GIRL

Margaret Way
THE WILD SWAN

Violet Winspear
DESIRE HAS NO MERCY

Harlequin is pleased to offer these six very special titles, out of print since 1980. These authors have published over 250 titles between them. Popular demand required that we reissue each of these exciting romances in new beautifully designed covers.

Available in April wherever paperback books are sold, or through Harlequin Reader Service. Simply send your name, address and zip or postal code, with a check or money order for $2.50 for each copy ordered (includes 75¢ for postage and handling) payable to Harlequin Reader Service, to:

Harlequin Reader Service

In the U.S.
P.O. Box 52040
Phoenix, AZ 85072-2040

In Canada
P.O. Box 2800
Postal Station A
5170 Yonge Street
Willowdale, Ontario
M2N 6J3

PAE-1

An epic novel of exotic rituals
and the lure of the Upper Amazon

THE TAKERS RIVER OF GOLD

JERRY AND S.A. AHERN

THE TAKERS are the intrepid Josh Culhane and the seductive Mary Mulrooney. These two adventurers launch an incredible journey into the Brazilian rain forest. Far upriver, the jungle yields its deepest secret—the lost city of the Amazon warrior women!

THE TAKERS series is making publishing history. Awarded *The Romantic Times* first prize for High Adventure in 1984, the opening book in the series was hailed by *The Romantic Times* as "the next trend in romance writing and reading. Highly recommended!"

Jerry and S.A. Ahern have never been better!

TAK–3

Share the joys and sorrows
of real-life love with
Harlequin American Romance!™

GET THIS BOOK
FREE as your introduction to
Harlequin American Romance —
an exciting series of romance
novels written especially for
the American woman of today.

Mail to:
Harlequin Reader Service

In the U.S.
2504 West Southern Ave.
Tempe, AZ 85282

In Canada
P.O. Box 2800, Postal Station A
5170 Yonge St., Willowdale, Ont. M2N 6J3

YES! I want to be one of the first to discover
Harlequin American Romance. Send me FREE and without
obligation *Twice in a Lifetime.* If you do not hear from me after I
have examined my FREE book, please send me the 4 new
Harlequin American Romances each month as soon as they
come off the presses. I understand that I will be billed only $2.25
for each book (total $9.00). There are no shipping or handling
charges. There is no minimum number of books that I have to
purchase. In fact, I may cancel this arrangement at any time.
Twice in a Lifetime is mine to keep as a FREE gift, even if I do not
buy any additional books.   154-BPA-BPGE

Name	(please print)	
Address		Apt. no.
City	State/Prov.	Zip/Postal Code

Signature (If under 18, parent or guardian must sign.)

This offer is limited to one order per household and not valid to current Harlequin
American Romance subscribers. We reserve the right to exercise discretion in
granting membership. If price changes are necessary, you will be notified.

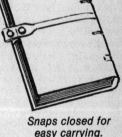